EROT

MW01002194

Warlock

A novel of possession

BY
PERRY BRASS

Belhue Press

Belhue Press, First Edition
Copyright © 2001 by Perry Brass

Published in the United States of America by:
Belhue Press
2501 Palisade Avenue, Suite A1
Bronx, NY 10463
Electronic mail address: belhuepress@earthlink.net

ALL RIGHTS RESERVED: No part of this book may be reproduced in any form without written permission from the author, except for brief passages for review purposes in a newspaper or magazine.

The following is a work of fiction. All the characters, specific settings, and events in it are purely fictitious and have no relationship to actual specific personages, living or dead, or business entities except when described as part of a fictional narrative.

Cover and overall design by M. Fitzhugh.
Cover photo by Gilberto Prioste.

ISBN 1-892149-03-6
LIBRARY OF CONGRESS CATALOGUE CARD NUMBER: 2001088277

"And the sudden, sexual laughter of the man, so strange a sound of pain and desire, obstinate reluctance and helpless passion, a noise as if something was tearing at his breast, was a sound to remember."

D. H. Lawrence, *The Plumed Serpent*

With great thanks to Hugh, and to Robert and Peter, and to Patrick Merla. And to all of my readers beginning this journey with me.

Other books by Perry Brass:

Sex-charge (poetry)

Mirage, a science fiction novel.

Works *and Other 'Smoky George' Stories*

Circles, the sequel to *Mirage*.

Out There: *Stories of Private Desires. Horror. And the Afterlife.*

Albert *or The Book of Man*, the third book in the *Mirage* series.

Works *and Other 'Smoky George' Stories*, <u>Expanded Edition</u>.

The Harvest, a "science/politico" novel

The Lover of My Soul, *A Search for Ecstasy and Wisdom*
(poetry and other collected writings)

How to Survive Your <u>Own</u> Gay Life, *An Adult Guide to Love, Sex, and Relationships*

Angel Lust, *An Erotic Novel of Time Travel*

ONE

My shame, my shame;

my bitter, punching, screaming shame—my God, he'd be so incensed if he knew I were telling you this. But what else can I do? I'm torn up with grief. He's gone. I get up at three o' clock in the dark and pace back and forth through these big empty rooms waiting for him. This luxurious place, that he's given to me to live in near Central Park, is a prison. I have never been in such splendor, luxury, style and pain. My insides crawl for him. I feel a loss inside that resembles tumbling down a yawning elevator shaft. Down, down, down to the bare hell of my existence. This is stark love. I know it. I rage sometimes. I get up angry. Why did this have to happen to me? What is so unique about me to feel such twisting, frantic helplessness? I can't control it. Is it organic? A part of my very self that he recognized and pulled out of me, as it waited stupidly, mutely, for him?

I had waited. Without even knowing that I had waited.

And now I know.

I can only humiliate myself to him. Did you know that the words "humility" and "humiliate" come from the same root, *humus*? Dirt. It means to make *dirt* of oneself, yet isn't dirt what we all come from? The products of dirt. The grain. The fruit. The solid, life-sucking, bitter roots. The animals that feed on them. And then, finally, feed us. So to be humiliated is only to go back to the source from which we came—the dirt, the mud—returning to our own ... oblivion. That's what I sought from him: my oblivion.

7

That dreamless rest from my own burdens of being. Of knowing.

And, even worse, of *not* knowing.

He's hairy. He has this wondrous, dense covering of the finest body hair I've ever seen on a human being. In bright daylight, if you saw him naked—and, in daylight, it would be rare to do that—the hair appears so intensely pale that light shines directly through it. Then he seems unworldly; fetal, like some primitive, just-gestated mammal; some burrower of the underground of your own dark existence, that you don't expect to see at the surface, in the path of light. But what I've said does no justice to him because he is … the word is … gorgeous. He's startling. Though, truthfully (let me be truthful, now, with you), he's a bit paunchy.

He's no centerfold beauty with the "six-pack" roll of ab muscles, though he is so strong that he can pick me up with one arm. Literally. He has a middleweight prizefighter's ox-strong shoulders and a garbageman's upper arms that can knock the wind out of you. But the most amazing, most delicious, most arresting article about him is his mouth. It's not quite human. It's close to being a demon's, like an anteater's rippling, muscular, delicate tide of lips. Powerful, generous, caressive. They draw you in, tie themselves in a lavish concentration around you, and pull your very soul from you.

The way he talks, the way he utilizes that mouth, sends shivers through me. He can kiss me and threaten me at the same time and I know that I'll obey him, as I've never obeyed anyone before. I can hear his voice; that plaintive, slightly husky sound tattooed now to my organs; that voice that I can taste inside my mouth like I can taste his own tongue. Nubby, large and fleshy. Coarse, okay, he's coarse. Definitely vulgar.

Disgustingly real.

A voice from the back streets and the gutters; with no deception in him, yet there are moments when we want to deceive ourselves—truly. When we'll pay to do that, and we know we'll pay. "I got you," he told me. "You belong with me. You're a piece of shit and a piece of heaven. I swear I need you." His lips were all over me. Male, beefy; like exploring, lubricated little fingers surrounding a fluttering tongue. All over me. Everyplace. "You ain't goin' no place," he warned me. I started crying from sheer, exhausted, uncontainable relief.

He was right … the shame, the wanting, the loathing, too, of it! I gave up my pointless job in the low-paying back tunnels of a bank. In a "financial institution" that was like a mental institution: really, I swear. No lie. Just "with benefits." And my daily routines, I relinquished those, too. And my apartment, yes—all those nice little New York things. The merciful, pointless friends. The little possessions that you hoard away carefully, so no one can rob them from you—almost twenty years worth, sitting there, looking at me. I just walked out.

He said, "Come with me," and I did. His big car was waiting. I had spent enough time with him in that towering space of an apartment that took up a high floor of a wing of an old West Side building. Views. Clouds. Distant boats, chugga-chugging up the river, then chugging down. Almost the whole, transparent glittering island of Manhattan. And those endless big closets and storage areas; in New York storage becomes important. And locked rooms.

He had his own locked rooms.

And carpets, he collected carpets. Soft Persians and lustrous Chinese silks and old muted Indians, like faded madras shirts. Those colors, when the light hit, they dazzled your eyes. But there were few lights. Bad for the colors, he said, of his beautiful things. He would take his shoes off a lot. Or even, for that matter—when we were totally alone, just the two of us—all his clothes off. Then he was free to be himself, and he wanted me naked, too, he said.

Sometimes he wore just a dressing gown, but there were still closets and closets of his clothes. Dark suits. English, French, Italian. Some American from the pissy-rich stores on Madison Avenue. And then sports jackets in warm toffee-brown shades or clear marine hues; some in brilliant Irish tweeds, some in cashmere. I wish I could show them all to you, but, even now, I can barely touch his clothes.

9

I do wear the things that he bought me. A really beautiful, impressive suit. A pair of coal-black jeans that feel almost like suede. Some brilliant white shirts. He gave me a buttery leather jacket and I wrap myself in it, so that the thick, creamy shearling inside hugs me. The way he did. The soft silkiness of the hair on his body. Even his strange dark large toes, with the thick, grayed, nacreous toenails, were hairy; hair crept from his wrists all the way to the first joints of his fingers. I've sucked the hairs on his hands, licked them, wet them with my own explosive tears.

I have to tell you this. I have to warn you. I'm in love with him, and I am dirt. I would kill you if you came between us, but I need you. I can no longer face this alone. He has taken so much from me that at the moment my own suicide would mean nothing to me, and probably—the way everything's been so miserably left—less to him. What can I say? Time can reverse itself ... sometimes. This is blank despair talking, but can't you still detect the danger? I am falling down that open elevator shaft. Down, down ...

I had no idea it would be like this. Not when we met.

That was different.

It was, I've got to tell you, in New York, at the baths, that flashy, noisy sexual pinball machine on the West Side. I'd just arrived, and, as usual, was all anxious, nervous anxiety. I'm not a great looker (understatement), someone to whom other men are immediately attracted. I am short, slightly built, mid-winter pale. I have a small penis. My "endowment" has always been my Achilles' Heel ... or hell. Men are for the most part disappointed by it. It's a small boy's dick. It never grew up and became a real, honest-to-God man's dick. One of those down-on-your-knees, "Yes, sir!", hot 'n' ready, big ol' swingin' acres of cock-flesh you see fully-charged in slick magazines and glistening wet dreams.

10   I'm aware of that.

You learn either to live with it, or not. Okay, maybe I can't. I've been in situations like this before: hot, exciting, totally pumped. And men have walked into my room and two minutes later, after inspecting the sad state of my genital packaging, simply walked out.

To make matters worse: I am, perhaps from fear or nerves, or maybe even a cruel trick of heredity…prone to impotence. Or, in TV lingo, "erectile dysfunction." I can get "junior" up, nudging him cautiously awake, then with no warning, he stops paying attention. He (okay, *it*) goes limp. Numb even. Like it's only an extra piece of flesh down there where my stomach ends. I have hated the crap out of my little dick for years. It's like a three-day-old dead minnow.

So why was I there that night?

I kept wondering that myself—you always do in situations like this. Why was I there: just to embarrass myself? Did I ask for it? Who wouldn't ask that; but who wouldn't hope, either?

What I really wanted was … (okay, I admit it) someone to hold me. I mean … really hold me, and make me feel like a man does with another man. Warmer; larger; full: that feeling of rising so very far above yourself that you can barely hold on to the earth. Yeah, true, it's like joining something way, way beyond your own paltry limits.

(Or, as the club boys would say, just swinging 'round and 'round on a wonderful piece o' cock.)

O great hammer, lightning thunder-dick itself: the gonadal, full-lipped god with his star-hot, veiny arm deep, deep inside us.

Strength, throbbing excitement. Lust swimming, pushing its way all the way up to the very brow of power. I wanted that. Waited, like a singer who has forgotten his song, but knows that he must, at the very least, bring himself to sing it. You get out there on the stage, the band's all ready, you open your mouth and … I stayed alone in my dark little room, shaking. Like I was pursued by rejection already. Slapped by it. Kicked in the nuts. Savage sex noises exploding around me. *Uh-huh uh-huh uh-huh uh-huh uh-huh.* The grunting. The jackhammer breathing. Ear-splitting sound system. Big naked feet beating the floor as men marched by, peeped in, disappeared. I tried to relax. I wanted to. I needed to force myself to separate from where I was.

I started to drift off... the sound system finally began to click down, taking with it the hard breathing, even those feet beating down the industrial carpeting on the floor.

The edges of my brain, so tense, began to ease up and move away from my dumb work at the bank, and my expectations—the truth being that I'd probably leave as untouched as I had walked in. My brain left that; and, for a moment, I felt myself rising into that glorious ether of sex itself. Of celestial abandon; beauty; escape. I was there, back in some tiny innocence before I had learned to be afraid, back where we were all the children of the true Spirit, all-numerous in its Oneness, in that Paradise that accepts each of us exactly for what we are.

I floated, drifting in my head, as the loud, thumping music died off ... so that I was no longer aware that it's piercing volume had been designed specifically to get anxious, designer-drugged customers in and out of these Halls of Empty Promises as quickly as possible, without ever really touching, except on the most fleeting level. I was relaxed enough so that I was no longer a part of that. I could touch, really: now... as I was trailing through a heaven of my own delight, pulsing, alive with my own spirit, imagining myself out there, naked, free, with my equipment no longer a disappointment to anyone; that is, if it were really, at that moment, truly mine.

Who knows? Perhaps we can remake ourselves more than we think. Perhaps you can go through a once-locked door, and then...the door, which I'd left slightly ajar, mysteriously opened. With the strong, outside light behind him, I saw almost nothing of him: just that crystalline fine hair, lifted like a glowing field of airborne dandelion puffs on top of the high, silhouetted landscape of his broad, beefy shoulders and his arms. In that sharp, sudden, dazing yellow light from the hallway that he grabbed with 12 him, he strode in. My eyes, forced into immediacy, swallowed him whole.

There was this single, instant glance between us—like a flare fired above a dark ocean—point-blank, intense, disarming; then he dropped the white towel that he wore and snapped the door closed. He dove on to me, his mouth finding mine, his hands kneading my neck. That mouth, the mouth I told you about: I thought it would pull my whole soul from me. I became all goose pimples, shot with this freezing breeze that traveled down to my toes, as his hands followed it, warming me, stroking, caressing and holding me. He licked my shoulders and chest, my tiny erect nipples; my stomach. Then his hands reached for my small organ. Just pulled it gently to him and I found myself completely, unrecognizably... *yes*, hard ... as nails.

I know that's totally porn magazine crappo, but how else can I put it? Some ready-to-be-disentangled, captive animal in me had been awakened, and now it responded to him more fully than I had known myself capable of doing: Was I *really* this? He began to lavish me with his strong tongue, his supple lips, the whole intoxicating seduction of his warm eager mouth, his unannounced being. I was drawn into him as if I were entering the densest forest, that manhood in full leaf that I had waited for without hope on my side or warning on his. "Who," I wondered, "is this?"

His arms pulled me up over him, lifted me, so that he was now under me, supporting me with his strength. I felt as if I were floating in some amniotic sac, attached to this deep, spreading hairiness around me, like the bubble-rich stems that hold the white faces of water lilies to the thick muck below. And I was just drifting among these deep stems; with this thing sucking me, pleasuring me, as babies are given to pleasure, without thought, or boundary, or, even, self.

He stopped. I was trembling. My own "stem" was shot with heat. He started to stroke me. I was big now. I knew it. *BIG.*

It was impossible.

I must have been going crazy; but I knew it: it, *I*, was big. About as *big* as I was ever going to get.

I held his head and pushed my fingers through his thick hair, as he clutched them, gratefully, I could tell—but how could such a thing be, that he really wanted to suck tiny me that way? Then I felt this odd, sudden,

13

painful pinch, very instant, like a fine tooth, on my scrotum. It was no more than a pin prick, really—like an alcohol sting on a cut—but it hit my left testicle with the precision of a stereo phono needle on an old black 33-rpm record. Maybe the record was jazz, because after the pain subsided (and it was gone quickly, really fast), it was like Ella Fitzgerald was serenading with Billie Holiday; they were doing it for me. Suddenly I felt so calm that all I could do was stroke his curly head at my crotch. I was at peace. A peace I had only dreamed about before, but which was now floating purely, instinctually, over me.

Then the old bath noises, from a hazy, mental distance of about a mile away, started to resume. I did not want to listen to them, but tried to drift in that oblivion that he had brought me to. I have no idea how long that paradise lasted, but afterwards I felt as if I had gone through the most intense, explosive orgasm—a full battalion of release—without coming. I had not, as they used to say, "delivered myself." I knew that. And I was now soft again: I could do nothing about it; the thing started to shrivel back up. It might disappear virtually—my worst fear; and he'd get bored and leave, as so many others had.

I opened my eyes. He was now lying next to me. His body seemed so much larger than mine and the vast, downy-soft hairiness of it, a glowing, late-sunset pink in that dim, dim light, made me sigh with its luxuriant power. I reached out and pulled the back of his hand to me, and kissed it.

"You're kinda good looking," he said to me. "You just don't know it."

I sighed. "Think so?"

"Yeah. I have a thing for pale men. Funny, ain't it? And I gotta tell you, I like your dick. It's like a seashell. Small and really pretty. I bet you don't know that either. Lemme tell you, I could suck on you for an hour. You got perfection in you; you just don't know it. You're not stuck on yourself, like so many queers in New York are."

I shook my head. "I don't know about being stuck on anything." I reached down and felt this residue of shock in my balls. They had drawn up. They felt, I can only say, vulnerable and tender, in their sensitive sac.

14

"What did you do to me?" I whispered. I only wanted to know; I wasn't trying to challenge him.

"Lemme see. Sometimes I get carried away a bit."

He pulled me to him, lifted my legs, then my scrotum up. He switched on the small, low-watted wall light that came with the room, and examined me like a surgeon. "No problem. Maybe I pulled a hair or two, that's all."

"It felt like you bit me."

He lowered me gently, turned off the light, and then kissed me with that incredibly warm, pliant mouth. "Would y'be mad if I did?"

What could I say? "No, I wouldn't."

"Good. I don't want you mad at me. I want you to like me. I gotta tell you something." He paused and smiled. This genuine wry glow came to him. How could I not like him? I wondered. "You're gonna think I'm a crazy shit. But you're the seventh guy I been with tonight. I been horny as a spring ram. But none of 'em gave me any satisfaction. Except you. You know that?"

I shrugged my shoulders and smiled. How could I know? Seven? A sexual athlete; a male nympho. I was hoping, beyond even my dumbest hopes, for one encounter; I could never keep up with anything like that. "Seven?" I asked. The man was all eros certainly. He drew his knees up to his hairy chest and began to talk.

"The first had a real, super-size schlong, and those big-guy, kinda gym muscles, too. He had a chrome cockring on so tight, I'm surprised it didn't kill him. I don't know why people are like that, like just dick machines. He thought he was God's gift to faggolas, and tried to shove his cock into my mouth, then up my ass. I let him think he could do it, then slapped the crap out of him. You should have seen his face. He was one of those big pretty boys with salon-tanned skin and the right face. A magazine face. Nothing behind it, see? I grabbed his head, and ended up making him suck me off. 15 I shot right down his cute throat. You should have seen him—kind of shocked, I think—but happy. I slapped him on his ass some more, then left.

"The second was in the steam room. He was a fat blond with glass-es that got fogged up. He sat on my dick and asked me back to his room. He had rubbers there, and I fucked him like a horse. He was a sweet kiss-er. I took the rubber off and threw it into the garbage and left. The third and fourth was a threesome, an older black man and a young white guy. They were good. I came with them, too. The black man had a nice tool, but they often do. I liked his attitude. It was totally cool. Neither of them was something I would want to keep with me, but then why should I? Sometimes I get lost in the moment. Know what I mean?"

If only I did, I thought. I was so deliberate. So fearful.

"Number five was this nervous guy with bad breath and a funny long cock, kind of twisty, like a piece of spiral macaroni. Sorry, not for me. Nice bod, but...number six—"

"Why are you telling me this? I didn't really need to know it. Do you want me to feel you're—" I hesitated, then said: "Cheap?"

He smiled. His teeth glowed slightly bluish in the light. He had a kind of "urban skin," slightly pitted in places on his cheeks. The mouth, that mouth that rippled and could do such amazing things, lifted up slightly at each corner. It was like the insistent curl of a wave coming on to a beach. I liked his grin. "Cheap I'm not, you'll learn that. On the other hand, sexually, satiation is something I really don't understand. Perhaps because of my age—"

"How old are you?"

He smiled. I liked him. I could not help it. "We don't know each other enough for me to answer that." He leaned over and kissed me. "You don't kiss like other guys. The last one I popped into wouldn't kiss me at all. I walked into his room. At first he had his head hidden by his sheet. He looked like a big whale, with a whale-sized dick standing up under there, waiting."

16   "Did you bite his balls, too?" I asked.

"Huh?" His neck stiffened, his smile dropped and he bolted away from me. The air in the small room got colder, and the noise so loud it hurt.

I tried to grab a handful of his soft body hair, but could not keep him close to me. He reached up and switched off the small light. His body darkened instantly within the small room. "You think you can just ask me anything?"

He stood up on his large bare feet, then moved a step away from me. I felt riveted to the bed. I was sure he was going to grab his towel and rush out, furious, looking for number eight. There was a silence between us, made worse by the thumping noise outside. I couldn't keep my eyes from him, but felt totally at a loss of what to say.

He looked away from me. I had been too stupid; what could I say to him? I was sure he was going to leave. My head fell in embarrassment, then I heard him say, very slowly, in command: "If you want me to pay attention to you, you must kneel. Right now."

At first—because of the loudness from outside; the shock of it—I wasn't sure what he had said. Then he repeated his command, in exactly the same, measured way. I hated the dumb, mechanical noise from outside. I felt as if he had given me no alternative. It was either the canned bar music and everything around it that rejected me; or doing exactly what he wanted me to do.

I got off the bed, feeling very tiny—very pointless—then prostrated myself before him, with my forehead at his ankles. He leaned down, patting my head, giving me hope, some immediate recognition, perhaps; perhaps some direction towards my surrender to his world. My fingers cautiously stroked his feet. I ran my lips from his ankles, up through his hairy, muscular calves, then to his knees. I rose up slightly to his cock, which flopped down and reminded me of something from a horse or a statue. Not that it was extreme in length, but it was imposing. He shielded its weight from me, pushing me gently, really gently, aside. "Not yet," he whispered. "I gotta get dressed. The truth is, I want you to come home with me."

Without showering, I met him just outside the lobby, where men were lining up—it was now Sunday morning at two. He was dressed beautifully. An expensive, nicely pressed white shirt; pleated, gray flannel slacks; loafers. A beautiful tweed sports jacket, perfectly tailored, made him look even more commanding. It was fall, and not cold yet. The earth was starting to go to sleep, but not the city. I asked him where he lived and he told me. I was impressed. We left the baths.

"I gave my driver the night off," he said casually. "He shouldn't have to wait out here for me. It's not right, know what I mean?"

Frankly, I didn't, but we were close to Sixth Avenue and he got us a cab immediately. He told the driver, who looked Bengali, to step on it. There was very little traffic. I rolled my window down a bit, and breathed in the air: it felt wonderfully fresh for New York. I got to look at his face now; the passing stream of lights outside slid over the contours of his features as he turned to me and then turned away, giving me both his full face and profile. His nose was just a little too large, his neck too big, his cheeks sunken slightly. His eyes were deep in his face. They had a hard, glittering surface; I could not tell their color. Maybe it changed with the surroundings. I wasn't sure.

There was little, truthfully, "photo handsome" about him. But his mouth, even at rest, had this commanding presence. It looked like it might say something at any moment that could change my life, if I let it.

"What's your name?" I asked.

"What does it matter?"

"My name is Alwyn. Alwyn Barrow. But it's easier if you just call me Allen. That's what my friends do."

He looked over at me. "They were Irish trying to be English?"

I smiled. "Close."

"It's okay. We all try to be something we aren't. So if you aren't anything to begin with, it's easier. Nobody knows who I really am. I like it that way. Why'd you decide to come with me, do I seem trustable to you?"

I shrugged. "Maybe it was just destined."

18   "Good answer. I wanna drink. I can't wait to get home and have a scotch. Do you do scotch?"

I could, I told him. I asked him what he did, if he would not tell me his name.

"I make deals, and, lemme tell you, lotsa money. There's a lotta flashy, grabby money out now. Total greed—it wants to know others like it. It's like at the baths, all the big dicks want more big dick. I find it kinda revolting. Vulgar, y'know? But it's easy to work with. They think I'm a stooge. I love it. Men who have so much money that they crap dollars, feel good about dealing with me. I used to wonder why; now I don't."

The driver asked him which entrance he wanted. The building had two. He told him, and we got out and he paid him. The doormen—there were two, even then—looked at us and smiled at him. One of them took us up in the elevator to his floor. There was no door. We walked directly into his apartment. There were soft lights and that infinity of carpets, and then a series of windows that looked out onto the city and the Park, and, then, with a turn, even the distant deep silver of the Hudson River. I had never been in anything like it.

"How long have you lived here?" I asked.

"A while, but not too long. Maybe five years. You like ice in your scotch?"

I told him sure. He went out into the kitchen and left me there. My heart started to beat hard. I felt so outclassed—I'd always had diddly-shit jobs that went nowhere, but then so many New Yorkers do. We can't all be infinite money people. Why would he want to have anything to do with me? This was probably just another amusement for him—a one-nighter. Suddenly I felt bad. Really bummed out. He came back in with the two scotches, having dropped his clothes in the kitchen. "I like being naked when I'm by myself," he said. He handed me the scotch, and I sipped it.

It was very good. I had never tasted scotch like that: how could I? This was that eighteen-dollar-a-glass scotch that I had read about in the *Times*. It came from little estates in Scotland where you brought special clothes to go trout fishing, and you pretended to be just a normal person who liked to fish in funny clothes. Not totally rich. The scotch had that quality of having almost no scotchy "taste," or bite, just a golden hint of

19

subtle, nutlike sweetness. It was cold and warm at the same time. It went icily down your throat and then lingered just at the top of your chest, warming you. It reminded me of being out on the beach. In the spring. At night. Wearing a sweater, how good that felt.

"You're thinking about a beach, aren't you?"

I nodded. He put his drink down on a marble coaster on a table, and then began to strip me of my clothes. He did this very softly and sweetly, kissing me every time he released a button. I thought I was going to collapse from the sheer loveliness of him, all that power and softness. "I wish you'd tell me your name," I said.

"Why?" he asked, kissing me on my cheeks and then my throat. He licked my throat, back and forth, sucking at the Adam's apple.

"So I could"—I wanted to say, "not feel like such a poor relation here," but all I could say was—"say it. We like to hear our own names, don't we? Isn't that why we have them, the Bible and all?"

"If you know my name, you'll have leverage over me. I know about leverage, believe me. I work with these leverage shits all the time, so I don't want you to have that yet." He kissed me again; I forgot about his name—or wanting to know any more.

We were now both completely naked. He lifted me up and carried me into his bedroom, like I was a bride or a girl. With his powerful arms and legs, it was easy for him. There were a lot of rooms in the apartment and I was not sure if the bedroom he took me into was his room or not. But it was beautiful and softly lit, richly furnished with a big bed upholstered in studded, bronzy, dark leather. The bed was tall and I had to lift myself onto it. He jumped right on it, and then gave me a hand up. I felt really small now, and in a different world, like a child in an adult's room. I looked around in the dim light, trying to figure out what sort of person would live there, and what type of person my mysterious host was.

20   Suddenly he appeared over me, smiling. "Do you like it here?" he asked.

I did not want to offend him, but I was frankly intimidated. I nodded shyly and he smiled at me openly. Everything that I saw in the apartment, its richness, its size, made me uneasy. Sure, he was wealthy but ... unpolished. Despite his beautiful clothing, there was something raw and noticeably ugly about him, as if his torn edges had never been smoothed back and the loose threads carefully snipped. I noticed that his fingernails were jagged and his feet really callused, like he went barefoot too much in the wrong places. His feet were clunky, "peasant" feet, not handsome at all. The toes were too big and gnarled. They looked like potatoes just dug out of the ground. The nails were thickly ridged, gray as graphite, and dull like beach glass. They were almost like hooves.

But, strangely enough, this excited me. In my inconsequential world of polite little gay men with polite little jobs, who went out to lunch and split the check with a razor blade, he would not have fit in at all. They would have found him ungainly, *nouveau*, someone to titter at; someone they could immediately allow themselves to feel—no matter how insecurely—superior to. He got on top of me, and started nuzzling me, licking me; I forgot about his repulsive feet, except for my desire to kneel at them again. I forgot all of my qualms. It was easy to do that—he left me defenseless, just his amazing mouth, his big hands, the way he reached suddenly again for my small, tender testicles. I felt warm, or perhaps it was just the wonderful scotch.

He touched my forehead gently, and started to stroke it so that I became truly relaxed. His mouth explored my smooth, hairless stomach until it reached my penis. He then performed what he had done at the baths, but slower, much slower, and with more care and tenderness. I felt suddenly—how else can I say it?—taken care of by him; loved even, if you can use such a word in such a context. But why not? Can't love emerge at any moment, just as violence can and does? Both seemed to be flip sides of the same archaic coin, one whose origins we can never totally trace.   21

So now I felt as if he were simply hovering, weightlessly, over me, perhaps because I was so relaxed. His weight did seem like nothing at all. Maybe in some ingenious trick of strength, he was hanging over me; or, perhaps, I was just imagining him doing that, in real space, suspended like a distant, gray planet. But there he was: all warmth, softness, duck's down hairiness, in that deep weediness of my own brain. I relaxed now, except for my own small organ, which was about to "cream," like the kids say. It was totally blooming. It felt like a fresh bouquet of daisies, or the young, fleshy, snow-white buds of the magnolias I remembered from my childhood, in the spring when all was fertile, newly wet, and rushing to the surface after so much winter's sleep. With his lips down at my testicles once more, I felt as if I were also rushing, pouring myself out to him.

Gingerly, he took both delicate balls into his mouth, then pushed one out with the tip of his tongue. He was so expert. So loving. Still I tensed up: I could remember that *zing* of past pain, even if I were sure nothing would happen now. I was safe; he liked me. I *was* sure. I could not really see what he was doing, but just closed my eyes. Then, I felt it once more— that instant electrical *zap*, like some wavering, probing hypodermic needle, extracting some precise fluid tissue from me ... with, I admit, only a passable element of finesse.

The pain, I admit, was more from surprise than actual harm—it was like a wasp sting felt through a gauzy layer of cotton. It shot all the way through me, up my spine to some waiting point in my brain. There the sensation, like an arc of lightening, doubled back and whipped down again until it hit my crotch. My penis pulsed, throbbed, became deliciously heated with a desire to release its raw, new energies in orgasm.

But it did not.

Something had happened; I knew it, but could not take myself away from it. He had brought me there for a purpose and I had allowed it. I was desperate for him. Weak. Empty. I assented. I softly stroked his curly head with my hand, then ran my fingers to the pits of his cheeks, and held his face to my scrotum.

I did not know how long I could take this; I wanted him to *take* me, to suck me dry with that mouth that was so good at what it could do. But he was really doing nothing to my cock. Nothing. He seemed to have lost interest in it. Then it was over. The stinging; the mysteriously painful, strange act. My penis became thin, hopelessly small again; it sank like the bloom of a white summer flower, after the first frost.

Flaccid, dead, impotent: I was. And he sat on the side of the bed, away from me. For a moment, I thought he was disgusted with me. All I could see was the back of his head, but his spine and shoulders were straight up, squared; like a military man.

"My name is Destry," he announced. "Destry Powars. It's spelled P-O-W-A-R-S, but pronounced 'Powers.' Would you like to sleep here with me?"

I could barely catch my breath. I closed my eyes. There were warm tears in them.

"Yes," I answered.

TWO

The next morning,

a middle-aged Swiss man named Karl, dressed in a dark, pin-striped suit, served breakfast formally to us at the end of a long, polished dining room table. We had shirred eggs, small pork sausages, home-made muffins, English tea. Not what I usually had for breakfast, which was more in the lines of a Post cereal, but it was a nice treat for me. No one ever made breakfast for me—unless of course I went out with some friends and we talked about work and split the check, like I said, with a razor blade. Karl was unobtrusive, hardly said a word, like he was not there. Occasionally, he asked me if I wanted something else. "More tea, sir?" he asked. "More muffins, or toast perhaps?"

My host ignored him, sometimes waved or pointed at something— he did little talking to him. Karl had a perfect, precise, North Atlantic way of speaking English. I had worked for a Swiss banker once who had had a university education in Bern and he spoke like that. Mr. Powars, or Destry (it was hard now for me to feel very close to him, I felt so removed) did not speak that way. At all. He leafed through half a dozen newspapers—I counted the *Times*, the *Post*, the *Daily News*, the pink *Financial Times*, and the *Wall Street Journal*—and drank a cup of coffee and several cups of tea, while wearing a freshly pressed dressing gown of puckered blue cotton. I was given a similar robe, and felt well-taken care of, distantly happy. And ready to leave.

24

I needed to go back to my small apartment downtown, the one in a nowhere neighborhood, near several gas stations where taxi drivers hung out and where there were diners and coffee shops and places to eat greasy and cheap. That had been my life. I did not argue about it. I was happy. Like most queer men I had escaped my parents and that itself had been one of the central successes of my life: that I had survived my own childhood and had come to the city, had been a part of the "gay diaspora," had seen things happen. A liberation movement we had made, or some of us had made; a disease that had been thrust on us, that no one could talk about for almost a decade. Now, here I was, in this amazing luxury that some people took for granted, like life were merely a shopping mall and they could go through it with no limit on their credit.

"I should be getting back," I said to my host.

He nodded at me. "Makes sense." He went back to one of his papers. He laughed at a joke in the second section of the *Times*. One of New York's richest old women was now marrying a much younger man. Likewise, one of New York's richest men was marrying a younger woman, for the fifth time.

He smiled, excused himself, then went into his bedroom. I heard a bath door close. I looked up at Karl. Despite his formality, our eyes engaged for a moment; then, quickly, he averted them from me. He asked me if breakfast were all right. I told him it was.

He nodded, then turned slightly towards me. "Mr. Powars is happy you are here," he let out, his voice barely breaking a whisper. "So am I."

"Thank you," I said. "Does he have," I hesitated, then said it, "other guests, who stay for breakfast?"

He did not answer me, but only said, "He usually has breakfast alone. May I take your plate?" I told him he could. As he took it, he said, "He is smiling, that is what's important." Karl smiled, too. He had a long, bony face, all tense dimples and ridges, like the hard skull beneath begrudged the flesh stretched over it. He nodded at me, then Powars came back in again.

25

"Nothing like coffee and tea in the morning," he announced. "It's like getting a bunch of those Israeli movers working inside you. Ever seen those guys at it? Everything with them is like the Six Day War. I got them to move me in here—mostly what I had was books and clothes. The rest came straight from the store; you know how it is in a new place? You want new stuff. I decided I want you to come back here and have dinner with me. Tell Karl where you live. I'll have the driver come by and pick you up at eight."

He smiled briefly at me, then got up and went to the bedroom. I felt now like I'd really been stung—and it hurt very badly; then heard a shower going. I felt dismissed, like an employee who's been asked to come back at a time when it's convenient for his employer. Karl looked at me patiently, then went into the kitchen. He came back with a small notepad. "Your address, sir?"

"Don't bother," I said crisply. "I don't want to come back here."

He lowered his eyes. "You really need to," he said quietly. "I know you don't think I know it. But you want to come back; I can see it on your face. In my work, one learns to read faces. He's tired, and he has much business to do. I know it."

I gave him my address, then went into the bedroom where my clothes were ready. At some point, mysteriously enough, Karl had folded them neatly and placed them on a polished side table. Powars came out of the shower, wearing a terry robe now. "If you want to shower, Allen, do it in the guest bath. I don't like others to use my bathroom. Sorry. It's a funny thing. We all got quirks, right?"

I decided I did not want a shower, especially in his *guest* bathroom. I barely had a bathroom, much less a *guest* one. I put my underwear on, and then the rest of my clothes. I stood up and looked at him, while he sat at a small writing table, turned away from me. "Who are you?" I asked. "And why do you act like such a jerk?"

He turned to me. "That's real nice. I brought you back here, and you already think you're better than me, don't you?" His eyes left me, they followed the parquet floor away from me, all the way up to the doorway and then into the hall. "I had to earn all this, Allen. I had to wipe the floor with people. That's what jerks do, isn't it?"

He was so strange, the hairy body, the ugly feet. What was he?

"You won't have to wipe the floor with me," I told him. "Because I won't be on your floor again. I want Karl to tear up my address. Thanks for breakfast, and the lift."

He suddenly stood up. He made me feel very small now. A dark shadow crossed his brow, and I realized for the first time that his eyes were actually brown. This rich chocolate brown, flecked with the most amazing gold; like amber. He walked over to me. I was shaking. I hated him the way a child would.

He took my hand and impulsively kissed it. He was trembling. I had not expected anything like this. "I have had to relearn everything," he said, releasing a huge sigh. "I've had to relearn and relearn and relearn. I would like very much for you to have dinner with me, Allen. I would be very pleased if you did. We'll go anywhere you want to go."

"I'll think about it," I said. I was hurt. I walked out. I passed Karl in the hallway. He was in a white workman's apron, dusting and polishing the furniture. He looked up at me. If he could read faces, as he said he could, he could easily read all the tension and anger and confusion in mine. "One day that man will die alone," he said. "His heart will turn to ice. He will be made so small, and he doesn't want to—you *must* come back for him."

He put aside his polishing cloth, then rang for the elevator and it was brought up. The elevator man, dressed in a dark uniform, discreetly ignored me, and I went down into the street. Everything there was so chaotic, so real and alive. I felt as if I had been swept up into an obscene, immoral world and now I was in love. I knew it. I got the subway at the narrow station at Seventy-Second Street and Broadway. Everything around me seemed silent. I was inside myself, locked tight, bewildered. I knew I shouldn't see him again: he would hurt me, belittle me—and completely make me his own. I had to find out the secret of Destry Powars, but how would I do it unless I met him for dinner?

THREE

Back at my small place

downtown, I felt like one of those little escargot snails that had been removed from its shell and was now stuffed back into it. The place was familiar, but suddenly it seemed too tiny and too jumbled. Pictures of me and my friends covered the walls and lay about on my desk, which was also where I ate a lot of my meals alone. The pictures retold the story of my life—leaving the South, coming to the city when I was young; getting my first jobs, always underpaid but comfortable jobs. I was always somebody's assistant, somebody's do-this/make-that-right person. I guess that has been the position of multitudes of queer men for the last thousand years. We were the assistants, the consorts, the escorts, the "walkers." We did not call the shots, we just made the reservations for other people to have power dinners.

I felt suddenly small and a bit frightened. My life was now laid out to me, in all of its tawdry smallness. My apartment was so real, so familiar—such a part of my own limitations—and the huge spaces I'd been in only an hour earlier were not. I went into my bedroom, hardly as big as one of Destry Powars's bathrooms, and saw my clothes neatly lined up. There were work clothes, cheap sports jackets I had got at various men's discount places, polyester ties, and, of course, shirts, the kind that came in plastic packages, that you did not have to iron. I did not have a Karl working for me to iron things. Even Powars's table napkins had been beauti-

28

fully hand-ironed. I could tell that.

I started to take my clothes off, they still smelled of the baths, of me, of the night before, but not of Destry Powars; no, he had a different smell. I could feel in it my nose, the memory of it. I could even *hear* that smell, as you might hear a distant song or just remember it. The scent had a slightly tangy, cool spiciness to it: clove, musk, some grated lemon rind and even a note of gin in it. Juniper. It drifted through all the fine silky hair on his big body. The strong legs. The kind of horsy chest. The cock. I was naked now. He had an animal cock. Horse; that was what it was. It was not human. I realized that. The head of it. Big. Fleshy. Dark. I shivered. I felt slightly nauseated from the rush of memory that hit me. I got into the shower—my shower, never ever hotel clean; mold at the rusted metal stall corners—and turned it on. I used plain Ivory soap and lathered my hands with it, and then rubbed the lather over me. My hands went to my genitals. My dick felt pathetic—I was under-endowed. I was a kid, who just passed as a man, a little pisser; a piss ant, that's what I was.

I remembered boys sizing me up at school. "Wee-wee wienie!" one kid joked. "You gotta toy peeshooter. Next time get a real one!" I felt so tiny. I remembered the public showers at gym, feeling pitiful, scared as hell to look at the equipment of other boys. I started to have theories. I noticed that boys with small asses seemed to have big dicks. I wondered, was my ass too big? Then I saw Ralph Sweeney, this huge oomph of a guy, butt like a dump truck, who was equipped with a bazooka. Bazooka, that's what a big one was like. No wonder they named a popular bubble gum for it. All kids wanted to have a big one in their mouths. It was the absolute fear, mixing with the total desire. The forbidden; the disgusting. The thing you wanted so much it that made you throw up with desire. Made you sick with desire. Next theory: Feet. Boys with mountain-sized feet had way-big meat. So I started noticing the boys with big feet all over the place. In the hallways, in the boys' room, waiting in line to catch the school bus. It became a fun game.

Then, in the locker room, again, I'd stare down at the feet. Feet are wonderful. I was a prodigy of feet. Smooth, young, big, excellent feet. The kind that led up to large calves with pubescent hair already on them, then on to thighs, pale, dripping sweat sometimes, dripping shower water, then the edges of that fresh young meadow of pubic hair. The kind that eager diligent rabbits might munch on had the body become the true landscape of desire that it was for me. Then the test: yes, big feet often did mean big equipment…but not always. Sometimes there were these prancing little creatures, who had dainties to walk on and what dangled between their legs truly surprised you. Fat, long, luscious tubes that just hung there. Casually. Cool as … *shit*, maybe. (How do you like that for one of those contradictions that make no sense at all?) And you were supposed to pretend that it wasn't there, just waiting for you to examine it; to want more than anything else to suck it. Yeah, man: it don't exist. Dicks among boys are like God: you pray to the Deity silently.

The big dick in front of you was supposed to be fuzzied out. Like TV computer editing. Your eyes were supposed to do it, and if not your eyes, certainly your brain. You were supposed to talk in the locker room about—shit!—baseball, while they stood there. Just dangling. Playing with it, *maybe*; but not *knowing* they were playing with it maybe, too.

No wonder people went nuts.

Normally, *you* were supposed to do all that funny fuzzying business: the mental act that made the cock unseeable. But Nature had already done that for me. My short-changed equipment was pre-edited. No one had to fuzzy up the old brain screen. I was already fuzzied, minimized, censored. When you have almost nothing to start off with, who's going to stare at it? Even worse, it had taken me a long time to grow pubic hair, so for a long time my little wienie was bare. It was small, and right out there, and still unseeable, like a six-year-old kid's. I started crying in my shower. Just sobbing. I couldn't help it. I wasn't feeling sorry for myself, just frightened of my own smallness. What did Powars ever see in me? This man, this weird bigness: I felt trapped in my own inadequacy.

Stupid. I was stupid. I had this teeny, dumb-ass, kiddy twiggy between my legs, with two petite acorns for testicles. What the hell did Powers see in me? And what did he want? I soaped up my groin and felt almost nothing there. I pushed the white soap around the small, tapering head of my cock—if I can call it a cock; it was a pee-pee, that's what it was—and then, past the dumb numb, bashful little void that was my kid dick, to my little balls. They shrank in pain. Just RANG all over me. The pain made a noise, like a scream in my ear. I slid to the floor of the stall, the water drifting over my back now as I curled up, fetally, to hold on to myself.

I cupped my scrotum in my hands as delicately as I could. What had been done to me? Was it maybe just the bristle on his cheek, or the way he went about sucking me? He was coarse, okay, I knew that. He was not like the forever boyish men that I associated with, men who in another era would have been selling ribbons to ladies in elegant department stores with pneumatic tubes. Sure, that all sounds like paleontology to most people. But I had read that in the olden days, queers worked in department stores, where they politely waited on well-dressed ladies. They were not allowed to handle "filthy" money. It was always sent up and down these air-driven tubes to the top office where the "real" men counted it. The queers worked with "girls," a.k.a. spinsters. I felt like a throw-back to that—me and my friends. We were all so pleasant. Dinner in the Village, at safe little reasonable restaurants, while the "real" world of "real" men ate at those steak palaces on Park Avenue, lined with the type of big cars that I was sure Destry Powars rode in.

I eased my way back up. The ringing pain, it was a shock. Okay, I knew that. Maybe I was just being hysterical, another disgusting "female" term. I was a loser. I had no dick. I should have been a ribbon clerk. I washed all the soap off me. Dried off. Then I took a small hand mirror and looked under my balls. I could see nothing. Really. I had a small viewing glass, I used to take it to museum exhibitions, when I wanted to see detail. It was wonderful for Durer, or Persian miniatures. Sometimes I felt like a Persian miniature. I placed the glass between the underside of my genitals and my mirror. I could see nothing. Then I decided there was not enough light in my tiny john to see much.

I took a towel, the mirror, and the looking glass and brought the whole thing over to my bed. There was more light there from a barred back window and I had a good light for reading. The bed was in disarray. I had not made it from the night before. I rarely made my bed. It was a prerogative, I thought, of my adulthood. Now that I no longer lived "at home," I did not have to make up my bed. As if the place where I lived was not *my* home. But then, what was it? Maybe it was like my life: just some temporary arrangement that led to…

The magnifying glass, directed at the mirror, showed it. This minute incision, like a razor cut, very neat, into the thin, dimply-skinned sac of my scrotum. Nothing like a bite, just a perfect little cut—you could see it between the roots of two hairs, that now looked like slightly dark, beige bamboo shoots. I touched the place, and felt this irritating, stinging wince of pain. Where did it come from? How could something so small, so precise, cause this kind of reaction?

I cupped my testicles in both of my hands. My hands were now shaking and I started to stroke the skin to relieve the pain. I was crying. Mostly from this awful fear that I had fallen into something … ugly. I released my balls. They rested on my white sheets. I should have washed the sheets; a tiny amount of what they call "pre-cum" came out of me.

That produced an unexpected swath of relief. I could not be so damaged. I was still "pre-cumming"; right? I relaxed, then I saw Powars's cunning, almost adorable face smiling at me. The immense flush of his smile overwhelmed every cell of being I had: I could not bear it. What was he doing there, in some remote corner of my brain? The pain, regardless of my pre-cum; he was taking *something* out of me—but what was he offering me in return? That flood of release, peace; satisfaction…the great, terrifying "whatever" (?). I began to tremble. This—charlatan. I felt welded to him, and didn't want to be.

Not at all! I took the magnifying glass and looked again. Deeper.

Harder. Then I dug my thumb hard into the location where the incision was: I had to. I had to feel what was happening. He was taking something out of me—and doing what? *What?* The immediate sensation was like the steel point of a long, slightly flexible straight pin, scraping back and forth over the entire sole of my left foot.

My own small left foot. Back and forth. The pain felt—as I rocked through it—almost ecstatic. It was so sharp, intense, and centralized that I started to laugh. It was like receiving a tickle in the worst way. You laugh until you shriek!

I closed my eyes, just to feel it without any visual interference. I pressed down again on it—and held my breath. That cold, stabbing nerve sensation, that started at my left sole, raced up my leg. It went straight up the thigh, then right into my heart—my chest—and back down again, directly into the groin. It stayed there for a moment, inside my testicles. My legs felt numb, paralyzed.

Both of them. The pain vibrated in me—there was no longer that peaceful, orgasmic (okay, you dope! "cosmic") relief. No, this was awful! This was full scale agony…what the hell had he done to me?

I started shrieking: "*God! God! God!*" The hand mirror exploded against the wall of my room—I'd thrown it spastically. I was no longer in control. That sound. CWwww! … then splinters of glass from the crash. I had to control myself. Get up. I knew it. Just to see that I could. I felt weak; uncertain. I wanted to call someone, but who? No one would believe this, and what was it? Should I see a doctor? Some kind of urologist, dick-doctor? And tell him what?

I looked down at the floor, to spot the splinters. They looked like diamonds and cast their reflections all over the walls. The bright reflections swam about me and I saw some of them on my arms, like a passing school of tiny silvery fish traveling up the stream of my body. They were reflecting light and my own anxious state … I eased myself off the bed. My legs no longer rang with pain, maybe the pain was all in my head: total anxiety. Pure and simple. I had a pair of rubber flip-flops close by; I managed to get to them. I had a task to do: I was going to do it and just forget about the pain. Or the discovery of what I had seen on my scrotum.

I made myself breathe again slowly. And swept up the glittering shards of broken mirror and put them in a big plastic sack from the Jefferson Market on Sixth Avenue. I liked to splurge and go there sometimes and buy a take-home dinner. I'd rent a movie and eat good for the night. It was cozy; it was the New York way now, as well as, I was sure, most of the country. You lived in the regular, routine misery of yourself, with some expensive intermittent delights if you had the money. I took a couple of extra-strength Tylenol, changed the sheets on my bed, made it up as neatly as I could, and then relaxed.

The sun was down. It was getting close to eight. I had not given Karl my telephone number, and I did not know anything about the strange Mr. Powars. But he was the only one who could answer the questions I had in my mind. I got up and shaved carefully at the mirror in my bathroom. I felt unexpectedly handsome. Slightly "wounded," tired, but handsome. Truly. It was Sunday and I had been invited out for dinner. I got dressed in a pair of dark khakis, one of my nicer shirts from a plastic sleeve, a presentable striped tie, and good shoes. I put on a V-necked sleeveless sweater and a sports jacket. That seemed right. It was from a discount store, but a nice herringbone tweed. I thought: without a lot of difficult questions, I could pass muster as someone of substance.

It was raining, just slightly, but windy when I got downstairs. My building has a stoop, and I stood on it and looked out. It was a dismal night. A man came up to me. He was in his fifties, neatly but not expensively dressed, in need of a shave. He wore a dark driver's cap. "Mr. Barrow?" he asked.

I nodded.

"This way, please. Mr. Powars is waiting for you in the car."

I went with him down about a quarter of a block. The car was big and dark. That's what I remember first. Big, polished, black. This shining, quiet, luxurious presence that both threatened and promised. It reminded me of big, dark Cuban cigars, those aromatic phalluses that made Wall Street men, masters of capitalism, smile when they lit up. The driver opened the back door for me.

There was a small reading light and a *Wall Street Journal* was wide open. The *Journal* snapped closed. He looked up at me. He needed a shave. He smiled. The reading light hit his teeth. They sparkled with this diamond quality, like the bright reflections from the mica on ocean beach sidewalks in the moonlight. I'd seen those reflections once. Years ago, in Miami. Now I could see the delicious, beard-stippled dimples on his face. His eyes, brown with that lavish infusion of gold in them, lit up as he looked at me. "Hi. Glad you could do this. I wanna take you someplace fun. Okay?"

FOUR

He was wearing

a leather suit, but not what you'd think. No garden variety S & M gear. No, this was gorgeously, artfully tailored. Beautifully cut, black leather pants whose side pockets flared out deftly, like a well-cut English suit would; with a fetally soft, anthracite-black, leather sports jacket, to match. The jacket draped fluidly, like another skin. It made my herringbone tweed look like a piece of dreck from the Salvation Army. His was maybe Armani; who knows? With it he wore a simple, very fine, white cotton T-shirt; its simplicity, I realized, only called attention to its expense.

"You look good," he said. He kept smiling at me. But the smile had a funny quality. It was stiff. "I didn't want you to get so dolled up, but you look good. Hey, y'know, it's good you could do this. I thought we'd just go and have some fun. Kick back maybe. Know what I mean?"

I nodded. I did not know what he meant. At all.

He pulled me to him. It started to rain more outside, but next to him I felt this incredible security and the headiness of his smell—his leather, his muscular skin; the subtle, spicy cologne that he wore that I could not place—I'd never smelled anything like it—and then the smell of the car: clean, marshmallow-soft leather; gleaming polished wood; his breath, that scotchiness with a slight, distant hint of garlic, maybe. Something in his mouth, something in him. I wanted to fall all over him. What could I say? He kissed me. His cheeks slightly scraped me. I loved their slight bristle. I felt overwhelmed and yet definitely, sadly, awfully apprehensive. "You like me, don't you?" he said.

I nodded.

He pressed my crotch, then rubbed the khaki. "I like that," he said in a low voice. "I wanna take you away. Wouldja let me?"

I tried to smile. "Where?"

"Why ask? When you trust someone, you don't ask questions. You're like me: I know it. You're gonna trust me, Allen. You're gonna give me everything. Please, I'm asking you, will you?"

"But I don't have anything," I protested.

The rain got harder, and the car glided through it like a black swan. I felt like I was no longer in New York. I was in another place, one of those places you read about in the "Style" section of the *Times*, where people are beautiful and life is effortless and no one ever thinks about the right-hand side of the menu, where the hard prices wait with a coy wink. He pulled me to him and started kissing my neck. His tongue rolled over my Adam's apple and he softly sucked on it. This little arpeggio of coolness rolled down the nerves of my spine. My neck prickled as he sucked delicately at me, then bit lightly, creasing the skin. Yes, I thought, I will give him everything ... but what does he really want?

The car was now on the East Side and we were going all the way up Madison Avenue. The temperature in it was perfect, not a drop lower or higher than comfortable. I heard the driver's voice ask, "The same place, Mr. Powars?"

"Yeah," he said, drawing away from me. "Y'know, my club!" he started laughing. "Wait'll you see this place. It's such a hoot! It's called Toyland. It's fun. Just like the song, 'Toyland, Toyland, little girl and boy land!'—I take guys from Europe there all the time. Europe. South America. Hong Kong. You won't believe it. They got good steaks, too. Wait'll you taste 'em."

37

The car stopped in front of an anonymous commercial building on a side street off Madison, somewhere in the blocks above Central Park, in a neighborhood of bodegas, take-out joints with flickering signs in Spanish, housing projects, and tenements. It was dark, wet, with big cars around, looking like sullen whales at a feeding ground. The driver parked, then got out with a large black umbrella to open the door for us.

"Thanks, Winchell," Powars said. "I'll call you when we're through. Go get yourself a pizza or something. Just don't get out of range, okay?"

"You got protection?" Winchell said in the rain.

"You think I'm gonna carry protection in there? You think I'm nuts?" He smiled coyly. "Sure, I got it."

He opened his jacket and I could see a slight budge in it, hardly bigger than a child's hand. I swallowed hard. Winchell escorted us with his umbrella to a canopy, where a group of doormen, dark-skinned with very dark glasses waited. A small sign with discreet white letters said, "Private Club." I wondered how the doormen could see anything, but they smiled at Destry Powars and then ignored me, like I was just a little tail that had been attached as an afterthought to a powerful dog. As soon as the black door began to open, Winchell disappeared. I looked out into the rain as the big car turned and neatly cut a slice of water in its wake.

"You're gonna like this place, Allen," Powars promised me. "It ain't got the kind of stuff you probably dig, but once you get into it, you're gonna think it's—"

Inside, it was very loud; we were in a huge room filled with tall poles and suspended catwalks and almost naked women. About a dozen of them were either strutting on the walks or churning around the poles. They were dancing, gyrating, bending way over, bouncing up and down, or were on the floor. Some were crawling around down there, or kneeling. Men would pet them like dogs, and stick wads of bills into their bikini bottoms. The women wore pasties over their nipples, but sometimes even those were transparent. "They keep trying to clean this place up. The girls used to be—well, you could see everything. Pussy, the whole thing. But now it's a bit more wholesome." He laughed.

"How you doin', Mr. Powars?" A big man with a tiny, smooth, dark olive complected face, wearing a baggy Italian-style suit that still looked like a stuffed duffel bag on him, approached. "Nice outfit you got on tonight. It's—" The big man placed his forefingers and thumbs together to form neat little circles. I noticed that his small hands had several large rings on them. His bejeweled pinkies were extended. He could not quite find the words.

"Thanks, Baby. Allen, this is Baby Zoula. He runs the place. Baby and I go *back*—not a lot go back, but, hey, nowadays, you know, go back can mean something like a year. I love you, Baby. You got a good crowd tonight."

Baby beamed and rocked on his heels as he spoke. "Sunday here is good for us. Nobody likes t'leggo of the weekend. The Wall Street dudes, they gotta work their butts off, so they wanna come up here, eat good, drink good, have some fun. Some action, maybe. A guy needs his right t'do that, don'cha think? The guvment always wants to watch ya ass. But a man's gotta have that right, ya know?"

"Sure," Powars said seriously. "I booked a table. Is it ready?'

Baby led us into an adjacent dining room. It was low-ceilinged and intimate and smelled of thick cigars from a bar and hefty, char-broiled steaks from the kitchen. We sat down at a table on the side that seemed to have been made for the two of us, or three of us. I noticed there was an empty chair. We had menus, but Powars ordered for us. Two large rare Angus steaks, baked Idahos, salads, blue cheese dressing. He ordered a single malt scotch for himself and I had a red vermouth with a twist. The drinks came. They looked as if each should have had a couple of goldfish swimming in it, they were so big. Along with the drinks, and later the food, came a line of girls. They would come up and smile, and ask if they could sit down. Powars would pat them and kiss them, feel them up a bit, give them a squeeze, then they'd leave after being tipped.

He cut into his steak and forked off a big red chunk of it that he stuffed into his mouth, while drinking scotch and talking. "I love women," he said, swallowing.

"You do?"

"Sure. Who doesn't? They're fun. They never ask as much from you as guys. You give 'em a little squeeze and a hug and they're happy. I mean I could fuck 'em, but no girl wants to get fucked if she can get the dough without getting fucked. That's a universal law, don'chu think, with girls."

I shrugged my shoulders, and then ate some of the steak. It was actually very good, but why not? The place was expensive, despite its location and the sleaze factor. But expense and sleaze seem to go together now. I tried to smile at him and not hear a word he said. The cigar smoke was bothering me. I wanted to get the hell out. I hated the way he talked about women. It upset me. Did he talk about me that way?

Suddenly, a tall, drop-dead gorgeous young woman breezed up to us. She looked like she'd popped out of some big Las Vegas revue (all sequins, ostrich feathers, and bleached, beefy gay boys who do magic) and had very dark black skin that shimmered with a tawny-red North African glow. She had long, perfect legs, like a dancer, and perfect breasts, too. They reminded me of lustrous little crème brulées, but black-licorice flavored. I could imagine them glistening, standing up neatly by themselves, on white French café saucers.

Her little nipples, like candy flower buds, peeked out of the narrow silver halter top she wore. She had on a black leather microskirt—and had amazing hair. It cascaded down her sylphic neck to her shoulders. It was sable-black with real, sparkling highlights, like something Diana Ross would have envied. In Miss Ross's photos, her hair always looked too chemical, but this wasn't. She was young and fetching. Okay, she fetched me. She shot a porcelain-white smile at Powars. "Bambino! *Comè sta?*"

"I'm good," he said. "How 'bout you, Felicia? You're the prettiest girl in the world. Allen, this is Felicia, the Queen of Sheba. I mean it. She's African. And from Italy, too. She's from all over the darn world. She's special, really!"

40   "*Tu è kind*, bambino." She made little kissing noises as she spoke, stringing her consonants together so that they became extra hard. "*Noi faciamo bella*," she cooed. "I leev once in Rome. I make friends weeth a nice Ee-

talian count!" She giggled and ran her long fingers through her hair, like she was untangling wet spaghetti. Her supple neck seemed to have about fourteen vertebrae in it, and she had gorgeous wide shoulders, like a channel swimmer. Okay, she was boyish, but also girlish. She had a tiny purse. She took out a mirror about as big as a teaspoon and looked at herself. Destry watched, mesmerized. He winked, all grizzled dimples, at me.

She smiled at her reflected face. Her large, almond-shaped eyes were outlined in lapis blue. When she smiled, her face lit up; the light extended all the way to the ends of her hair. Baby Zoula came up to us. "Hi you, boys? Is Feleesh givin' you a good time?"

"Baby, she's my girl," Powars said. "I could eat her pussy right here."

Felicia pretended to be embarrased. "Bambino, *tu è bad!*" she pouted. She demurely dropped her mirror into her purse, then covered her face with her slender fingers.

"You want your private space, Mr. Powars? I could arrange that. You know we allow the lap dancin' and stuff like that all out at the bar, but we got our private spaces. You'd like that, right?"

"Sure."

"You want any other entertainment for your friend?"

Destry Powars looked at me. His eyes twinkled. "I told you you'd have fun here."

"I'm okay," I said. "I'll just—"

"He'll come with us!" Powars insisted, when what I'd wanted to say was that I'd just leave. I was out of my depths. The money. The cigars. The sleaze. Of course, was it any different from God-knows-what on Christopher Street, or in Chelsea? Here it was straight men with too much money. There it was gay boys with too much time. I looked at Felicia, and she looked at me and then winked. She smiled as if we had a secret together, just the two of us.

Her long fingers ventured to my face. She brushed my nose coyly. "I know what you want, bambino. I do." 41

I felt the color rising to my cheeks. "You do?"

"Sure, Baby," she turned to Zoula and said dryly. "The three of us are gonna go up t' have some fun. Just let us have Room B and shut the door for 'bout a hour. Okay?"

Room B was on a floor directly above the action. We saw other men walking through the hallway, with girls from the floor or the catwalks. The men had their shirts unbuttoned and their ties tossed anywhere around their necks or over their shoulders. They looked like young football players or firemen. It was a look that I had seen enough. It was hot, really. Kind of brain-dead but raptorial, like they'd eat anything once they were hungry enough. The girls smiled broadly but looked hollow, their tits inflated like giant Macy's balloons at Thanksgiving. I did not feel quite so nervous now. I'd been really anxious before, following the three of them with Baby strutting ahead at the lead. Felicia turned back and playfully took one of my hands, then Powars grabbed the other. I decided then that, no matter what, I could at least make the decision to turn around and … suddenly Baby stopped and, very ceremoniously, let us in. I looked around.

The room was a dump. Kind of like something at the baths, but even more drab. These men, the customers, were not into décor. It was just a cot, a sink and a chair. I'd expected better, but I guess everything was kind of fly-by-night, despite the river of instant money Toyland floated on. Now I felt strangely deflated. Not nervous, like I said, just disappointed. I felt oddly sad for Felicia, and wondered what sort of person she really was.

She smiled at me. "Bambino, we're gonna have such a nice time. Three can be *molto* fun, you know." She shot a look at Mr. Zoula, whose fat beringed fingers were clasped in front of him. "*Ciao*, Baby. We'll see you in the bye-'n'-bye."

"Sure, Feleesh. Hey, Destry, you want anything, you just gimme a toodle." He let out a big grin. "You got my cell number?"

42   "Sure, Baby," Powars said, smiling and nodding. "I got it. How 'bout some scotch? You got that Glen Harris, Glen Campbell, Glen-whatzit-called?"

"You mean Glenfiddich? Yeah, we got it. You wanna bottle?"

"Sure," he answered. "And send up a lotta ice." He looked at me seriously. "You want water?"

I shrugged my shoulders.

"Bring 'im some water, too," Powars ordered. "I don't know why people need the water—" Baby Zoula disappeared. We were alone now; there was almost no light in the room. Felicia unsnapped her halter from the back. She did have beautiful breasts. Each one would have filled up a crystal champagne glass, with their tiny little candy nipples at the top. She had this lovely fresh darkness to her. I could see why men must have gone crazy over her.

She sat on the edge of the cot, and closed her eyes, then reopened them. The delicately drawn blue around them, then the liquid darkness within, pulled you in intensely. She was shiny, exotic, elegant; like a jewel-encrusted pin I had seen once in a window at Tiffany's in the form of a crawling lizard. Yes, she was reptilian; but in a hard, glittering, jewel-like way.

Powars came to her immediately, running his hands over her breasts, kneeling, putting her girlish, button-like nipples into his mouth. I could hear his mouth softly sucking and her sighs. "Ohhh, Bambino, *facia bella*. You are somethin'...."

He turned to me. "You should try this."

I was off to one side, just watching. I could not figure out what was going on, or, frankly, why was I there.

"Get more comfy, Bambino," she suggested to him. He looked at me for a moment, then smiled. "Sure," he said. He got up and took off his soft leather jacket, then his expensive T-shirt. He looked all satyr now, all big shoulders, hairy chest, and big arms. I watched and knew my eyes were glowing. I desired him so much, yet everything about him threatened me. He continued smiling, then approached me and ran his fingers through my hair.

43

"I told you this is fun, Allen." He got to a chair and removed his expensive shoes and socks and then unbuckled and pulled off his beautifully cut leather pants. He was wearing only bright, fire-engine red bikini underwear. Kind of like a thong, a jockstrap, something out of a splashy California men's catalogue. It looked lurid next to his hairy thighs. His cock was curled up in it, like a jungle snake rearing to uncoil. His feet were big, with those oyster-shell thick, gray toenails; kind of bestial, really. Without his elegant clothes, he was a different thing. A beast, yes. Some apparition out of a swamp, a …

"You're so cute," Felicia cooed to him. "I never met a guy who looked like you."

He went up to her and bent over and kissed her. She was still on the bed. She pulled the red bikini briefs down, then got it off him. He was now naked, and shamelessly erect. She played with his big dick, licking it with her tongue, getting her tongue down into his balls. She turned him around, and kissed his hairy, muscular ass. "I never met a girl like you, either," he said, his voice low. "Hey, Allen, I want you to see what Felicia's got."

"Oh, Bambino, it ain't nothin' that nobody else ain't got," she said, dropping the coy Euro breathiness along with her unzipped leather microskirt. Powars dug his fingers into her small pink pantie; she squirmed and kissed him, then he fished out her dick.

It had, somehow, been tucked in there, and once it came out it was actually bigger than mine. Not a lot bigger, I thought, but bigger, anyway—despite the hormones that I was sure she was taking. He pulled the briefs off her, then went down on her, sinking his face into her pubic hairs. She cooed and gurgled, then did the same thing to him, sucking him expertly. I just watched now, like you would a show or a movie, or something on the sidewalk at Times Square, something you could not avoid but did not know what to make of. Once by accident I had seen a man who'd been stabbed in the arm and people just watched. The guy ran away, and the man lay on the sidewalk, bleeding, despite cops all around him, waiting for the EMS medics. He was not going to die, but the blood was there, and people simply watched.

She was still working on him when there was a discreet knock at the door. Powars motioned for me to go to it, since I was still completely dressed. A tall blond waitress brought in a black lacquered tray with a new bottle of Glenfiddich, three high ball glasses, a small crystal water pitcher, and an ice bucket. She presented me with a bill, and I signed it using Powars's name. She looked into the room. She smiled blankly, kind of like an Avon lady, then left.

I went back in.

Felicia got back up and smiled at me. She walked around now, naked except for a pair of pink patent-leather sling-back heels. I looked down at them. They made a kind of glow in the dark room. Strangely, her cock, demurely half-hidden in the black sparkle between her slender thighs, did not seem out of place with the heels. It just seemed like another part of the show. She went to her purse and pulled out her compact and redid her lips with some transparent gloss. She put a little on her cheekbones as well. She was beautiful. Black as Sheba, but not a queen, at least in that way.

"Open that for us, Allen," Powars said. I cracked open the seal on the bottle, and poured out ice and scotch for him. I made one for myself with water in it.

"I'll have a teeny one," Felicia said. "I can't work on the job, you know." She took Powars's cock in her hand, as he drank crisply from the scotch. "That's something you don't have, bambino. A teeny one!"

"Allen, you heard her. Give Miss Felicia a small one. She's quite a lady, isn't she, dick and all?"

She giggled and ran her fingers through the hair on his chest. "Dick. Clit. The nice thing about this place is that there are guys here who don't care what you've got, as long as you know just what to do with 'em. I get some of these guys. Macho, married, Wall Street. The first time they see it *boing*! Then they can't wait to get their mouths on it, just like you, bambino. Your friend, though, I think he's more uptight than some of the straight dudes. Are you that afraid of my surprise?"

I looked at her ...Yeah, she was right. I was kind of put off. Right over the edge, you could say. I'd been a garden-variety queer all my life, the type who hung out with polite young men who talked about their jobs and their mothers and now here I was—in this weird place. I knew that New York offered everything for a price, so I guess this made sense.

Destry looked sympathetically at me. "Why not get comfy, Allen?"

"Because I don't feel 'comfy'!"—I was about ready to crack right then. "Maybe I should just leave."

He got up and approached me. He was bigger than I and his raw hairy nakedness jumped out at me, especially with Felicia waiting behind him. All I felt was threatened and all I wanted to do was get to the door. I started for it. He stopped me and pulled my tie out from the sweater, and then pulled the tweed jacket off me. He threw the jacket down on the floor, then began to rip at my tie until it hurt. It was choking me. "Where would you go?" he demanded.

"To my place," I said. "I don't need this. It's just too—" I looked on the floor and then kneeled down to pick up my jacket. It was cheap, but he had treated it like garbage. Then I felt this sharp blow to my face. He had slapped me hard. The room rang around me, as if a bell inside my head had gone off.

"You think you can just leave—like everything I do is bullshit?" I hated him. I managed to lift my head up and look into his face. I really hated him. He turned from me. "Felicia honey, let us alone for a while, okay? Tell Baby I'll be right back down there and settle up the bill."

She smiled coldly. I glanced quickly at her. I hurt for her; I hurt for me, too. "Is that what you want, Bambino?" Powars nodded his head. She lifted her handsome shoulders, then dropped them. "Something tol' me you two *ragazzis* were cooler with each other than with I."

He took some of the water and swallowed it. "That ain't it, Felicia. But you know, real smart people *know* just when not to wear out their welcome."

"That so?" She crossed her arms in front of her, they glowed like polished ebony. "Shit! I see. Well, nobody tol' me I had any welcome!" She laughed bitterly. I clenched my jacket in my hands. I could not look directly at either of them. My head throbbed. Out of the corner of my eye, I saw

Felicia quickly slip her silver halter back on. Then she looped her panties over her heels, then pulled up her microskirt. She zipped it closed. "No sweat, honey. When you're tired of playing with him, I'll come back up."

"Sure," Powars whispered. "I'll let you know."

I heard the door close, then put my jacket back on. I tried to ease my tie back into place.

"I just wanted to show you something," Powars said, his head turned from me. "Why don't you just take your clothes off? I'll make love to you right here."

"No." I felt hurt all over. I started for the door.

He turned to me, grinning shyly. "Okay. So, you don't like black beauties with dicks." He broke into a big smile. "Lighten up. 'Life's a cabaret, old chum!'"

"Think so?" I looked at him. He was still smiling. "What do you want from me, Destry? I have nothing to offer you. I just want to get the hell out. I'm not like this, I'm—"

I wanted to say that I was in love with him. Right there. That was the truth. It was the rotten-shit, awful truth: I hated it. I felt humiliated. Overpowered. How had I stumbled into such stupidity? I didn't admire him, I didn't envy his stake in life, even as glamorous as it seemed. Then I saw what was going on. I could not turn away. No. I could barely believe it. It was stupid. He was crying horribly.

I could see it. He had crumpled to my feet and he started kissing the ridiculous cuffs of my pants. They were just khakis from the Gap. How could he be doing this? He made this sound like a beaten dog. I hated it. I hated hearing it. I would rather he just slapped me again and again. It was better when he slapped me. I had to say something. "Do you want some more of the scotch?" I whispered.

He did not answer. He went over to the cot in this room that seemed more like a prison cell. He slumped himself down on it, face down, covering his face with his big hands. His back, covered with hair that looked dark now, like a dog's, jerked with spasms of remorse, of choked and then 47 released tears, as they shot through him.

I hated it. I hated that sound. To me it was worse than the snap of a belt. There was a knock at the door. I heard Baby Zoula's voice. "Hey man, you guys all right there? Feleesh is waitin' for you."

I went over. "We're fine," I said. "We'll have some more of the scotch and then come down."

I joined him back at the cot. I took my tie off and then my jacket. I stroked his back and then took my shirt off. I don't know what happened, but I started crying, too. "Why'd you say that?" he said to me, his face still buried in his arms. "I'm a piece of shit. I have to keep relearning what I am. That's all. I want to eat you. I'm powerless with you. You just don't know how much. Please see it. Would you, please?"

I nodded my head, though he could not see me. "I'll try to see it," I said. That was all I could say.

I took off the rest of my clothes and then joined him as fast as I could.

FIVE

He was covering my face

with his mouth, sucking the very air out of my lungs. "I want to worship you," he whispered. "I want to offer you everything."

"Why?"

"You can see inside me. I think. Maybe. I don't know. But I need you. I mean it. You don't know what loneliness is, when you can never be what you really are."

I was puzzled. Completely. He was this odd mystery. Fatal, maybe. I felt like I had fallen into a trap, but who had set it? I—"I have nothing," I said to him. "You're a winner. The world likes winners. Look at the way they act towards you here. What have I got?"

He ran his mouth over me, covering my bare chest—pale, hairless— with adoration. I ran my fingers through the fine tendrils on his chest and his shoulders and then into the thick rushes of dark hair on his head. He lapped at me, softly sucking at me, making this noise like birds eating, like seagulls or hungry cats. It was eerie. I had never heard any human make such a sound.

Then, that strange feeling on my testicles again. It came. He was down there, and I could feel the skin make this little pop as he sucked the fine membrane into his mouth and his teeth—more like a straight pin, like a ... I can only say, a very deft fang—opened it. The sensation at first was kind of ... ingratiating. What else can I say? It was warm and oozy and,

49

oddly, seductive. "Like a patient etherised upon a table," Eliot says in Prufrock's famous love song: that was how I felt. Passive, enraptured. He was doing this to me: this big man with the ungainly animal feet and the hair all over him, and the shoulders like a NFL player and the big chest—and I dug my hands into it, stroking his chest, doubling about so that I could knead his shoulders and stroke his head as he did this.

Yes, until the sensation became arched with pain. Lurid, furious pain shot out of me. My balls were on fire. I had to push my fist into my mouth to keep from screaming. I knew now what I had to do. I doubled as much as I could on the narrow cheap cot, and pulled his cock down into my throat and sucked him as he ate at me, like a rapturous animal, his dick so hard and big that I could barely handle it. It was like sucking a bull, the taste as gamy and male and forbidden.

I was now not even hard. I couldn't get hard. I could not tell if it were just my old problem, getting hard when I needed it, or it was what he was doing to me. But there was blood, I knew, down my leg. He came into my mouth, like a river engorged by a storm, then eased away from me. "Thank you," he said. He got up and took the Glenfiddich and started drinking it straight from the bottle. He pulled me to him. "Want some?"

I nodded, and he took some and then spit it directly into my mouth. I was delighted; really, just suddenly crazy. Never had I done *anything* like that before, and I held the warm, kind of honeyed bubbliness in my mouth and then swallowed it, so that it took some of the sharp, zincy flavor of his cum away. I smiled and suddenly belched. He did it again and again, until between the two of us, we'd finished a lot of the bottle. Since I, very sensibly, hardly drink, I felt stupidly close to drunk.

"Let me clean you up," he offered. He took the water from the pitcher and found a towel and dabbed the blood from my leg. There wasn't much really. I don't know why I had thought there was—hysteria, sure. I was just a bit nauseated. I was not used to huge steaks and way, way too much expensive scotch, and ... all of this.

He sat up on the bed then, his knees pulled up to his big chest. I sat

50

next to him, then crawled between his knees. I put my fingers behind me, on his strange toes. I sighed.

"Why are you doing this to me?" I asked. "I have to know, what have you done?"

"If you don't like it, you can leave," he said. He was now at rest. He had his arms around me from behind. It was a lie. I was trapped, held, willing or not. Leave? Impossible.

I turned my head to him. "You know I can't leave."

We now faced one another, intertwining legs, arms. He kissed me, sucking the soul right out of me. "Good. Let's get dressed. I'll pay these stupid shits, and we'll go someplace else. Do you like the Box? It's a leather place downtown. I'll talk to you there."

He jumped off the cot and put his clothes on, but told me to stay where I was. He would dress me, he said. He put on his expensive T, the red briefs, the pants, his socks and shoes, then lifted me off the bed. He sat back on the cot and examined my groin. Gently he lifted my testicles up. The odd pain of it; the strange, drained feeling I had from there—this was real. I knew it. He kissed my small cock reverently.

"You're the most beautiful flower," he said. "I knew it the moment I saw you. You make me tremble. For real. I love you."

He started to dress me like a child, putting my white Fruit of the Loom briefs on, leg by leg. Being very careful with me. Then opening the khaki pants for me as if I could not do this myself. He helped me with the shirt and buttoned it for me, then tied the tie for me. "I want you to wear my jacket," he said. "I don't need it." He tossed my jacket away. "Leave this shit here; I'll get you more clothes. I want you to like me. Will you? We'll go to the Box."

We left the room and went down into the raucous club with all the men from Wall Street and the girls. Baby met us. "What happened to you guys up there?" he asked, concerned.

"My friend got a stomach problem. Too much steak and scotch. You know how some guys are—wussies at heart, right?" He winked at Zoula and then me. I nodded. The room was starting to do this funny wobble.

Baby winked back. "No problem. We get guys who do all sorts of things in here. But that's what we're here for. We make friends and keep 'em, right? What'd you think about Feleesh? She's special, ain't she?"

"She sure is," Powars said, twinkling, his eyes slightly glazed. "She's my kinda girl."

"Thought so," Baby said. We were now at the bar. He handed him a bill, and Powars signed for it. There were men all around us. They had this funny way of looking at you and not looking at you at the same time. They were wearing expensive Madison Avenue clothes, with all those little tell-tale things to let you know that they had money. A flash of alligator belt; Swiss watches; the gleaming white stars of Mont Blanc pens. I felt like I'd worked around these men all my life. They always seemed older than I was, no matter what age they were. I had to go pee. I told Powars I needed to be excused. Felicia came up and started nuzzling him. She was followed by a very fat-hipped man in another dark suit, who looked like he had no balls but a lot of money.

"Honey," he said. "You're the prettiest little black thing I ever seen."

She smiled. "*Grazi*, Bambino. You wanna go *facia bella*."

"What does that mean, honey? I'm from Texas. I only know one language." He winked.

"It means have a good time in Italian. Make pretty. Make nice, y'know?"

"Sure, honey," he said. "But I told you, I only know one language."

"That's all right," she cooed. "I know it, too."

I found the men's room. Like the private rooms upstairs, it was ugly and utilitarian, with big, open stand-up urinals. No matter what Toyland thought of it's "friends," the customers, it had certainly stinted on the men's room. But then, what were men anyway, when you got down to it? Here men were just dollar bills, right? I stood up and peed. I admit, I liked the kind of numb, drunk little feeling I had.

At first, a slight bit of blood came out in my urine, then it was clear. I smiled. So what? Nothing hurt, at least then, right now. I was wearing Powars's beautiful, expensive black leather jacket—it was too big, but it felt immediately right. One of the young, very beefy NFL-looking Wall Street types came up next to me to pee. Very ceremoniously he managed his cock out, then pitched himself back so that this thick instrument was directly in my view and let go a stream. "Beer," he said. "I really needed this."

I smiled, but not at him.

"These girls can give you a nice blow job," he said. "But, y'know, it takes a man to know how to do it."

I nodded. Zipped myself up, then said, "You're right."

"Yeah?"

I stepped back from the urinals. "Yeah," I said, putting on the kind of quasi-threatening, deep, offhand voice he had. "You can blow me any time you'd like."

I did a quick, hundred-and-eighty-degree turn, then left. I was now back out in the action. Baby Zoula saw me and nodded to me and pointed to the door. There was Powars, waiting. We walked out. It was now pouring even more, but Winchell was there, again with his big umbrella. "We're going to the Box," Powars said to Winchell, as the driver escorted the two of us to the back of the car.

Inside, the reading light on, I saw that Powars's T was wetter than expected. He stripped it off and put another on. "I always keep extra clothes here," he said. He had another leather jacket and he put it on, too. This one was more motorcycle than Madison Avenue. We headed downtown in the rain. "Did you have a good night?" he asked Winchell.

"Yes, sir," the driver said. "How was the club?"

"Good. It was a lotta fun, but we had enough for the night." He turned on a small TV and looked at the stock ticker reports on a news channel. He leafed through some newspapers, as if I weren't there. I got pissed and flicked off the TV and took the newspaper away from him.

53

"Some man in the men's room," I laughed suddenly, "made an improper advance at me."

"Sure. Happens all the time. They get tanked and want a blow job. Every straight man wants it. They wanna man to do it. Or they wanna do him. They'll suck your dick. Just don't ever remind 'em of it. That's why I like that place. They get a chick like Feleesh in there and they go nuts. You know, a chick with a dick? She's so pretty. Nice personality, too. I should have her up to the house sometime, but I don't like to mix my personal life with that kind of stuff."

He was inscrutable to me. He turned the TV back on, but with the sound off. He just watched the ticker, then cut off the reading light and pulled me to him and kissed me. His mouth tasted really wonderful, like it had some essence in it that overpowered me. It was not simply the garlicky, steaky, scotchy flavor, but the way his whole juices ran through me. I cupped his face to mine, the slight bristle of his cheeks pressing into my palms. He loosened my tie and unbuttoned my shirt, then started sucking my right nipple. He stopped. "You ain't looking right for the Box," he noticed. I wasn't.

"Take the shirt off," he said. I did. "Now, if you just wear this jacket"—he meant his, the leather blazer—"the khakis don't make it, but don't worry. We ain't gonna be there that long." He called up to the driver. "Winchell. We're just gonna have one drink at the Box, then we're gonna go home. Okay?"

"Sure, sir," he said.

The rain had stopped when we got out on West Street, off Twelfth. I had not been to the Box in years. I find S & M people too—well, they're either for real and too frightening, or just for show and too ridiculous. I guess Toyland was not a whole lot different, except that the underpinning of violence there was for real; thus Powars's taking "protection" with him. He must have forgotten about it. Suddenly I realized it was in the pocket of the jacket he'd given me. Just before we got in the door of the bar, I fished out the small black revolver and handed it to him.

"Put that thing away," he ordered. "It's licensed. I'm not stupid. Just keep it, okay? And keep your mouth shut about it."

I smiled. The strange Mr. Powars could be funny at times, I thought. Inside the Box we went through a series of dim little corridors, then into the main bar. It was really dark with little pins of light poking through it. And also full-blast loud; throbbing with house dance music and crowded with men in full leather. I recognized some of them—men I'd known by sight, like extras in the film of my own gay life. They were there, but they had almost no real part. I guess that's a function of belonging to this diverse community. It becomes like a small, even reassuring village within the anonymous tension of the city. All these people entering and leaving and not actually seeing each other; then I go to the Box and see familiar but unnamable faces, wearing leather outfits that they would not even dream of wearing in daylight on the subway.

"You want a beer or something?" he asked.

I nodded and he went over to the bar. A short thin man came up to me. He could have been me, almost. I mean, he had one of those little jobs that mean nothing now. Like I had. I'd met him at a dating social at the Community Center. He'd been interested in me, but we really had nothing to talk about, and did not seem to get very far at the social. "Hi, Henry," I said to him.

He smiled. He was fairly shy, despite the macho costume he wore: a black leather, state trooper's jacket, with snug, black leather jodhpurs. The jodhpurs' tight crotch emphasized his packed genitals, which stuck out like a squirrel's head from a hollow in a pine tree. He had small, wire-rimmed glasses and a close-cropped head. His face had nice, even features and little teeth. He might have been some kind of forgotten bureaucrat in the Third Reich, or a paper cruncher in one of the back offices at Chase. I admit he had a beautiful chest and large nipples that had been very "worked on." You could see this through the skin-tight gray uniform shirt he wore. His tits were outlined in the fabric.

"I didn't expect to see you here," he said. "I didn't think you went in for this kind of scene."

I looked at him. I wasn't sure what to tell him. "It's nice to see you," I said.

"Nice t'see you." He had a beer in his hand, and then coyly ran it up against my bare chest inside Destry's jacket. "I mean it. Do you play rough?"

I wasn't sure what to say, but I did not have to say anything. Powars came back with two Coronas. He looked at Henry. I introduced them. He did not smile, but just said: "Allen and I came here to talk, so—"

"Sure," Henry said. He looked at me. "I guess that answers my question." He walked away.

"What question?" Powars demanded.

"He wanted to know if I played rough."

Destry laughed. "He doesn't know from rough. Maybe you should have showed him what you have inside your jacket pocket." He laughed really loudly. "It's not like you're glad to see him. At least not with it in that pocket."

"You were rude to him. I don't like rude people, Destry."

"So? I don't like people who barge in on you; who think they can just barge in on your life. That makes us even, right?"

I thanked him for the beer and took a sip. Then I said, very close to his ear, because it was loud in there, "Destry, what *do* you want? I mean it. What are you trying to do to me?"

He shrugged his big shoulders. "Nothing. Why would I want to do something *to* you? I wanna do something *for* you, Allen. I wanna take you to Switzerland with me. I've gotta go in two days. We'll take a night flight to Zurich, first class. Swissair. You ever sleep in first class? It's"—he shrugged his shoulders, he became wordless for a moment, then said, "Great. It's so ... you'll like it. You'll need some clothes, so I'll buy you some. I'll pay for everything."

56

I looked at him. My mouth started to make that "W" sound that ended in "Why?" but did not get that far. I'm sure he could see it.

"You'll like it," he said. "I mean Switzerland. It's nice. Really. The people I work with—they have this thing once a year, and it's—"

Now I did say it. It was hard for me to talk over the music, so I whispered under it. "*Why*—why would you want me there? Why would *they* want me? I mean, why—"

His face became tense and sad, like I'd hurt him. I hated myself. "*Why? Why*—why're you asking questions, Allen? I mean, something like this happens about once in a lifetime. I know about once-in-a-lifetime shit. This could …" He went on talking, but I could hardly hear a word he said above the explosive din of the sound system. I thought he was talking about holding on to his life, or explaining it. His face went through a number of expressions. Kind of desperate; humorous; comically defeated. Then he smiled. He made a few jokes over my head, certainly over my range of hearing; then he did say, seriously, and I heard him: "I'd like your company."

I was quiet. I looked at him: this fascinating, chameleon-like creature. Suddenly the loud music faded. I'd been trained, I think, since childhood to question anything that was just handed to me. I worked with men who grabbed what they could, and then simply watched things fall into their laps: things that they had expected all along, and automatically grabbed for. But I was still trained to—"This is nuts," I said, interrupting my thoughts. "I have a job. Friends. An apartment. You think people can just drop their lives for you?"

He sucked at the long neck of the Corona. Belched a bit, then said, "No. Come on. I'll even pay you if you need the money."

"That's not the problem. I have work, I have—"

"Tell 'em at work that you're having a problem, if you want to. I mean, I'm not asking you to burn all your bridges. Say you need to go do stuff. Take care of a sick mother or something. Most companies will let you do that, right?"

"My mother's dead. Both my parents are dead. Everyone at work knows that. I don't make a lot of money, but I have friends there. We talk to each other."

"Sure. You go out. Have lunch. Spill all of your lima beans, right? All four or five of 'em." He smiled. "I'm going to let you change your life, Allen. Can you take that?" He paused for a moment, then said: "That's what I call a 'flight into change.' Know what I mean? I did that years ago. I had to relearn everything. I told you that. I know I seem funny to you—I can be a real asshole—hey, don't repeat that! But my feelings for you are good. I need you." He took some more beer. "I mean it. Do you have a passport?"

"No," I said. "I *don't* have a passport." The truth was, I'd never been out of the country.

"No problem. I'll get you a visa from the Swiss. They can be real good about these things. I do enough business there. Don't worry about that. Just give me a couple of pieces of identification. I'll get my girl Gwinny on to it."

"Can I think about it?"

"No. You can't *think* about it. Just go, all right?"

I drank some of the beer, then looked around. There were men in leather all around me, milling about, doing their little courtship dances that usually led to almost nothing. Henry was talking to another guy, an older daddy type. Daddy was kissing him, and had his hands in Henry's shirt. Something told me that a minute later, Henry would walk on. Shy as he was, he just wanted the attention. There were guys all around who looked totally professional at being queer. Very comfortable at it: I had never been. It was the only life that made any sense to me, but I had never felt myself to be a real part of it.

"I'll go."

"You're smart. I knew it."

"Why do you keep … hurting my balls?"

He smiled at me. "I'm not hurting you," he answered. "I'm hurting me."

I wondered what he meant. It made no sense to me, then he started kissing my neck. He did that better than anyone I had ever known. Just the lusciousness of his supple mouth on those nerves, on that part of my pale skin. I felt like I was walking into something. A cave on a beach. Or was I the sand on the beach already, and he was the ocean? He reached down and gently sucked my chest, my nipples. Discreetly, I looked up. Henry had left the daddy type and had gone on to someone else. My balls did not hurt anymore. Nothing hurt. The only thing I wanted in the world was now kissing my neck again. He stopped, then finished his beer.

He fucked me that night. I was HIV negative and he told me he was also. I believed him. I was ready. I was ready to take that completely captivating swan dive into ... what? The complete unknowability of another man? The thing that he was, all animal, angel, ape and god? I was enthralled by him, made thrallish, really. He fucked me beautifully, just working at it, I sat on top of his lap with his big dick right up me. I felt lost in him, and he looked at me in his endless dark way that seemed to be all windows, a line of them, each opening slowly then closing behind them, all the way finally towards that ... that last opening.

For a big man, he was supple and he could kiss me in every place, even on my cock, even sucking me some, as he fucked me. The strange thing was that I had a difficult time getting hard. I felt as if there were something missing from me: some final point in the electrical circuit that would do it. Some element within me that, as much as I responded to him—as excited, as totally turned on as I was—I still could not reach that single, out-of-the-way peak where I knew he stood. He was there, standing up, all cock, all dark, raging eyes; all chest and nipples; all savage hair and mouth and teeth.

But I ... I was still not there. I was someplace in my mind where I saw the two of us walking, hand in hand, into some dense, soaring primal forest of male connectedness. There, each animal was totemic. Had wings. And dwelled within us. He was the ancient winged bull from Assyria— and I was the questioning sphinx, the winged lion, sprawled at his feet. But whose head was on me now? More windows opened. Closed. Opened. Closed ... Then one slightly cracked open—

And that was the very last window we call the brain. It was now only snow. Like a TV set with the tube busted. Pure drifting snow. Then I saw Felicia's face, the deep-black, almond-shaped eyes lined in cerulean blue: her face with that grin that was blank and ecstatic at the same time—yes, that face with its cunning, positive expression—was stuck on my head. On my shoulders. I was the sphinx, with Felicia's long swan neck and Ethiopian face. And he came inside me, like a shotgun going off. He leaned back. Flopped; satisfied. I was soft, lost, wandering somewhere outside of Destry Powars's tempestuous desire, waiting, as Felicia had said, for a "welcome."

He fell asleep, the large mass of him, muscle and hair, collapsed there. He looked like one of Picasso's hunky bull-horned Minotaurs with their engorged cornucopia cocks, flush from sex, now in tempting repose. I had been turned on often by these creatures: Picasso is pornographic as hell. He used to masturbate over his own drawings. I had to admire that: you create what turns you on. It may scare you a bit, but doesn't real excitement have a bit of the scare in it? I could see Picasso in his younger (but still approaching middle age), vastly horny incarnation—the one in love with young, blonde, totally *shiksa* Marie Thérèse Walter—drawing these forbidden, erotic images—the virginal girl, the Minotaur ravishing her—then taking out his bronzy, uncut Spanish wee-wee, and, yes, laughing at our Girl Scout-cookie prudery towards sex.

You create it, then you suck it. You taste and lick what you make. Powars had done that to me. He was creating me: the thought was genuinely nauseating, the way birth is. Don't you get morning sickness all the way up to it? Destry nodded his curly head, then smiled in his sleep; he was drooling a bit and snoring. I went into the bath to clean up. It was his bath, but what the hell? I flushed the toilet and finished. He came in. I must have woken him. He seemed so huge and naked. He scratched his dark, hairy butt and farted loudly, half awake. "You wanna shower?" he asked.

We got in together. The shower was large, white and tiled like a steam room, with wonderful fine jets of water. He had a big expensive bar of imported Spanish soap. It was a gay, saucy yellow and smelled of spicy carnations with hints of orange and vanilla. It was like being washed in money. I could imagine handfuls of silver coins being washed down the drain. He soaped me down, getting it all over me, inside my arm pits, on my chest and back. He knelt down and worked the thick, foaming lather through my crotch and into my asshole. He assiduously cleaned my feet, using his big fingers to lather between each toe. He lifted each foot, and patiently massaged my soles.

The water fell down on us like a fine rain. It dispersed the lather. I was clean. He licked at my feet, sucking my toes, then went up to my crotch, and sucked my cock like it was a kid's lollipop. He played with me like I was a plastic doll. I wondered if he had done that before to Felicia at Toyland. I felt small and deliciously passive as this huge, hairy man, Minotaur, beast, destroyer, sucked my small boy-dick. I got hard now. He stuck a finger up my ass, then pulled it out and licked the finger and stuck it back up there. He stopped sucking me, then ate my ass some, just getting his tongue up there. I squirmed from delight. He had found the key, and was now winding me up. He withdrew; giggled a bit. More water came down.

"Lemme have your cock again," he ordered.

I did. He played with my feet at the same time as he went back to sucking me. Tickling, caressing, touching them. The hardness of my cock was wonderful: I wanted my whole brain to flow into it, the way his did. He could be only a penis, the surest, purest gay fantasy of life, without borders around its boundless, childlike sensuosity. I could not. I ran my fingers through his thick hair, then he spit my dick out, like it was a peach stone. He grabbed at my tender balls and chewed them lightly with his teeth. It was still painful. I started crying, just whimpering a bit, and he slapped my ass. Really hard. I mean, punishingly hard, and I cried more—I kept trying to pull his hair to get his mouth away from me, but I could not. He had me in his teeth. I was frightened. What could I do or say? He had me … yeah, I knew it: the Minotaur had me. He stopped. He put my scrotum next to his cheek, the beard bristles—it was no longer just a four o' clock shadow—announced themselves to the tender, reactive skin there. He cupped the little bag, then ran it delicately up to his ear.

It was quiet. Just the water. Completely still. Did he hear something, inside me—there? I managed to grab his hand, and just get him away from me. I slid down, until we were both kneeling, holding each other on the big tile floor. I clutched at his big, clunky hairy feet. The fine water, slightly larger than a mist, got into my eyes and I closed them. He leaned over me and then went back to my balls once more. He sucked at them, and then I knew—I felt nothing, really, I was so hypercharged, so past any objective reality that I could recall—but I knew, that he had taken something out of me. Instantly. Just sucked it right out of me.

That tongue, those teeth ... facile, quick; part shears and part scalpel ... had gone in and done it. He had eaten my own cum before it had even become that, and had filched my testosterone from me before it could drive itself into sperm. But all I felt was this strange peace. He had me now; and what I was left with was really the most complete orgasm I'd ever experienced. It made me wonder if I had ever had one before; he held me.

He sang softly into my ear, "*It's a grand night for singing / the stars are bright above / the earth is aglow / and to add to th' show / I think that I'm falling in love*—" I could feel his warm breath, kind, penetrating, holding me—"*Falling, falling, in love.*" I felt as if I were on a vast, cosmic merry-go-round. As if I had been lifted up, up, up, and a ring of slowly revolving lights was taking me through the night, above treetops and house roofs, all the way into ...

SIX

The next morning,

I woke up in Powars's beautiful, leather-boarded bed and for a second
berated myself. What was I doing? I had bills to pay, rent—I was one of
those little people who still paid rent; I owned nothing really—and now I
was sleeping late, on this amazing mattress that seemed to hold you
exactly as you wanted, on a bed fitted with the kind of sheets I only
drooled at, from places I could not walk into. You know, those stores that
have a buzzer outside and no prices posted. I had once been in one of
those Madison Avenue stores and the turd who waited on me, when I
asked him how much a tie cost—just a tie, that was all—shrugged his
blazer-clad shoulders and sneered, "Whatever we feel you need to pay for
it," then laughed. I never went into another place like that again, and here
I was, sleeping on it.

Karl walked in. "Are you ready for breakfast, sir? Mr. Powars has
been up for several hours."

He withdrew the curtains and raised the blinds behind them. Sunlight
streamed in. I wasn't wearing anything and felt self-conscious. Karl pulled
a dressing gown from a closet and handed it to me in the bed, then left.

Powars was still there, reading a newspaper with a notepad next to
him, when I arrived, in the robe, at the breakfast table. He was dressed
casually in a pair of nice brown corduroy slacks and a beautiful, blue-pin-
striped shirt of a very fine cotton that I was sure Karl had just ironed.

63

"Karl!" he called. "I'm gonna make a list of stuff I need for Switzerland. You can get it, right?"

Karl was in the kitchen and grunted something. Powars turned to me. He was sipping a cup of black coffee. "You better get back to your place and get some underwear and a coupla changes of clothes. Winchell will take you. If you need toothpaste or stuff like that, just add it to Karl's list. I'm meeting with some people this afternoon—actually in about ninety minutes—at Rockefeller Center. I better hurry. I've got to change and do stuff. Got any questions?"

I poured myself a cup of coffee. "Who are the people?"

He turned to me, his eyes suddenly very cold. "Why?"

I felt small; I swallowed, then said, "I want to know something about you, that's all."

He resumed a more natural smile. "It'll just confuse you. But if you gotta know, one's the C.E.O. of one of the world's largest multi ... well, multi-everythings. They're into the whole shebang. Fertilizers. Chemicals. Drugs. Some big over-the-counter drugs; a coupla under-the-counter drugs. Metals. Electronics. A buncha military contracts. Y'know, parts for weaponry, vehicles, explosives; land mines, even. Kids get blown up." His eyes shut for a second. "That kind of stuff. And some media. Everybody wants media now. His problem is how to keep it all together, and yet separate at the same time. Heads of state come and kiss his big rear end. Does that answer your question?"

I nodded. It did not. I just looked at him.

I was confused—he was right about that—but he went on. "His name is real simple. Anderson. He's got some ... 'friends,' you might say. They're related to some of the people I work with. Distant ... 'cousins.' He wants me to send greetings to these cousins while I'm in Switzerland. So we'll talk about that. And we'll talk about money; you know, where to get more of it—they're always looking for more money—and where to put it. It's simple. These big schmucks like to talk. They just aren't sure if you know how to listen."

Suddenly he grinned at his own wit. I felt as if I had just asked him the price of the tie in the shop. Except in this case, he was going to give me the tie, *if* I didn't ask. He moved closer to me. He'd still not shaved, but he looked refreshed, though a bit edgy. "How you feel?"

I told him I was all right. My voice, I knew, got dryer. I felt kind of cut by him. Hurt. It was not just what he was taking out of me. It was something else. I wasn't sure exactly what, but that hurt, too.

"Karl'll get you a nice breakfast. And anything else you need. I gotta pack tonight, 'cause tomorrow I've got stuff to do before we get on the plane. That's the problem about these kinda trips, you never know how much clothes to take." His brow wrinkled. He looked a bit disturbed, then he said, "Oh, you might want to call your work people. Tell 'em what we discussed. Make up something." He smiled at me like I was a child who had to be coached. "You can do that, right?"

"Yeah." I hated him. Why was he such a … only one word came to mind: Shit. Why was he such a shit? The whole thing seemed impossible. But there was no way that I could stop it. It was inconceivable to me—how could I just walk out? To what? As totally self-involved as he was, as completely destructive and intimidating, he was also the most amazing man I'd ever met. He was that indivisible combination of lover, monster, and child; or were they basically the same?

He got closer to me and nuzzled me. His breath smelled of coffee—warm, rich, sweet. He used a lot of sugar. His unshaven cheek slightly prickled the tender place at my neck where my jaw met my ear. "You're not happy here, are you?" he whispered. "I want you to be happy."

"Why are you the way you are?" I burst out. "I asked you a simple question, and you just belittle me."

He started to kiss me, on the ear, on the neck and cheek. I thought I was going to pee all over myself. I was on the verge of crying. "If I tell you any more, Allen, suppose you run off and hate me? I don't operate in the nicest world. I don't want you to hate me."

"I can't hate you." I started kissing him, clawing at him. Karl appeared. He had a large, well-set tray of breakfast muffins for me, with toast, orange juice, and an egg in a cup.

"Is this—" Karl began to say.

Powars withdrew from me. "Thanks, Karl. Listen, can you get out my brown suit, the new dark one, and make sure it's ready? It may need pressing—okay?"

Karl nodded. I looked at him, and then thanked him warmly for the breakfast. My mother had never liked making breakfast for us—my father, my sister, and me. It was always an ugly, fretful time. She was ... okay, a bitch in the morning, until she'd had about an hour and a couple of cigarettes. You remember things like that. Now I had to put myself back together. I began eating, buttering the toast, carefully opening the top of the egg. Karl left and I realized that, for a moment, Powars was watching me, like a fascinated bird of prey. I had seen vultures on nature shows on TV with that same patient look. His head was cocked just a bit, and he smiled, opening his teeth.

"I thought you had to go," I said.

"No—yeah—I mean, listen, can't I just stay for a moment and watch you eat?"

"Why?"

He shook his head softly. "I dunno. What can I say?" He shrugged his shoulders. "Maybe ... I just want to pull everything out of you. So there's more space for me."

I nodded my head, as if I understood what he was saying. I didn't, but I felt as if I were on display—now *I* was the tie, the one without a price tag. But he had the money, anyway. Certainly the money, in whatever form it came, that could buy me. I looked into his eyes. They looked suddenly very soft. Golden amber. He knelt by my side. "You're like this kid," he said. "You make me feel like a kid, too."

66   I did not say anything. He reached inside my robe and began pinching my left nipple. It was not a hard pinch. It was just perfect. I realized that I was in love with his hands, his strange feet. I would never let him

know that. He was a monster. Really. I knew it.

His cell phone rang. He clicked it on.

"Hey!" He jumped up and his face became hard again. His eyes started to become darker, denser, the golden amber now replaced with a charcoal brownish-gray. "Come on, Gwinny. What do y'think I gotta let him know?" His mouth hardened. It no longer looked like the supple mouth he kissed me with. "Come on—I'm countin' on you. That's what I thought. Yeah, with these Anderson people, we stomp 'em—but we don't let 'em know we're stompin' too hard. Right?"

He paused. "So how much should I offer him? And what do we really want t'get out of this?"

He nodded. He started to pace about the room, but I could tell he was focused completely on what she was saying. "'S'pose he won't give it to us?"

He stood quiet for a moment. His jaw clenched. He released it. "Then I'm gonna have t'make him—stick his face right in it."

Suddenly he started laughing really hard. He was convulsed with laughter, though the hardness did not seem to leave his voice.

"Something must be funny," I said. I looked right at him. He ignored me.

"For a chink bitch, you're cool," he said. "I know! You're not a chink bitch. Your old man was an English colonel. Everybody's old man was an English colonel—except mine. He was a drug addict and sometimes a queer. Anyway, I'm glad we're having this talk. I was startin' to think that Anderson had me by the short hairs and I don't like that idea. You're right: we make him, but just add a little sugar to it." He glanced over at me and winked. I smiled. He smiled back, then he said to the phone, "You'll have all this stuff for the trip, right? Good. I'm countin' on you." He stood behind me now and kissed my hair. "Like I told you, I'm bringing a friend. He's going to need a visa. Can you do that for me?"

There was a pause. He jumped away from me. I could see that he had stopped smiling. His eyes closed; his voice got tougher. "I know. It ain't—*isn't*—something *they* want. But I need something too. Lemme tell you, I been doin' this long enough by myself!" His voice, naturally low, tough, spackled over with a thick, indifferent kind of maleness, cracked. "Shi-*tttt!*" he screamed.

That final "t" landed like a sledgehammer. Then he didn't make a sound for a while; he made this tense, wary walk around the room, with his gray-brown eyes glancing back and forth at various things, including me. Gwinny was saying something and he was listening and also fighting it, or maybe not fighting it, but just hating it anyway. Then he stopped pacing. I looked over at him, though he didn't look at me. He ran his large tongue over his lower lip and that wonderful, supple sweetness of his mouth returned. "I want you on my side, Gwinny. You are, aren't you?"

He smiled into the phone; she must have been saying something he wanted to hear. He looked over and smiled at me, then came and kissed me on the back of my neck. About ten seconds later, he said good-bye to her, then clicked off. He pulled a chair out from the table, and sat quietly. All the euphoria in his face sank. It looked cold and distant. I asked him, softly, carefully, if everything were okay.

"Sure."

"So that's Gwinny—the one you said is your 'girl'?"

He drank some more coffee. "Yeah, well, she's kinda like my assistant; I mean sometimes we collaborate. Hell, she tells *me* what to do. Her name's Gwendolyn Hong Rose. She's half Chinese, from way over there. Her father was a Brit and her mother was a smart lady who didn't take shit from nobody. Gwinny, anyway, she's stays on my side. She loves me."

"Is she pretty?"

"You'll meet her. She'll get your visa for you. She'll be in Switzerland, too. Not on our flight, but she'll be there. She'll come in with some of the others."

I wanted to ask him who the "others" were—but I didn't. Powars was
68 no longer looking at me, but drinking the coffee with his eyes tightly closed. Karl walked in, and avoided him. He brought fresh coffee, more muffins, and juice. Karl smiled at me in that stiff manner, like his face might peel off

if he smiled too hard. Then he disappeared back into the kitchen.

Powars sat a few minutes longer. He opened his eyes, then stared right at me. We looked at one another carefully. I didn't say a word. I really had no idea what to say. I could tell that he was under more strain than he was letting out. He tried to shrug it off, but it was there. I managed to eat a little bit. I felt like he was drilling a hole straight through me. It made eating difficult. I wasn't aware of what anything tasted like. The egg. The muffins. Karl had the most wonderful strawberry preserves, with tiny ruby-red berries in them. I love strawberry preserves. I wanted to feel the sweet moistness of the berries in my mouth. I didn't. They didn't taste like anything special. They could have been A & P-brand for all I knew. Powars's cell phone rang once more. He got up, pulled it out of his pocket and clicked it on. "Powars," he said dryly.

I watched him as he paced.

"Hi, Tony," he beamed for a moment. "You old fag. Sure. How could I not be there? Just gimme your notes before."

There was a pause. He looked serious.

"I'm not gonna make any...I will speak *verrrry* nicely, Tony. I know, you think I'm a *schmuck* from New Jersey. Right? Fuck you. Those people want something from me and I know how to give it to 'em. It's give and take, right? I been trained perfectly." He looked over at me as I watched him, and he smiled. But I could tell that the smile was not one of happiness, but of being discovered. Uncovered, truly. So, he was a *schmuck* from New Jersey? Well, everyone in New York was a *schmuck* from someplace. He stopped smiling. Then he came over to me, and put his hand on my shoulder. Then he said, "I'll see you there. Bye, Tony, I love you, fuckface."

He clicked off and took his hand away from me. I looked up at him. He was serious now. I knew I was treading on bad territory, but I said, "Who was that?"

"He's a guy named Tony. Kind of a funny queer, if you ask me."

"Why funny?"

69

He turned away from me. "It's not funny, actually. You'll meet him in Switzerland, too. He's part of the—" he closed his eyes and stopped talking.

"Part of what?"

He was now behind my chair. "The world. The whole miserable, fuckin' world, my friend. Which always wants more than you can give it." I felt his breath at the back of my neck, just above the collar of the robe. Then he kissed me right there—on the back of my neck—and placed his big hands on my shoulders for a moment. I put my hands on top of his. I thought I was going to stop breathing. Then without saying another word, he left.

I could still feel his hands there, a weight at my shoulders, like they'd been a lawn mower parting the grass. I bowed my head. It felt heavy, like a bowling ball. I wanted to hear something else. Chewing was too loud, and this awful depression settled into the room as I knew that I would wait, hour by hour, for him to return.

Karl came to clear the dishes. "Mr. Powars will take a taxi over to Rockefeller Center, so if you want Winchell, just let me know. I hope you had a nice breakfast."

I told him I did. "How long have you worked for Mr. Powars?" I asked.

"Oh, not so long. Five years perhaps. He's good. He pays me well. Some Americans only look nice but are not. They give you no"—he pronounced it, with great seriousness—"pri-vahsy." I smiled and so did he. He had a lean face and big, horsey teeth. "I will not work mit children. Here, they are too spoiled. They'll kick you. Bad behavior like that. Mr. Powars is lonely. His life is not so easy. I'm afraid he can—" He halted; I wanted to know.

"Be what?" I asked.

"I should not say this. All right. If you must know. Hurt. He can be hurt. Do you have articles you want on the list?"

He handed Powars's list to me. Most of the stuff was pretty pedestrian: Crest toothpaste, Q-tips, Pepto-Bismol, remedies for his acid stomach. Fascinating that he had stomach problems. There was something with fiber in it to keep him going, and something to stop him up. I did not think that men like Powars had those problems; I thought their problems were amusement mainly, or frustration. I added baby oil to it—I have dry skin. There were a lot of things I needed to do. I excused myself from Karl. He made me feel like I was a guest at his very exclusive Swiss restaurant. At any moment he might snap his heels together and offer me a bill. As an acceptable, responsible adult, I would certainly pay it gratefully, without arguing about any of the details.

Powers on the other hand made me feel like a bad child. Fitful. Frustrated. Dumb. A little obedient at best; but, mostly, too willful as children will be. I expected him to say: "Isn't it nice? He's sucking my big dick all on his own." After breakfast, I used the bathroom, then showered again. I had nothing fresh to wear after the night before. Karl offered me some clothes—one of Powars's good shirts, his socks, and underwear. The shirt was beautiful, a white oxford button-down, but very fine and silky. The buttons were pure oyster shell. I had never seen anything like them. Karl left and I just looked at the buttons and felt them in my fingers. Then I put the shirt on. It was too big for me, but I did not care. It was English, the label said from "Jermyn Street," very beautifully made, and I liked it.

I called the bank and told my supervisor that I was going away for a week. That was all. Just a week. I was having a family emergency. "This is unusual," Mrs. Dunwoody said. Eleanor Dunwoody was a portly, dignified, WASPish lady in her mid-sixties. She wore nice blouses, frankly artificial pearls, and genuinely tasteful, bland suits. She was from Bronxville in lower Westchester County, and had been educated only to marry. She had worked for the bank for thirty years and would retire soon. She was looking forward to it and talked about all the things she would do. Travel. Sleep late. Go to nice places she'd never been. She and her husband, an ad agency executive, had divorced years ago—it was just "one of those things," she said. "We got married because everyone else did. We had two kids. I'm not sorry for it. I like the kids."

"You know you're jeopardizing your vacation," she said to me. "I mean, I'm all for helping you. I like you, Allen, but Personnel gets funny

71

about these kinds of leaves. Can you document it? I mean, like a doctor's certificates, something like that?"

I told her that my sister was having a nervous breakdown. There was no way I could "document it." "How about a psychiatrist?" she asked seriously. "Can't you get a psychiatrist to write you a note about her?"

"Sure," I said. "I'll get him to write me a note." I put my hand over the receiver while she told me how nice that would be. "Just a short one," she said. "On his letterhead. That's all you need."

"Then I can stick it where the sun don't shine," I said, then took my hand off the mouthpiece and said, "I'll bring it to you as soon as I get back."

She became concerned, motherly. My job was rubberstampy and pretty—actually, *petty*—clerical. It was not the kind of job that led to great things. I processed certain checks and inquired on foreign letters of credit. I got to call people all over the world and find out how the weather was in Istanbul, but a chimpanzee probably could have done that. It would have had a hard time on the phone, but could have used the rubber stamps.

So, I wasn't a ball of fire and had not become a dot-com billionaire. Like Powars might be, for all I knew. It was funny that all my working life I had been stuck between men like Destry—ruthless, inevitable, invincible forces that they are in business—and the sweet Eleanor Dunwoodys of the world, motherly, protective, insecure, and, when driven to it, quite capable of razoring off your head and serving it tastefully back to you, with hard sauce over it. Eleanor could fire me just as fast anyone else. It was time for me to change: I knew it. I said good-bye to her while she was still in the midstream of her sympathies, and hung up. I left the bedroom.

I ventured out into the narrow hallway. It was painted a dark vermilion. There were no pictures, no mirrors, nothing usually seen in the hallways of New York apartments to let you know something had happened there. Usually, people could look at themselves in mirrors before they left, or make a quick glance at pictures of family and loved ones. The long hallway was quiet—sleepy almost—sort of like being in a hotel when the guests had left and the staff was out for a smoke. I could hear Karl in the kitchen, distantly puttering about. I was at a loss for what to do—I should have told him to tell Winchell that I wanted to go down to my place and settle things. Pack, like Destry had told me. I had no pets, no plants to water. My super could collect what mail I got. Mostly bills. People did not send personal letters anymore; I wasn't even "e-mailable" as everyone said. For the most part I kept to myself, even though there wasn't a whole lot to keep.

But, so what? What's so bad about that?

I looked up at the red ceiling and saw rubied patterns of light, like fluttering moth wings, dancing across it. There must have been, I guessed, a window someplace; then I saw a transom high above a closed door. Once more I realized there were rooms here where I had not been. Beside the door with the transom, there were two others. Closed. Most probably locked. Suddenly, I thought, if I were really going to stay there for any amount of time—the idea vaguely visited me—I should know something. Okay, maybe, I should know *everything*. That seemed right. I did have a sister: I was telling Mrs. Dunwoody the truth. And she could have had a real breakdown; they were fairly common in our family. That was the truth. So, I thought, maybe I should know a little more *truth* about this place, this mysterious little palazzo in a West Side apartment building.

I walked up to one of the doors and put my hand on an old pewter-looking knob. It was cold, a bit slippery, like it had just been oiled. I felt nervous, the way you would the first time you tried masturbating in the bathroom, praying your Cyclopean parents wouldn't notice the too-long locked door. I squeezed hard; my hand sweated. The oily knob turned to the left; opened. It was big, dark, and simple in there. Filled with brooms, mops, polish, lamb's wool dusters, and a wooden ironing board straight out of the Smithsonian. I was an idiot. I shut the door. It made this snap like bubble gum popping. Karl could have heard it a mile away; he'd be   73
out in a yodel, or whatever the Swiss call a quick second.

I raced around a corner, into a dark little bathroom I had no idea existed, then watched. No Karl. The john, very monk-like, smelled of cheap supermarket soap. Maybe it was Karl's. I'd better get out; I did. Then I saw those mothy lights flickering up again on the red ceiling. I edged out until I was again in front of the door with the transom. I tried the knob in either direction and got no result; it was a type of old cut crystal you don't see anymore. I felt really funny: maybe he was hiding dead wives in there. I half expected the door to explode and a stiff wigged body to jump into my arms. I was crazy. Then, still curious but dumb enough not to know any better, I took out a plastic credit card—I'd seen this trick before; it seemed to work—and I quickly slipped it under the lock, then slid it very smoothly up.

My heart jackhammered. *Ka-boom, ka-boom.* People have a right to "pri-vahsy" certainly. The cut crystal turned by itself, and I slipped in as easily as the Visa card had. "Visa, there when you need it." The lower part of the room was manhole dark. But acrobatic slivers of light trapezed over the ceiling, past a few dented slats at the top of the blinds. I must have seen their fugitive brothers through the transom. The blinds looked as if they were never raised. Mesmerized, I watched the light do odd figures above me, until the darkness below became possible to see in.

I saw everything. It was just an old office, kind of like a doctor's "professional space," when they used to live above the stairs and saw patients down below. It was kind of homey, with a very old desk, oak, I guessed, and a desk lamp with a thick, green glass shade. It had a beaded pull chord. I pulled it. The light was low-level; kind of sickly, yes, that was the word. It was *sickly*, but it worked, throwing a soft, hazy green stillness over the room.

Old, heavy-wood filing cabinets stood around the desk and dark, wooden bookshelves climbed up above it. My eyes saw them now; and then the things on the desk. Not many. Mostly papers, in neat piles. Brittle-looking, tissue-thin airmail letters, with faded purplish Swiss postmarks. They looked kind of … medieval. Then I saw something quite strange on the desk. I wanted to think it was just a paperweight, but it was fashioned from some kind of yellowish, translucent skin; like old parchment. It had the brittle, faded look of the letters. I got closer to it. Even in the greenish light, I could make out thin, swirling veins of a denser substance, like hardened roots, pressing furiously at the surface under it.

The skin took the form of a lizard, perhaps a very small alligator-like creature, but definitely with an odd, humanish face; infantile; sleeping. With soft, innocently babyish features. The face had upturned lips, a little squiggle of a nose, and pinkish ears pinned back to the sides of its slightly flattened head. Its papery eyelids were closed, but I could detect, under them, the distant spherical presence of actual eyes, which might … somehow open and follow you. Its darkened little front claws were bent before a pale, slightly curled underbelly. The veiny depths of this stomach seemed capable of breath; that it might stir even momentarily out of its dreamless sleep gripped me with fear ….

And some fascination. I watched it, dumbfounded, came close to picking it up, but knew I couldn't. Suddenly I didn't want to look at it anymore. I admit I have a way of avoiding unpleasantness. I dislike like rude people and don't like repulsive things. There was something about this curious object that seemed too morbidly strange. A fetal, human-featured reptile … I shuddered, then turned.

I spotted a bunch of old leather-bound books. I like old books. If I ever wanted to collect anything, it would be old books. The truth is, I collect nothing. I have friends who collect—mostly glass paperweights, baseball hats, refrigerator magnets. Stuff like old Broadway records. None of that interests me. But these books were right there in front of me on a lower shelf. I started to pull them out.

Some were in German, which I don't know. Then I saw a thick one in French, and I opened it, saw the title: *Les Secrets d' Immortalité Égyptienne*. Date: 1842. There were gorgeous, hand-tinted, engraved pictures, and the paper had that kind of faint, barely captured aroma, like dried cherries, that good paper has.

I started to leaf through the pages. The paper felt rich and nubby to my fingers, heavy with rag content, which I knew was important with old books. I had taken enough high school French that I could read some of it. I could never actually speak it, with all those funny vowels that never really come out of your mouth; they either stay in the back someplace or bleep through your nose. But reading some of it was easy. Then I saw this picture. It was a diagram. It showed the body of a man in Egyptian face drag. The eye make up, the wig; but he was naked. No loincloth. Then there were notes, with arrows pointed at various parts of his body, showing which area was sacred to which god.

I used to haunt the Egyptian section of the Metropolitan Museum, so I knew a little about this stuff—about Horus, the god with the hot young T-square body and the hawk face, and Anubis, the jackal-headed god of the dead. And Thoth, the god of magic. You knew him by his ibis head. He was stationed at the head in the diagram. Ra, the sun god, was at the heart. Horus was at the arms, and Anubis at the liver.

By the genitals (which were nicely detailed, I have to say, and shown in three-quarter view, as if turned to one side) was a long arrow which led to a cartouche, "a little box," tinted a lovely purple, all by itself. The descriptive writing was in fairly dense French, hard reading for me, but at the bottom of the box was a tiny picture of a mummiform man I realized had to be Osiris, the famous resurrection god, who was usually shown as being either a mummy or a regular man, colored all in green, the color of rebirth. It said something like the genital area was "sacré du Osiris" and his followers revered this as the Source of Life. There were secret rituals for this area, and in terms of immortality it was known as …

I tried to read more. The ink was smudged, like some hand damp with perspiration had gone over it too many times. I squinted hard, until I could make out what it said: that the genital area was "la source distinguée du secret."

There was not much light in the room and the dimness was starting to make my eyes hurt, especially looking at the yellowed paper; but I turned the leaf. And saw another illustration with, again, a diagram. This—how can I say it?—showed the testicles being opened. Very carefully. You could see little marks on them. Tooth marks … I thought my heart would stop—I raced to the next page. A sequence of drawings showed a man, well-drawn, from the front, kneeling, also naked, "eating" at the body of another handsome young man, who was lying supine and naked. Not exactly cannibalizing him, but disfiguring him, so that his testicles were now being … the only word is "sliced" by the kneeling man's teeth. The sequence revealed intimate "close-ups." You could see everything in beautifully rendered detail: the testicles themselves; the veins; small drops of blood coming out.

Then the door opened slowly. Just a crack.

I almost jumped. It was like opening a tomb.

I dropped the book directly on the desk, and the little stuffed lizard suddenly bolted directly at me. I had to grab it as hard as I could. I tried to keep from jumping myself, then I turned around.

"Mr. Powars," Karl said, shaking his head sadly, "would not like to see you in here, sir. It would make him sad, I believe."

He walked up to me and took the reptile from me.

"It's interesting," he said with that lean, dry smile on his face. "A mummified animal; from the jungles deep in Peru, I was told. A child's pet, we think. It is not to be touched. Oils from one's fingers can cause it to disintegrate. I only come in here now and then to dust."

He put the thing that I had thought was a paperweight carefully back on the desk, and reached to switch off the desk light. I got in his way.

"What's in here?" I asked.

"His books. Papers. All business. They go back a long way. Usually the room is kept locked. Even the cleaning ladies are not allowed in here. Mr. Powars must have forgotten to lock it properly."

I nodded. "Yes, he must have forgot, but this old stuff"—I was referring to the book—"why's he interested in it?" I tried to smile vaguely. "I mean, he seems more up to date." I turned to take another look at the 77 bookshelves. "I didn't know he liked to read this kind of thing." I must have been sweating, just grabbing for words. "I mean, I thought he was more Wall Street, or"—I knew Karl wanted to get me out of the room as quickly as possible—"finance. Yes, I thought he was more finance."

Karl smiled. "It is only a hobby with him. Mr. Powars is interested in many things." He made a quick visual inventory of the room. Nodded his head—I guess he was satisfied—then smiled at me again. I felt as if I'd been accused of shoplifting, then acquitted. Karl must have thought I was simply stupid. What did I know? He straightened up a few other objects on the desk. A polished brass letter opener; a few pyramids of fine crystal—maybe Steuben paperweights, I don't know—and then some writing instruments. "I think everything is all right," he said; then he leaned over and switched off the light. "Please, come with me now. Winchell is ready to drive you."

He took my arm firmly and led me away, closing the door and locking it quickly with a key from his pocket. "Please don't tell him you've been here. Like I said, it would make him sad. You wouldn't like that, would you?"

At first I was glad to be back in my apartment, where I could be myself, and then I realized there wasn't a lot of myself to be. When you become used to a life that is not much of a life, you don't realize what you've been missing. People who live in areas where the only connection they have to the outside is, say, a big Walmart, will tell you how wonderful it is to shop in a place where everything is under one roof and nothing is left to chance. What relatives I have are those kind of people. They will come to Manhattan and decry that we have no Red Lobsters for them to eat in. There is a Red Lobster in almost every town in America, and they want to come to the teeming bustle of New York and eat in one. Not that I am that kind of snob—gracious, no—but suddenly I realized that there was really nothing in my house, or my life, that I would miss if I left it.

I had dispensed with just about any source of identification, except what I carried in my wallet. My credit cards were my identification. And maybe my library card. I realized then that I did need some piece of I.D. that I could give to Powars for my visa. By pure luck, I had a copy of my birth certificate. I had lost my Social Security card once, and they had asked me for my birth certificate. I called the small town where I was born and had grown up, and they sent me a copy. That was enough, I thought. That showed who I was, who my parents were. My age. What else was I, or anyone for that matter?

I no longer identified with my clothing, or my furniture, or even the nice men who'd been my friends. Some had left messages on my answering machine and I quickly called some back and left messages on theirs saying that I was going out of town for a week. I did not have a lot of time to spend. Winchell was waiting outside, and I was to meet Powars for dinner that evening. Karl said it was important, and I knew I could not disappoint Destry.

As I put clothing together in one of those little suitcases on wheels, I wondered about that office. For such an up-to-date person like Destry Powars, the office seemed archaic. Two sweaters, I decided, would be a good idea; and some of my presentable but cheap shirts, jeans, of course, another of my discount house sports jackets, and a nice pair of slacks. I threw in a few pairs of underwear and knew, for certain, that I needed to go back into that office. I needed to, before we made this trip to Switzerland, just for my own peace of mind.

I was willing to leave my life, now, for Destry Powars and what he might offer me. But I wanted to have some idea of what I was really getting into.

SEVEN

He came back

at four o' clock, smiling. I was in the bedroom, watching the news on Channel One. He jumped on the bed and pulled me to him. I asked him how he felt.

"Great! It was a good meeting." He smiled and kissed me impulsively, like there was nothing between us now, nothing to hold us apart. There was just the unguarded exuberance of that kiss. I thought I was going to pee all over the bed, I was so excited, but I couldn't let him know that. I nodded my head and looked into his eyes, all brownish and gold. "These guys can play rough, lemme tell you, but they're nothing compared to us. I'll—I mean we—we'll walk on 'em and they know it." He winked. "But I won't walk too fast."

He was wearing a beautifully cut, bittersweet-chocolate-brown suit—the new one?—with a beige, spread-collar shirt and a deep blue tie that was perfectly knotted in a four-in-hand. I'd seen lawyers who tied like that: I could never do it, but then I did not buy ties like that. He had on brown suede shoes I was sure Karl had just brushed before he left. He had the shoes up on the bed, but was careful to keep his feet away from the bedspread. He was shaved and had a fresh haircut. He looked very handsome, very successful. I took his hand suddenly and put it over my mouth, palm down. I liked the way his wrist, decked with hair, smelled. Perhaps it was the Spanish soap, or just him.

"How was—what's her name?"

"Gwinny? She was fine. She's good. I kinda lost it for a moment, and she got me back on track. See, people have a funny thing about money. They don't want to use their own money. That's how the rich shits stay rich. They wanna use *your* money. So these guys, they want our money." He smiled knowingly. "They just don't want to know where it comes from."

"Where does it come from?"

He looked into my face and smiled, but it wasn't a good smile. "Why do you wanna know something like that?"

I shrugged my shoulders. "Okay," I said. I felt small, like a dog who gives up and shows you his belly to be rubbed. "And Tony, was he okay?"

"No. He's an asshole and a queer. He's not happy that I want you in Switzerland. Maybe I shouldn't tell you that. But I want you there. Hell, I done enough for them." His eyes suddenly looked sad. He turned away from me. I asked him what was wrong. I felt bad for him, though I had no idea what he was talking about. He turned back to me. "You know what the worst thing in the world is?"

"Wanting what you can't have?" I ventured to say.

"No. That ain't it, believe me. I got what I wanted. No, it's when people want to take *everything* out of you, just to get at what you don't have. Know what I mean? They know what you don't have, and they keep taking more and more outta you, just to make sure it's not there. Me—I go nuts at times; I want things to add up too fast. Gwinny says my balls kick aside my brains." He smiled. "I know I lack polish and a lotta warmth. I'm always gonna lack that. It's just not in me to have that—I know it. Just like I know this doesn't mean much to you. But it's the only way I can say it."

"It's all right," I said.

"It is?"

I nodded. I had no idea what I was actually saying, but it had to be all right. Just had to be. He kissed me again. But this time, I only let him. I became frightened, feeling that I was sinking into something deeper, more ugly, than I knew; and I had to hide it. I had to pretend that all of

81

this was just a lovely game.

He stopped kissing me. He reached over, untied his suede shoes, and tossed them lightly onto the floor, several feet from the bed. "Did Karl do everything for you?"

"Yes," I said. "Winchell drove me back. I got what I needed from my apartment."

"How about the rent? You need me to pay the rent?"

"No. Why should you do that? I'm getting a free trip to Switzerland." I got up and gave him the copy of my birth certificate. Now I really felt as if I were placing myself in his hands. He smiled and took it without saying another word, except, "What would you like for dinner? I can ask Karl to make it, or we can go out."

I shrugged my shoulders. "Going out would be fun. As long as we don't go back to Toyland. I think I'm over that place."

"Sure. I see what you mean. It's straight. Kinky but straight. You like gay people, don't you? You like being around them, I mean. You're more comfortable, right?"

"I guess." I didn't really feel like answering his question. Just about all of my friends were gay. And poor. Maybe not Appalachian poor, but by the standards of this city of rich people, poor. I did not want to have to apologize for them.

"You won't want them after a while. You'll want what I have to give you. Really, I mean it. I like queers sometimes, but not always. I mean, you go to places like the Box and that's what you get. But they ain't the deepest people in the world."

"Who is?" I asked. He smiled, then winked at me.

He got off the bed. "Are you all packed? I mean, I gotta get Karl to do a few more things. Why don't you just stay here for a coupla minutes and watch TV, and I'll go see him."

82   I told him that I'd go with him. I began to get up, and he playfully pushed me down. "No, you just stay. Okay? I'll be back in a snap. I feel like a drink. Want an aperitif? They say 'aperitivo' in Italy. I like the way

they say that."

He left and shut the door behind him. I waited a few minutes and then followed him. From behind a closed door in the hallway, I could see him speaking with Karl. They were talking German. It was strange, for a man who could barely handle English, I could hear that Powars spoke fluent German. I spoke no German at all. The language always seemed too galumpy and thuggish for me. Just a prejudice, I'm sure. I decided then to barge in. That would keep them from talking about me.

Destry looked at me, shocked. "Hey! I thought I told you to stay in the bedroom."

"I missed you. That's all." I smiled. "I wanted to be with the grown-ups."

"Get us two schnapses," he ordered Karl. "A little Goldwasser, maybe."

"Very good," Karl said. He went into the kitchen.

Powars looked at me, his eyes squinting. "You're not very good at doing what I tell you to do."

He had the jacket of his suit off, but the tie was still on. I ran my fingers up his expensive beige shirt that felt more silk than cotton and started to untie the tie, no easy task. He was very good with knots. He pulled my hands away. "Will you punish me?" I asked seductively.

"I might. Or I might just suck your cute little dick until your balls came off. How about that?" He gave me a slap on the rump, and then pulled me into the living room. Karl came in a moment later with two cocktail glasses filled to the brim with thick transparent liquid. It was ice cold and tasted kind of like licorice, but very dry instead of sweet. I thanked Karl and told Powars that I liked it.

"It's good, yeah? It's nice sometimes, just at this time of the day. Karl'll finish my packing. We'll stay in here while he does it. He doesn't like an audience when he packs. Then we'll go to a place near Lincoln Center that I like. It's Italian and good. We'll be flying out tomorrow, but it's gonna be a really full day, you better know that. So you might want to hit the sack early."

Dinner was fine. There was candlelight and beautiful wine and well-dressed people. The women wore cocktail dresses, like the kind you see in *Vogue*, and the men wore nice, expensive suits. Not Italian showy, like at Toyland, just nice. The menu was physically huge. I have noticed that good restaurants like to have big menus, with the large prices in very small print. You don't have a lot of choices—not like a diner, what I'm more used to—but you get big menus. This place had white tablecloths that I could have slept on, all perfectly starched and ironed. So were the napkins. I had some wonderful veal that tasted like heaven (if you could imagine heaven tasting like a part of a dead young animal) and he had some chicken or something like that. It was a small bird and very "free range." The menu called it a "Poussin."

He drank a lot of wine—I could hardly touch the stuff without falling off the chair, but he polished off almost a full bottle of red Italian, then had a demi-bottle of Burgundy. We had some beautiful fruit custard tarts with just a hint of almond for dessert, then he called on his cell phone for Winchell to pick us up. He was tipsy and he kept clutching me and running his fingers through my hair, which seemed to make the too-stylish waiters at the restaurant a bit nervous. If they weren't gay—some were Italian, so who could tell?—they should have been. The young hostess, or whatever she was called, in a black stretchy outfit that made her look like Morticia, with an accent straight out of Queens, asked if the "Gentleman is gonna be all right?" I said, "Sure."

Although I was hardly a number of years younger than Powars—I don't talk about my age, but I remember the 1960s—anyway, people always treated him like the "gentleman" and me like … "the friend of the gentleman." I understood that fast enough.

Winchell waited for us. It was a nice night, and I could have easily walked back to the apartment in that tower on Central Park West at Seventy-fourth Street, but I was not sure that Destry could have. "I needed to drink," he told me in the car. "Those guys—they kinda took it outta me today. But sometimes they do. Know what I mean?" I nodded. He kissed me. "You ever think you could fall for somebody like me? I mean, you know, like—" He stopped talking.

"Maybe," I said. "Why do you ask?"

"Don't be like that." He held my hand. He seemed so vulnerable, so impossible to understand. "It's bad enough I gotta be a shit. I know that's what you think I am, don'chu?"

I hesitated. We were almost there. It was a very quick ride. "Sometimes."

"I ain't. I mean, I'm not. Really. I gotta be the way I am. I learned all this, you just don't know how."

We were there. Winchell opened the door of the car for us and an old, very dignified elevator man brought us up without a word except, "Good night, sir."

I knew I was not included in that "sir" business, too. Maybe I was just along for the ride. Or was I? Karl did not come out when we entered the almost dark apartment. Powars stumbled a bit and kind of grabbed for the walls of the living room. I was afraid he was going to break an expensive lamp or something. Then his legs buckled and he fell to the floor, like a large sack of potatoes in very nice clothes.

He no longer had on the brown suit. He'd changed to dark, charcoal-gray slacks and a soft gray cashmere sweater. I had tried to look nice for the restaurant, but nothing like him. I leaned over him, carefully, concerned; then he grabbed me and pulled me to the floor, smiling. "This is … sure fun!" he drawled. "We should get naked." I smiled directly into his eyes, which quickly closed like a puppet's, when the right string is pulled.

I wasn't sure what to do. His mouth opened, and he let out a funny, kind of ripply snore, the kind you make when you don't normally snore but you're drunk. Was he out cold? He was too big for me to pick him up by myself. I thought about calling Karl, but did not. I got a couple of sofa pillows and put one under his head and one under his feet. I slapped his cheeks lightly—I had seen that in a movie—and he came to for a moment, smiled at me, then went back under. He lay there, his head straight up, his

85

eyes closed, his mouth open ... and I walked away, carefully turning back every few steps to look at him, to make sure that he stayed that way.

Once more, I was at the heavy old door to the office. In total darkness. My eyes opened up as much as they could. A thin splinter of light, hazy gray, emerged from the keyhole. It was so narrow and soft that you might have missed it unless you stood there as I did, barely breathing. I pulled out my Visa card and slipped it into the lock.

The sound was deafening as it disengaged. Ever so gently, I tried the crystal handle. It turned easily, but nothing happened. I tried several times, rotating it slowly to the left, then to the right, then—a hand slipped around my waist. "Thank you for being so nice to me."

"Are you all right?" I asked.

"Sure. I musta passed out. I used to be able to hold my booze, but, God, you get older and then all sorts of things happen. You wanna come in here, don't you?"

I did not answer him.

"Karl told me that you were in here."

"He did?"

"Yeah. I made him tell me. He didn't want to. He thought it would upset me, like, y'know, dealing with some of the most powerful men in the world is ... okay, so you wanna come in?"

I held my breath. Then exhaled. "No, I mean, not unless you want me to."

"Come on. Cut the shit. You want to. Don't you?" He took out his key, it was large and filigreed at the end—it looked antique—then put it in the lock. He turned it and the door sprang open. "I must have forgotten to deadlock it this morning. I was in there, before you got up. Anyway, *entré, mein herr.*"

We walked in. There was a small standing lamp on, near the entrance of the room, probably the source of the gray light. It's weak glow made the place feel even gloomier, stranger, than total darkness would have. "Sometimes I get a notion to come in here, so a timer pops the little light on," he explained. "Whatchu wanna see?"

I looked around. The books, the odd things in the room. Perhaps it was the single standing light, or the still radiating tenderness of the night itself; but I was a bit more at ease than I had been earlier. This made me notice things more. I looked again on the desk at the "mummified" infant reptile; in the shy light my eyes traced the veins, dark as ink, swirling under its crisply translucent skin. The effect was still close to nauseating. Maybe it was the expensive wine that I'd had at dinner; or, maybe, it was simply the appearance again of those tiny, dark gray foreclaws, curled sleepily at its stomach. Or the thinly lidded child's eyes, with the opaque spheres of death under them.

Destry picked it up, smiled, then passed its stiff, half-furled "fingers" up to my cheek. He pressed them in for a moment. I shuddered. "Do you like it?" he asked.

"No." I hated it.

"I should give it to you as a present," he joked. His brown eyes glowed.

"I told you I didn't like it."

He grinned. "I thought you didn't. I could tell by the way you looked at it. Presents are funny things; you gotta be ready for 'em. You find it kinda repulsive, right?"

I didn't answer him, but started to look around. I don't know why, perhaps it was some insistent curiosity towards that which—

"Funny about repulsive," he went on.

I tried to listen with one ear, and look closely with both eyes.

"What the French eat, Americans find repulsive. Frog legs, chopped and fried. Calf brains slowly cooked in milk. Stomach parts. The Swiss— now what *they* eat, you should ..."

I had stopped listening. The one ear went silent, as both eyes stopped at a trio of little brownish statues, standing halfway back, towards the end of one of the middle shelves. They were quite primitive- 87 ly rendered, but with nightmarish, intense faces and naked bodies. One was female, with large, young, exposed breasts; but her face looked sad, creased, and haggard. Her arms were clutched tightly to her sides. Just below her chest, her forearms were extended straight out, her fingers cupped, as if she were offering herself to the world.

The second, male and human in body, had a reptile's aggressively snouty, elongated face. Strangely enough, the body reminded me of Powars, in the posture of it; that always-attentive tension. The third figure was truly gruesome, grotesquely thick-bellied with short but powerful legs and deep-set eyes that looked into you. It had small ears, like the lizard, and almost no hair; big nipples hung from a large chest, and it— *he*—had a cock that looked wrinkled, thick and shriveled, and, yes, was definitely elephantine in size.

I was trying not to stare. I went back to the female figure, then the reptile-headed one. But I couldn't keep my eyes from them. There was a strange buzz around them, a noise with no sound emanating from it, but definitely some emotional vibration. There was something fecal about them, and altogether strangely self-gestated, as if the primitive material itself, with little human intervention, had made them out of some kind of oily, fertile mud dug from a ditch, or coarse clay. They were ugly, but had a savage power. I am not sure, odd as they were, how I'd overlooked them earlier. Maybe I'd been too nervous, with the immediate threat of Karl bursting in, or perhaps there'd just been too much to see all at one time. But the standing light was now on them, and its soft beam directed me to them. I could not help watching them—a trio of questionable, strangely compelling witnesses.

Powars's voice came back, loudly, into the vacuum of my concentration. "You must find this place really funny!" He chuckled, and then, like an arrogant magician, leaned over and snapped on the old greenish desk lamp, throwing that emerald haze, with its queerly threatening aura, over the room. It picked up everything again: the lizardy infant mummy, the crystal paperweights, the desk letters with their medieval Swiss postmarks.

Suddenly I hated being there with him. I shrugged my shoulders, pretending I could smile. I looked at him; the truth was, I was frightened

88

speechless.

"Come on," he demanded. "Whatcha wanna see? Open up, just say it."

Maybe the wine had got to me. Maybe I was … okay, I admit it: I was much more scared than drunk; I had drunk so little wine. "I, I, I—I want to go back."

"Go back where?" He held me in his large arms. "Where you wanna go, baby?"

I put my head on his deep chest. I wanted to bury myself there. I wanted to be protected by his body. "Bed."

"Naw. Come on." He lifted my chin up. "You're curious. Aren't you? You wanna know all about me. Who I am. The whole *megillah*, as the Yids say, right?"

I started crying. "No, I don't."

"Of course, you do. Don't lie. You think I'm sick. I have these funny little things—those statues that you were staring at; that funny mummy thing. Really weird crap, right?"

"I want to sit down. Would you let me sit down, please?"

He told me sure, and led me over to a chair. I sat on it. I guess it was just the tension—I had been so tense. Who wouldn't be? I had just met him, really, and he was … strange; yes, he was strange. If only I'd had a little more time with him. I was repelled by him, and also crazy about him. Time was falling in on me. He made me feel both bigger and smaller than I'd ever felt before. Suddenly everything started to do this jiggly little dance in front of my eyes. Time was screwing me. The books, the strange little statues, the dead reptile.

I clenched my eyes closed, then opened them. Tearily, I looked up at him. "Would you do me a favor?" I asked.

"Sure." He smiled knowingly. He could do me any favor, he was so sure of himself.

"Kiss me, please. Just kiss me."

He squatted down on his haunches, and kissed me. I was shaking. "I have something for you," he said and got up. "I want you to have this."

I nodded. I was so frightened and relieved at the same time—I mean, I was alive still, right? Yes, that was true, I was still alive: I thought my stomach was going to heave.

He took out a little brown paper bag from his desk, and a teaspoon. "I want you to take some of this in your mouth and just swallow it." He scooped out some powder. It was a deeply pigmented purple with a kind of reddish-brown tint. It was mealy looking; it reminded me of worm cast-offs. If anyone else had offered me this, I would have thrown it away. But I opened my mouth, and passively took it.

It tasted simultaneously hot and sweet, like cayenne pepper mixed with honey and cinnamon. But it felt grainy, like dirt in my mouth. Or maybe like dried pellets of tapioca; but not hard. Soft and powdery. I had difficulty swallowing it. He offered me no water. He rubbed my throat, then kissed me again. That kind, supple mouth; it lavished me. It was like being kissed by Zeus, if you'd just happened to meet Zeus next to Macy's. "Come on," he coaxed softly. "Get it all down. That's nice. I know it tastes kinda funny. But it's something you gotta do...."

I swallowed again. "I'd like some water."

"Naw. Water just dilutes it. You got enough water inside you. They been taking this for thousands of years. You know what it is?" I shook my head. "It's the dried blood of an insect, kind of like a beetle, that feeds on desert cattle somewhere in the Sudan. The Egyptians used it. Very powerful stuff, lemme tell you."

It was. I felt my stomach rise. I threw up a wad of something—mostly purple spit—into my hand. He took out a hankie and cleaned off my mouth and fingers.

"I think it's time for me to show you some things," he said.

My vision was now blurry and the room started to do this circular, elliptical motion, like a tilt-a-wheel. I grabbed at him, and he held me for a moment, then let me go. "How 'bout the books? You wanna see them? Karl said you were looking at that French one. That's nice. That's something, that book. I can read French. I can't speak it worth shit, but I can read it. When they were training me, they taught me how to read French and German, and what to say and how to act when I do what I have to do. They taught me a lot of things, you wanna see...." It was just his beautiful mouth moving.

I tried to rise, just to stand so that I wouldn't throw up again. I couldn't sit anymore. He was pulling books down and opening them up for me. Page after page of diagrams and strange charts and lists. They were only a blur, like the ink was running after being rained on. Then he started to touch the strange statues, that looked like they had been made out of mud. He stroked them, smiled, talked to them the way that people talk to dogs or cats, knowing they can't talk back, but they talk anyway. "Hey, buddies," he said, grinning. "How're my little friends, you sweet little bastards?" He closed his eyes. Suddenly I saw he was crying. "You are sweet little bastards!" Tears fell from his eyes.

I did not want to see this. Even with the blurry way I felt, it was painful to watch. He rocked a bit. Put his head in his hands, and cried and rocked. I wanted to approach him, but was scared I would throw up on him.

Then he calmed down. He was sober now, and that controlled quality came back to him. He carefully lifted the third and most revolting of the mud creatures, the squatty, muscular male one, off the shelf.

"This was a real gift. I treasure it seriously." He looked right into my eyes. "It protects me, Allen. It gives somebody like me, I guess you could say, power. Some people, some smart people, know that a part of your soul is inside something like this. That's what a gift is all about—you've just got to feel it. It's all about the giving and the treasuring. And also the taking. It's about how it got to you, and how you received it. And it's not just about the way it looks, but about what it's made out of." He halted, then said: "See him?"

Up close, the strange, plumpish creature was even more disturbing. Exaggerated muscles bulged all over it. The jaw had this threatening calm in its rigid set, that went down into its neck and shoulders, then into its massive thighs. A slight, almost benign smile on its face became lost in the darkness of its eyes; it had bizarre, clawed, animal-toed feet.

"It's called a pupè," he said. "It's like a tiny...psychic engine: it performs some—how can I put it?—some intense *work* of the soul. It's not your usual run-of-the-mill fetish, lemme tell you. It's a"—he paused; a slight, almost beguiling smile whose expression resembled, for an instant, the object's itself bloomed on his face—"an amazing gift. Entrusted to me. I took it and went from being a screw-up to...what I am. You don't know the power a gift like this has got!"

Passively, I looked at him as he spoke.

"That's how the dead come back to life," he continued. "I mean it. If you're fuckin' smart, you don't underestimate something like this, no matter what anybody else tells you."

He brought the statue close to my face, as he had with the repulsive infant reptile. He made me touch it, bringing my trembling fingers to it. It felt oddly similar to skin, strangely soft, yet muscley-rigid and bumpy. I had not expected that almost seductive texture from the coarse powdery way it appeared. The skin felt close to alive, though dead. My hands were freezing; my heart pounded. The soft red, tapioca-like grains were bad enough, but this...

It was horrid, this dwarfish creature. It—he—like I said, had this huge phallus, this dick that trailed close to its knees. When you're small, you envy well-endowed men, but this was not human.

"Funny, ain't he?" Powars asked. "He's called Nicky. They all have a name, though that's not his real name. His real name's—well, somewhere they know what his real name is. But, as Juliet said, 'What's in a name?' Huh? What's important is the soul. And this thing, it's got some kinda soul inside it. I know that; know what I mean?"

I did not know. I did not want to know.

He put Nicky on his desk, and looked at him. "I wish I could tell you 92 a lot more about this thing, this power, this...anyway, one day—"

My knees went wobbly. I fell on the floor. All I could say was, "No, no, no!" I did not want him to go on anymore. It was too upsetting, but he continued talking softly, this strange gibberish about what he could do and how he could make me do anything, while at the same time he pulled my shirt off, then my shoes off, and my pants down; then my underwear; my socks. I was now naked, like that horrible dwarf, but strangely enough, my cock was, like they say in the porno mags, "rock" hard.

I mean, I was sick to my stomach, dizzy, totally out of it—and my dick was like iron, like it belonged to somebody else. It wasn't even mine anymore. I didn't feel sexual at all, just removed and scared and yet distant at the same time. Like there was some real part of me there—a third part—watching one part that was frightened and another that had this huge erection, bigger than I'd ever had.

"Nice," he said. "I like it when your little dingy-dong's like that. I like your sweet little dong, you know that? I like the fact that it's sweet and nice and so suckable."

He started stroking me and then put me into his mouth. He was still dressed. I felt like I was a doll that he was playing with, and, I admit, I loved it. The sheer passive wonder of it. He kept jerking me and sucking me and stroking me and then his teeth—wise, yes, they were so wise—found my balls.

My balls did not hurt very much that time. He had my big, hardened, engorged cock cupped in one of his hands and my scrotum in his mouth, and there was a little blood, just a little, I could see it, coming out, dribbling down his chin while he sucked at me, as a bee would, hovering over a flower; or perhaps a soft, fluttering, furry-tongued moth.

I watched. His eyes were closed, but he had this totally blessed look on his face. His shirt was stained. All sorts of stuff was coming out of me—some of it even had that brownish purple color from what he had given me to swallow. He was messy. It had dribbled on him. I could see that. I felt so worn out, and yet with no pain at all: nothing. My dick was still hard, but I was in no hurry to climax. In fact, I wasn't sure if I could.

He stopped. This diabolical laugh came out of him. The kind of grating laugh you'd expect from some … psycho; but no, I couldn't say that. I loved him.

I kissed him. I could taste this sharp, organic flavor in his mouth, like something pressed out of a freshly dismembered organ. There was also another taste, vaguely familiar, reminding me of the burning, powdery pellets he had given me. Some of it, like I said, had dribbled from him. It looked like … a worm. Not a live one, but just the funny, kind of screwy shape of it. It was thin, white, and shiny, kind of like cum itself, but denser. It slid and he caught it in his hand and then sucked it back into his mouth.

"I'm making a mess," he said. "I shouldn't be wearing this shirt. It's gonna be pretty hard for Karl to clean it."

He got up and pulled the shirt off. I realized he did not have the sweater on now. He must have taken it off in the living room. The shirt was beautiful—it had that real magnificence that his shirts had. Luxurious. Expensive. I would never wear shirts like that. That was the truth; and there I was, wading into some depth that had never been allowed me before. That had always been declared out of bounds, out of my league.

I thought about that. Or maybe I just understood it. The understanding made me feel a little better. I could do this. My head slowed down: it stopped feeling like it was going through the spin cycle of a washer, or trying desperately to escape a pendulum with the business end of an ax attached to it.

He pulled me to his hairy chest. "I gotta tell you something, Allen," he said, the words now clear to me. A moment earlier, it had all seemed muffled, like I was slogging through water. "Any harm I do to you, I'd do to me. I'd just as soon chew my own arm off as harm you."

I nodded. "Okay," I heard myself say. That cock—the one that belonged to me but felt as if it were attached to a doll—was still hard: I was so out of it. "Thank you," I heard myself say, "for telling me that."

"No, baby. Thank you. I wish I could just tell you the whole shit; but we're gonna have such a good time in Switzerland—that's what I want you to know. The Swiss are the most hospitable people you're ever gonna meet. They'd give you the shirts off their backs, really. You should see; they're really nice. Believe me, they've given me enough shirts."

94

EIGHT

I don't remember

getting into bed that night, or even going to sleep. All I remember are a series of slow images that unfolded in my head and then passed out of it. He made me shower with him in his big bathroom. He soaped me down gently, and placed this wonderful, fresh-smelling French lotion on my raw balls. It felt very soothing. Then we got into bed and Destry held me, and kissed me. "You should have seen me before they got to me," he said. "I was just a snot-nosed shit from the boonies in New Jersey. My parents—they were like white trash. Sometimes you get these people—like generation after generation, they don't amount to nothing. White people can't get much lower than what I came from. I used to wander around thinking, how did I get here? Where was I gonna go? Then, they found me somehow. They just have this way of knowing you; they knew I was smart. They knew I came from the bottom of the bag, and they would pull me up.

"They brought me back to this house, where ... you shoulda seen that house. So, you think I got strange things? All the funny little things in it; the different, winding rooms. Old objects. Books. At first, I was scared shitless ... but that's when they started teaching me. They can look directly into your heart, and see all the way down through you. You don't know—you just don't know, Allen. They can turn you into a ... anyway, look what they did for me."

I remember nodding my head. I was buzzy with sleep and exhaus-

95

tion and a kind of fear that stayed right there on the surface, always touching me, no matter how much I believed I'd escaped it. I looked at him—it was dark, of course, and he was all hairy and intense and real now—and in my own way, I understood what he was saying. I did. I mean, I didn't understand it, there was no way I could. I knew nothing at all, really, but I understood what it was like always to be afraid, to always feel outside of it. He nuzzled me. Held me. I wanted his mouth on my dick again, it was now back to being little. You don't know what it's like to have a small cock—just a skinny wienie—and have a huge man adore you. Just ravish you. He had me. I was petrified with desire for him. Even the things he did to what was inside my balls did not make me want him less.

"You know what I'm saying?" he asked me. I nodded. I told him yes. I could see a smile blooming like a rose in the rain on his face. Sure, I *knew*. I knew nothing. But I did, in my own way. "We're gonna have such a good time," he promised. "You know that old song, 'Don't know much about history / don't know much about geometry. / Don't know much about French I took / don't know much from any book'?"

I nodded. I was very sleepy. Will-less, really. He could have read— or sung—the *Yellow Pages* to me, and I would have listened; or maybe not listened. But who cared?

His tongue went into my ear. "Well, you don't need t'know any of that shit. Because they taught me the real language—the language of"— he paused, then said—"circumstances. That's it: circumstances and pure intimidation. Money. Power. *Force*. Now I know it. Know what I mean?" I didn't answer him. What could I say? I was the twenty-first century version of a ribbon clerk. When a queer stops being a ribbon clerk, what does he become? I just listened to him.

"It didn't come free," he whispered. "No, baby, it don't come free. They always wanna keep taking something from you, until they find out just what you don't have. I know it's Greek to you, baby, but that's why I need you. See?"

I nodded to him, and then he began to make love to me again, like I was still a doll. I had to say that, it was the truth. He sucked me softly and sweetly, and stroked himself while he did that. His teeth went into my balls again, but I didn't feel it so much. I don't know what he was taking out of me. Perhaps it was the very hormonal essence of what sperm is, but I just drifted along, on this kind of odd, tender, magical music that was going on in my head. I'm a baby boomer and it was all this music from my youth, my kidhood. Old Stevie Wonder songs that evoked the beach and endless breezy summers to me, when I was a kid—and the Eagles and the Beach Boys—and I was drifting along on that and I knew he was taking more out of me; but I was no longer frightened. Maybe it was that strange gunk that he made me swallow; maybe it was just he, but though I was hard, I had no desire, no impetus, towards climax.

He was satisfying something within me. Something so primal and intrinsic that at that point I had no name for it, but it was there. I'd been too afraid of it before, but now I could give in to it. I died. I know, I just suddenly died—settling into this miasma of sinking delight, of some pure, delicious hunger being satisfied. It was like Jesus himself were feeding me, and tasting of me all over at the same time. I could no longer feel his mouth on me, his teeth at my testicles drawing from me some essential chemical, some force that I would only miss if I ever came back truly alive—that is, *if* I had ever been truly alive.

But at that moment, for that moment, I was there, curled up into it: with him. I was no longer conniving, inventing myself as we're all supposed to do, all the time, in this endless "opportunity" ahead of us now, that seems more like a guillotine's falling blade, slicing away at the real life in its path. There was some pain, sure, but no more than I normally felt in the course of living. I swear. I was just with him, and amazingly, miraculously, happy. He was taking me, drawing me into that vast darkness, where one flint-spark of light reigns supreme when it hits the soul. And he was that spark.

97

It was right there, at just the point where his wise tooth pulled something from me. Something I could not know, but which made me his.

Karl came in later. "I have breakfast ready for you, sir. I know this will be a difficult day. Winchell is ready for you, when you want him."

Powars nodded to him. I was already up. I did not sleep very hard after it was over; after he fell asleep. I just stayed awake in the dark and thought in a kind of low-grade way. No insights. No figuring it all out. I remembered, mostly, what my life had been like for the past twenty, close to thirty, years. I was one of that army of queer losers, the kind you see in bars nursing their drinks because they can't afford a second or a third. The kind who don't get on TV, who kind of scamper away from attention, because we associate that with getting exposed. Picked on.

The new big, mega-economy was rushing past me and I couldn't grab a fucking nickel of it. I had nice friends. Polite, sweet guys. We'd go out to Formica-tabled diners and eat, and worry about who owed what on the check. We'd see a Broadway play at half-price every now and then, and splurge on a vacation at some place like Provincetown, where we'd meet other guys exactly like us. We'd talk about how expensive things had become, while farther down at some other place on the beach, you'd see all the young hot-snot richies, who only smiled. They never complained. It was, after all, their time, and their world.

I didn't hate it. It was just the life that I had, a kind of constant kick in my little nuts. It was like seeing those big luxury car commercials on TV—you know, where you'll never be in that quiet, expensive world of country clubs and designer restaurants and golf courses.

Now, with no ticket of my own, I was suddenly in that world.

That's what I thought about, and then Karl woke us up. He drew apart the curtains in the bedroom a bit, and then, discreetly left. Powars grinned at me, sleepily. "Good night, last night, wasn't it? I mean, you liked that restaurant, right? I drank too much, didn't I?"

I smiled and shrugged my shoulders. Who was I to tell him how much to drink? We put on dressing gowns, and went in for breakfast. Some light started to come in. I never liked getting up in the dark, although some people do that all the time. I had coffee, muffins and an egg. Powars had cold cereal, and dove into the papers. He kept grinning and chuckling. The price of tin was going up. The price of oil was going to snap. "The boys won't let it go too high!" One of his Swiss drug people, he told me, was going to be "very happy. There are now some real opportunities all over Africa—closing for most people, and opening for them!" It sounded like some kind of religious jargon. He could have been speaking Japanese and I would have understood about as much. I went back to the bedroom, used the toilet, and showered. I was in my underwear when Powars came in. I knew we were going to fly off that day, but what else was going to happen, I had no idea.

"I want you to go out today and buy yourself something for the trip. Karl'll go with you. There's a guy I know, he has a place on Madison Avenue. He'll help you. Karl just phoned him. It's all set up."

I wanted to ask him what he'd be doing, but I was afraid to. "I guess you're busy," I said.

"*Busy* ain't half of it! Two meetings in the morning, at the Waldorf, and then one in the early afternoon, back on Park, that's going to be murder. You got any idea what those blocks on Park Avenue between Grand Central and Fifty-seventh Street are like?"

I shook my head.

"They're pure money! There are people who live between Connecticut and Park Avenue. That's the world for them. Gwinny'll be with me. Winchell'll take me over. Come on, just put on something nice and you'll get a whole lot of new stuff to take on the trip."

"What time will you be back?"

"Karl'll get you back in time. Don't worry." I looked at him, and he understood that he was not answering my question. "Okay, I'll be back close to three. I want you to be ready by then. The flight's at six, but we got rush hour, you know." He disappeared into the bathroom and shut the door. I knew that he wanted me to be gone when he was out. I could tell that. He had a lot on his mind, obviously, and he didn't want me fussing about things. At least that is what I told myself. I put on some slacks, one of my cheap shirts, and my sports jacket, and Karl was waiting for me by the door.

"We'll take a taxi across town, sir," he said, without anything that even resembled a smile. I nodded. I felt nervous now. More so than I had been with Powars. I felt that I had some leverage with Powars, some closeness, something to call my own with him. But I had nothing with Karl. I could not order him about the way Destry did. I could not avoid him either, or be friendly with him. Karl never allowed avenues for that. He was wearing a light, tan overcoat, cut in a slightly military fashion, and a matching driving cap. Both brought out all of his bland Swiss efficiency. The doormen downstairs raced to get us a taxi, and did, faster than I could even imagine. Alone, I would have had drivers avoid me like the plague.

It was a beautiful, clear morning; the park was beginning to lose its leaves. I lowered my window a bit and a fresh breeze rolled in. We drove in silence. I had this immediate feeling that I'd miss New York. I'd never really been away before, not even to Canada. People like me just didn't do that. Maybe Provincetown, or some beaches in New Jersey—I'd been to Key West years ago—but not Switzerland. Not just fly away. I felt kind of butterflyish, and also excited.

We turned onto Madison Avenue, drove past the Whitney Museum, and stopped at Eightieth Street. Karl paid the driver and I got out. The shop was called Jonathan Rune. It was very hip, all in dark, bronzy colors with muffled gangsta rap music hammering away in the background. The annoying hip-hop sound gave a staccatic heartbeat to the place; I thought it was almost funny, like Rune were saying, "Fuck you, rich people." But, in person, he wouldn't say that. No, not at all. Mr. Rune himself waited on me. He was in his late fifties, athletic and energetic, slightly short, slightly balding, dressed snappily in a three-piece English-style tweed suit. He looked like a well-paid accountant at a good hotel, the kind who knows to the penny how much money you have.

After a few minutes, he took his jacket off and tossed it on the counter; he and Karl already had a plan of what I should have. Karl held my old sports coat, as he told him that I was going with Mr. Powars to Switzerland. Rune nodded. "Great place! Those Swiss don't stand for monkey business. That's why the place runs like a clock. You know, they wouldn't elect the wife of a disgraced president to become their senator!" He chuckled over the threatening beat. "It's all that celebrity stuff; that's the only way the good people of New York could have done such a dumb thing." Like an expert bullfighter, he snapped open a waiting, autumn-weight, squid-ink-black suit jacket, so that I could get my arms into it. "I think you'll like this. It has just enough flare in it."

It did—it was almost poignant; I had never worn a suit like that. I did not believe it could exist for someone like me: it was single-breasted, fit with the precision of a fine watch; the buttons, like little stars, were sewn in perfectly, and the lapels draped so effortlessly... I can hardly describe it. I felt like a nobleman in a Caravaggio painting; like one of those self-insulated rich people you see strolling casually at the Metropolitan Museum. I went into the comfortable dressing room. The pants were artful, with minute pleats placed exactly where they should be and discreet side pockets, the kind in which a man might stow a single, pearl-handled pocket knife, but never show it. Rune and Karl came into the dressing rom. I did a little turn in front of a three-way mirror, trying to keep from sweating.

Rune jabbered on to Karl, praising Mr. Powars, the excellent Swiss air, and life on Madison Avenue. He bent over and did a few final nip-and-pin jobs in the right places; then both pieces were handed to an Indian tailor in the back, who did everything while I waited. "Tell Destry I envy him flying over there again," Rune said to me, while I sipped some coffee. We were out in the store now. "The Swiss don't have all those reg-ulations on business like we do here in New York—that's why that coun-try's always thriving."

Karl looked closely at him. "You seem to know a lot about Switzerland," he said dryly.

Rune smiled. "I'm a businessman. Businessmen always like a place where they don't ask questions." A woman in a large fur coat came into the store with a small dog. He rushed over to her, just as the tailor emerged with my suit. I tried it on in the dressing room again. I realized that I hated that man, hated Madison Avenue, but liked the suit. What could I say?

"Does it fit all right?" Karl called to me.

I told him that it did, then came out in my stocking feet. Rune broke off from the woman in the coat, and saw me. "Get your shoes on," he ordered. "We'll see if you need a little more in at the cuffs."

I put my shoes on, and he looked at me as if he were inspecting a dog at a show. I turned around and he gathered the waist of the coat in about half an inch. "When you get back, bring it in. We'll do a little more work on it. Is that all right?"

I did not answer him. I had no idea what condition I'd be in when I returned from Switzerland. Karl told him it would be fine, then signed for the suit, and we brought it out in a handsome beige box tied with cords that I wanted to keep for the rest of my life. Suddenly people looked at me differently on Madison Avenue, like I belonged there. We went into another store, where Karl bought me two white shirts that felt like silk; two handsome ties; and these gorgeous black jeans that felt like suede.

"How about a coat?" he asked.

I felt kind of numb. I had never spent so much money, even other people's. He grabbed my arm, and we walked a couple of blocks in silence until we came to a shearling shop, and there Karl bought me this wonderful coat. Or at least, Destry had; I wanted to believe that. Suddenly I felt tired and completely undeserving and stupid. This did not happen to people like me. We had lunch at a small Italian restaurant where the maitre d' tripped over himself to be accommodating. Karl mentioned
102 Destry's name, and it was like I was sprinkled in gold dust. I had a salad and little dumplings and squab. I'd never had squab—it was really like a small chicken, kind of like the *poussin*, but it tasted very good.

We took another taxi back. It was close to two when we got out on Central Park West. I told Karl that I needed to buy a few more things at a drug store nearby. "I would have got them for you," he protested, but I told him they were personal, so he brought my new treasures up to the apartment, and I had a moment to myself.

I walked into Central Park and sat down on a bench, dazed. This was really happening to me. Suddenly I was frightened again. It was not only that Powars was mysterious—and strange—it was that living like this could start to ... mean something. And then, it could just as easily be taken away. I went back to his building, and the doorman let me in instantly. I was taken up in the elevator, and let out into the apartment.

The apartment felt empty. I thought that Karl or Powars would have met me at the door, but instead there was only silence. Then I heard Karl puttering in the kitchen, and I walked softly into the bedroom, just in case Destry were there, grabbing a quick nap. I had hoped he would be. I wanted to climb onto the big bed with him, and just hug him, kiss him, undress him myself. But he wasn't there. I waited for a few very long minutes, circling the room with my eyes, then I walked out. The quiet of the big apartment could easily overwhelm me; I felt like such an intruder. Then, almost on tiptoe, I went to the old office in the back. I thought—well, did I really *think* it?—I just supposed that he'd be in there, perhaps with the strange books ... his hobby ... was that what it was? I'd already been in, so how could he mind me returning, unless, of course, the door were locked?

The light through the transom was playing its twisting, hallucinatory dance of shadows on the opposite red wall; I put my hand on the crystal knob and began to try it, when I heard this soft sound, halfway, I'd guess, between a low laugh and a compulsive sob, coming from within. It had a constant modulation, and seemed sort of animalish, like the growly, stomachy kind of sound a stalking dog sometimes makes. For a moment I could not believe it was coming from inside. It was too repetitious to be human. I was certain that it had to be coming from another apartment. Then the crystal knob gave, and I was inside.

103

The green lamp was on and the three little statues were on the desk, bathed in its strange morbid light. For a moment I was sure they were moving; I had to control a rush of fear knocking through me. I was afraid to look, but could not turn away. There was Destry, in his beautiful clothes, on the carpet, kneeling in front of them, making this awful moan that broke into funny, eerie pitches like waves within his throat. I could not see his face, but knew he was in a trance. He must have been. And a woman was with him, standing, stroking his hair. She seemed very kindly and warm, with lovely Asian features. She reminded me of some serene, caring nun in an old movie.

Her fingers were slowly caressing his head, in time to the noise. The sound made my blood turn icy. I managed to look up and watched her go to the desk and change the position of the statues, as Destry continued making the noise. Very carefully, she pushed Nicky back, and brought the reptile and the female forward. Then she turned, looking right at me, and I observed, instantly, a resemblance between the seriousness in her face and the nude female figure's expression.

"You must be Allen," she said.

Destry sprang to his feet. "Allen?" He turned to face me. I could see his shoulders tensing.

"It's all right," she said. She whispered something into his ear.

"He's gotta learn these things!" Destry exploded. "Man, when are you gonna learn a closed door *is* a closed door?"

My mouth dropped. I could not answer him. I hated him again. I felt powerless and horrible, I wanted to—

"Destry!" She strode towards me and apologized for him. "He didn't mean that, sweetheart." She looked back at him. "You know, it's *that* sort of attitude, Destry—" she broke off talking to him, then gave me a quick kiss on my cheek. "I'm Gwinny. Gwendolyn Rose, in case you haven't figured that out." She took my arm and led me into the living room. I felt like I had stopped breathing. I don't even remember going with her. But suddenly I was in the living room, alone with her.

104

Now I could really look at her. She was young looking, tall, and very attractive. Her shiny black hair fell to her shoulders, and she had warmly toned skin, like porcelain with blushes of peach in it. Her eyes were a vivid green; you could not help noticing them. She wore a simple loose, high-necked jacket, part of a conservatively cut dark suit, with a skirt. It did make her nun-like, sort of in an old 1940s, World-War-Two-movie kind of way, somewhat disguising her figure, her breasts. Except for her sheer stockings, short skirt, and high-heeled black patent leather pumps. These were definitely now. Real. She took my hand. There was something calming and natural about her.

"Destry was just doing some yoga. You know, chanting," she explained. "It relaxes him. You can't believe the morning we've had. Sometimes, the old tricks don't work. He's just managed to insult three people who conveniently control too much money—"

"With shit for brains!" Destry came stalking out of his office. "Three fuckin' bozo-assholes!" He looked exhausted. He put his hands to his head for a moment. His face had about six lines in it that I'd never seen before. He looked over at me. "You get the suit?" I told him I had. "Good. Let's see it. Was Johnny Rune okay to you?"

I told him he was, but Powars wasn't really listening. "Go on, put it on. Gwinny got your visa for you—so I've got it. Come on, chop-chop, I wanna see the suit. We gotta leave soon."

Gwinny looked at Destry and then smiled at me. "It's all right," she said. "He's a bit snappish from the day. Like I said, sometimes the old tricks just don't work. Things did not—"

"I told you to put on the suit," Destry commanded. "I want you to look good for this trip."

Gwinny shrugged and shook her head slowly. I walked out crushed, like I'd been dismissed. In Destry's bedroom, I put on the suit. I'd wanted to shower again just before we left; now I wasn't sure I'd have the time. Why did he have to treat me that way? All the sparkle and wonder of the morning left me. It was as if all of this money was …wrapped around those ugly little statues. I looked at myself in Destry's full-length mirror. I felt like a fool in an expensive suit; the beautiful giftness of it just fell away. I walked back out. He and Gwendolyn were seated, having a drink. Karl was there. Powars looked up at me.

"God, you look beautiful!" he exclaimed. He sprang up and ran his big fingers through my hair. Then he kissed me on the mouth, right there in front of Karl and Gwinny. I still felt icy. Shitty. I couldn't help it.

"He does look good," Karl said. "Mr. Rune did a fine job."

"He looks splendid," Gwinny agreed. She smiled at me sweetly. "We're sorry, Allen, about what happened. I mean—I should have locked the door. I know Destry hates to be bothered when he's meditating."

Destry shrugged sheepishly; deep embarrassment on his face. I had never seen that before. "There are things he's gotta learn. I had to learn 'em. I think he knows that."

Karl began picking up the glasses. "Can I offer you something to drink?" he asked me.

"Too late," Destry said. "We have to get this show started soon. You got me all packed?"

Karl nodded. "Yes, sir. It is all as you want it, Mr. Powars. In the bedroom."

Powars smiled; he looked at Gwinny and then at me. "Time just eats us, don't it? Thank you, Karl, you're a real *mensch*!"

Karl smiled. He began to laugh—I'd never seen him laugh—then he left the room. There was an awkward moment; I felt, again, kind of useless. I told them that I wanted a drink of water, and followed Karl into the kitchen.

He was sitting on a stool, finishing a cup of coffee, reading a Swiss paper. He jumped up when he saw me. "I'm only taking a moment," he apologized, as if I had caught him on the toilet or something. I knew that I shouldn't just help myself, so I asked him for a glass of water and he quickly got one for me, from bottled water in the refrigerator, with ice. I thanked him for going with me to Mr. Rune's; for everything.

He smiled with that dry, toothy face. "He would buy it for you, but you know his time is limited." He took another sip of coffee. "He told me what I should do. Everything was his idea. He wanted to give it to you."

I nodded. I hated to hate Powars. That was the truth. Then I asked Karl where would we be in Switzerland. He was Swiss and I knew nothing about the place. Audrey Hepburn had lived there—I remembered reading that once in *People*. It was where the rich, the famous, and the got-it-all people lived. The kind who did not have to bother mixing with anyone. "It's nice. You'll see. You'll be at a mountain resort by a lake. They always meet there. I know because sometimes I have to telephone him there."

"What will I do?"

"Why ask me? I'm a servant. You're his friend, but—" He stopped talking.

"But what?" I asked.

"Don't press him. It's important not to press a man like Mr. Powars. Anyway, *gute reisen*—that means 'good trip.'" He shook my hand seriously, then he got up and started polishing and cleaning again. I returned to the large living room. It was empty. Gwendolyn was gone, without even a good-bye. I sat down for a minute, thinking that Powars would be back and tell me what to do. He didn't, so I went into the bedroom.

He was in the shower, but one of his suitcases, in elegant dark leather, was open on the bed. Shirts were perfectly laid out in it, folded and fitted in with some slacks, another jacket, his underwear, his expensive cashmere socks. Another suitcase waited on the floor, but next to the suitcase on the bed was a smaller traveling bag made of some kind of impregnated canvas I wasn't familiar with. Like Louis Vuitton. Maybe it was German. Or Swiss. It was dark, sleek, very understated; almost threatening in its cool elegance. And closed.

I heard his water running, and thought about opening it. My first thought was that there'd be a gun in it, like the one he had taken to Toyland. Then I thought about the statues—the little mud effigies, as I called them—with that strange feeling like skin, that made my skin crawl. I wondered if he'd be taking the horrifying Nicky in it. I expected the lit-

107

tle thing's grotesquely big cock to pop out at me. I undid a clasp—it crisply snapped open—then carefully began to unzip the zipper. It made a noise like the teeth of a small saw ripping through cardboard.

I did it slowly, loathing every disengaging pop. Then I stopped hearing it—because my heart was beating too fast—and I thought: do I really want to know what's in there?

I did. The zipper managed its course almost all the way down. All I saw immediately were files, folders, letters. Then this silence, as his water stopped. I raced to get the zipper back up—and it snagged belligerently, about two inches from total closure. It looked like someone's open fly, with a bit of shirt showing. I jumped away from it, like it was on fire. He came in, drying himself. He smiled at me, his teeth dazzlingly white. I was taken back, mesmerized. My immediate impulse was to surrender to him. He had me completely. All of my previous storm of hatred reformed into this helplessly falling powder of guilt—and love. I wanted to kiss his big hairy feet; I wanted to be everything that he wanted me to be, even if I had so little idea what that was. Powars came over and gave me a big kiss. Then he looked over at the bag and smiled. "I bet you wanna know what's really in there. Is your curiosity running away with you?"

I tried to shrug off what he said. "It's none of my business."

"But you tried."

"I thought you might have a gun—I just—"

"I'm not that dumb, Allen. You don't take a gun on Swissair like that. What else did you think?"

"Okay." I had to come clean. "I wondered if you were going to take Nicky, or maybe some other things, in it."

"I wouldn't do that. Naw, they were gifts; I wouldn't take gifts like that on a trip like this. You're the only gift I wanna take with me to Switzerland."

He pulled me into his big arms and kissed me again. I could tell he was shaking a bit, nervous himself. I asked him if he were all right. "I'm okay," he said, smiling. "The day's been kind of a freakout. I'm glad you're here." He picked up the small valise. "Papers, really. I'll show you." He unzipped it quickly all the way and pulled out much of what was in it. He showed me his palm computer, then repacked the papers. "You must think I'm a dope! Jesus—trying t'bring a gun into Switzerland like that. I've taken heat into those mountains, but you don't do it in some bag with your papers and a palm computer. Would a gun scare you?"

"A little," I lied.

He put a hand on my shoulder. "That's okay. We all get scared sometimes. I know what that's about." His smile had disappeared.

He seemed suddenly deflated.

I wanted to be able to give *him* something. "Things aren't going well for you, are they?" I asked. "Is there something I can do?"

"Don't worry," he said, stroking my hair again. "You're here. As long as you don't leave, Allen, I'll be okay."

He smiled at me once more, drawing me into his soft brown eyes. He was so strikingly handsome now, fresh from the shower. He began to dress. He put on a pair of fresh boxer undershorts. They were white, neatly ironed, with thin blue stripes. He sat on the edge of the bed for a moment and told me how good I looked in the new suit. He asked if I wanted to shower again. I told him I'd do it quickly. I wanted to brush my teeth, too. "You should," he said. "Shower, I mean." He sighed loudly. "I'm glad you're coming with me. There's a lotta shit riding on this Swiss trip; stuff you don't even know about."

"I thought it was like a vacation."

"It will be, for you!"

He looked away from me and started to rub his fingers anxiously through his hair. He laid back on the bed and closed his eyes.

He looked wonderful—just the fresh white shorts with the blue stripes. The hairy body with that hair that sometimes looked almost trans- 109 parent, and at other times dark. I wanted to say something; I wanted to jump on the bed and suck him. But I felt blank.

He sat up. "You don't really know much about me. I wish you could understand what I feel about you. I wish even I could."

I took the black suit jacket off, and sat down next to him. I looked at him and stroked his head, the way I had seen Gwendolyn Hong Rose doing it. "I was afraid," I burst out suddenly, "you were going to take one of those statues. That thing scared me more than a gun, they're—"

"You talking about Nicky?"

I nodded my head.

"He's a gift, I told you. They're fragile. I wouldn't take 'em. The stuff they're made out of, it's just not something you travel around with. They break and—"

I nodded. "Yes, I see." I did not, but I was glad Nicky was not in there.

"It'll protect you, too, one day. Anyway, you don't have to worry about any of that. All I'm taking are letters, papers; a small computer. I'll have meetings—"

"Sure, meetings!" Suddenly the trip made more sense to me: he would have lots and lots of business to do; I'd just be a guest. I'd relax. We'd be together at night; romantic, lovely. I smiled. An idea popped into my head and I said, smartly, "I guess Customs would give you a hard time with the statues, anyway. Wouldn't they?"

He laughed. "Naw. Customs never go into your bags, I mean not people like me. That's what's so good about being rich. All kinds of people respect you. Cab drivers, Customs. They act like you're from another planet. Growing up, I had cops all over me. I was arrested once because some of my buddies stole a car and I was in it. I was innocent, you know, but guilt by association. Makes me understand what Negroes go through. Luckily, nothing remained as a record because I was a juvenile. But, hey, you've never been in trouble—right?"

"No," I said. "Never."

110   "Yeah. You're clean as a whistle. Of course, you never can tell whose mouth a whistle's been in, right? Or where that mouth has been. I know guys who are richer than ... anyway, they're real rich assholes. They'd eat

doody out of a cute girl's twat; I mean that." He chuckled.

I closed my eyes, trying to keep what he had said away from me. I hated his vulgarity, that sledgehammer humor. Why was he like this? He could be so horrible ... so demeaning.

I undressed, went into the big bathroom and quickly showered. I brushed my teeth, shaved again. I knew I could never come up to what Destry Powars was used to. But somehow—why, I didn't know—he needed me, and that alone could get me past the ugly, rough parts of himself he showed to me. He was in his trousers and a beautiful blue shirt with French cuffs, when I got out, picking at his large toes with the thick gray nails, and back on the phone, talking to someone about tin, then drugs. A new prescription drug was being made in Thailand and it needed funding. He grabbed my towel with one hand and dried my back. He kept kissing the back of my neck and my shoulders while he talked.

I felt like a king, or the young, forgotten prince whose lover is one. I put on my own underwear, and a new shirt Karl had bought for me, and then the new suit. Destry hung up, and finished dressing. He looked magnificent. He wore a gorgeous tie. This incredible, deep mauve silk, shot with threads of lavender and gold. He smiled as he tied it in the mirror.

"Nice, isn't it?"

I nodded. He brushed his hair and put an expensive lemony oil on it, just a slight amount. His hair glowed. "I'm ready for my close up, Mr. DeMille!"

I laughed.

"Hey, can you go out and tell Karl to tell Winchell we're ready? We are, aren't we?"

I told him we were. I went out and told Karl to call Winchell, who was in the car. Karl smiled. "Winchell is waiting," he said. "I'll go in and help Mr. Powars with his bags. Are you packed?"

"Yes," I said.   111

This is the nuttiest thing I've ever done in my life, I thought: going to Europe with a man I hardly knew; I had no money to speak of, he could do anything he wanted to me over there. Maybe this was some kind of white slavery ring, maybe...

Rush hour traffic was starting to thicken. Winchell drove us to JFK airport, weaving in and out of the cars like an Olympic swimmer in a pool. We sat in the back, and I watched everything as Powars spoke on his cell phone, read newspapers, glanced at a small TV for the news, and even napped a bit. When we got stuck in traffic, he got slightly anxious, but pretended he wasn't. When we finally arrived at the terminal, there were people to direct the car. Winchell pulled up, opened the trunk, and gave the luggage to a porter. Powars had three large suitcases—one just for his shoes, accessories, his overcoats—but he seemed completely confident that nothing would be lost. He kept the small valise with him.

The first class lounge was quiet and big and luxurious. The staff was so obsequious that I forgot I was in New York, where so many things operate on a "you-gottta-problem?" basis. In this magically cool, separate world was hot, excellent coffee and small tasty snacks; newspapers in all kinds of languages; plug-ins for computer equipment and fax machines. The reassuring, subtle buzz of polite rich people. Powars settled into a leather armchair and glanced through several papers. He chuckled to himself, looked up and smiled at me. "How you feeling?" he asked. "Excited? This is your first trip to Switzerland, right?"

I nodded.

I don't really travel that much, certainly not to Europe. Like I told you, I'd been to Key West once, a while back with some friends. We had stayed at one of those clothing-optional guest houses you see advertised in gay magazines, but since I have a small dick, I never took off all my clothes. Mostly I just watched. It was fun. I pretended that it didn't bother me that everyone else was doing something that I was afraid to do. Now here I was, flying off to Europe....

"But you been to Europe, right? England; France? You been before, right?"

"Yeah. A long time ago." I lied. "I don't really remember much."

"It's changed. Everything's changed. You'll love it. Now, we got them eating out the palms of our hands. You get all the nice things they got, and that European our-shit-don't-stink attitude's over. America's everything, because we have all the business now. You'll see. It's gonna be fun for you. I think you're gonna like it."

I smiled. A short while later, after Powars showed them the travel documents that he took out of a large black leather wallet, we got on the plane. It was big and smelled very nice and we were up front, in first class. My first impression, walking in, was how cold people were. Completely into themselves. That hostility you find in the back of the plane—all those people jammed together with their kids, trying to hog an empty overhead bin to themselves—was replaced with dry smugness. I looked around at the passengers, who did not return my gaze at all.

"You want window?" Powars asked me.

I shrugged. I had not thought about where I'd sit.

"Come on. Get the window. It's your first time flying into Switzerland. You're gonna like it."

I sat down first. Seats were only two across, so it made little difference to me really. I was in this completely different world, but it was a world Destry Powars was used to. There was a place for us to hang our jackets, and it was easy to get comfortable. Destry looked at the elegant little in-flight booklet. "They got some cool movies," he said, referring to the list of videos. You could program your own video, so you would not be forced to watch something you didn't want. The other passengers were not looking at the booklet. They were reading newspapers in German or French, or were at the in-flight phones. Some of them were at their computers. I thought you weren't supposed to use them at take off, but we had not taken off yet and the cabin attendants were too busy fussing to bother.

The other passengers were perfectly decked out and pressed and presentable, even though it was early evening and we had a night flight ahead of us. They looked like they could sleep in their clothes and still wake up perfect. Some of them were talking to each other in that discreet way that wealthy businessmen talk, in warm, hushed tones that could say anything—no matter how deadly—without ever "giving offense" to anyone.

For a moment I wondered what was going on in the other part of the plane, where the "real" people were; the ones who did not put on Madison Avenue clothes to fly in. I knew there would be whining kids, cheap luggage, people elbowing each other. But I felt comfortable now, in my new, expensive suit; who could tell that I was just a … johnny-come-lately? I eased down into my seat of glove leather, and it gently reclined into a comfy narrow bed.

It was all still so amazing to me: the truth was, I hardly knew Destry at all. When I first came to New York, I was in a bar in the East Fifties and I met a man who had been, I think the word is, "kept." He'd once been like me. Poor. He'd grown up in the style I would call "pig shit"; and then, when he was eighteen, he had met a man who just, well, did everything for him. "It was like Cinderella," he told me. "Except of course that I had to put out a lot. I liked him. I learned a lot from him—but it didn't last long."

I looked over at Destry. I was a lot older than eighteen—and I was certainly not being "kept" by him; but I did wonder what would happen when the novelty of me wore off. Or was I just a novelty? It was hard to say. Those things that he did to me with his mouth on my balls; even the strange way that I acted around him—maybe all of this was more than a novelty.

Was I really falling in love with him? How could I, seriously? There were times when I hated him.

Powars glanced at me, gave a funny smile, and closed his eyes. That anxious energy he had suddenly flaked off and what was under it, this sad softness, appeared. I hadn't realized how tired he was. At exactly 6:15, they announced take off in three languages—English, French, and German—and we started taxiing. As soon as the plane got off the ground, a pretty stewardess, or, as they call them, flight attendant, came around and offered us any beverage we wanted. Sodas, coffee, tea, champagne, Italian and French wines, aperitifs. Powars asked for a scotch. ("Why not?" he said to me. I nodded.)

I asked for a Bloody Mary and it arrived, very simple, with none of the celery and horseradish they use in bars to disguise the bad liquor. It tasted wonderful.

"They got good booze on this boat," Powars said smiling. He read some newspapers, then took off his shoes and loosened his tie. Suddenly I wanted to kiss him. But how could I? So I stroked his face. There was something about all these business people around me with their glacial, well-mannered indifference. I had to work hard to keep from feeling that I was imposing on their very special, very expensive air.

They had plush little slippers ready for us; Powars arranged a pillow, then napped for a while. I felt bored. There was almost nothing for me to read—most of the newspapers or magazines were about business and finance—and I looked around. I felt like I was in some kind of conspirator's beehive in the stratosphere: everyone was either buzzing on an in-flight telephone or fax machines, tapping at a computer, grabbing a nap, or conversing quietly in that very special "Don't you think it's time we chopped Alfred X's head off at the neck?" tone, in several languages. Dinner was served. It was very good for flight food: okay, I admit, it was fabulous. Heavy starched linen and silverware; lovely baby veal and parsleyed potatoes, with a chocolate soufflé for dessert. We had an excellent wine at dinner, and there was even after-dinner fruit and mints. But no one around us really said anything. There was just that low, hushed buzz. If I had not been there with Destry, I would have felt like I was on a well-fed prisoner ship.

After dinner, Destry looked at some papers, then got himself ready for sleep. He announced that he'd have a meeting in Zurich as soon as we arrived. "Gotta bunk down," he said, then went to the bathroom with his Swissair gift toiletry kit. Everyone in first class got one. He came back a short time later, reclined his seat and a sturdy, very stiff female flight attendant appeared with a blanket to throw over him. All the lights were out now in first class, except for a few reading lamps. There was no way I could sleep after the wine and the dinner, and also the simple excitement of being there, on my first flight to Europe. I selected a video. It was a new Julia Roberts movie. I liked her. Destry snored a bit. He had funny dreams. I could see them racing across his face, like the moving shadows of clouds over a mountain. At one moment, he started saying something in his sleep, although I could not understand it. Then he made that noise again, that funny half-laugh I had heard coming from the office. I hated it; I wanted to wake him, just to make him stop, but I knew I couldn't. I shouldn't.

I decided to use the bathroom. At least it would get me out of my seat. I removed my tie, then took my toiletry kit with me. I moved carefully through the aisles. First class was all twinkly and silent and upholstered. A young, very trim-looking steward with ash-blond hair passed me and smiled. He saw that I was looking for the john. He was handsome, like a fashion model in a dark uniform. "I'm sorry that it's in use." He spoke with a crisp accent, like he had learned how to speak at some school in England. "Can I bring you anything while you wait?" He smiled again, just lit up at me. He had beautiful clear blue eyes, dimples, and a nose like Montgomery Cliff. I couldn't tell if he was actually flirting with me, or just used to flirting with everyone.

I told him no, and then out of courtesy I introduced myself.

"Is this your first time with us?" he asked. I nodded. "Maybe your first time in first class?"

I nodded again. "How did you know?"

"Our first class passengers don't usually introduce themselves on Swissair. The Swiss, you know, are not the most forthright people. I'm not Swiss. I'm Danish. My name is Sven, Sven Martins, like Peter Martins. But we are not related."

I did not know who Peter Martins was and told him.,

116   "Ballet dancer. In New York I thought he was famous. I see you are with a friend. He travels with us often. I have seen his face before. I guess you're good friends?"

I looked over at Powars. He was sleeping; the dreams were still paddling around him, like menacing natives in canoes. I could tell. "Yes," I said. "Sometimes."

His eyes twinkled at me. "And other times?"

"Less friends," I said.

The man in the john left it. He seemed older, by about a hundred years, and Swiss and dressed too meticulously for me to describe. He looked like he came directly from that store where they refused to tell me the prices. He had a very satisfied look on his face, as if he had just performed a very personal function, that most people took for granted but for which he was to be highly praised.

"They're a constipated people," Sven whispered to me and smiled. He opened the john door. "Here, let me make sure the place is okay for you."

He went in, closed the door, so that the light would go on, then reopened it slightly. "See," he said and took my hand.

He led me in, then snapped the door behind us. "I just thought," he said with a kind of mocking shyness, "I'd give it a once-over." He beamed at me in the tight space, and I beamed back, giving him the full wattage of my smile. Then he was quickly all over me, and not exactly once. It was insane, but I was happy. For a moment, I could forget about everything. Even Destry. "Something told me that you wanted this," he whispered.

"I did."

It was over with quickly. To make matters brief, he blew me. He was good at it, and didn't even take his cock out of his neatly pressed uniform pants. It was, as the kids say, all about me. He was hot, eager, and didn't make me feel that he was disappointed that I was a true member of the "small members" club; he made me feel—anyway, I just glowed. I knew it. I'd heard about the famous "Mile High" club, and guessed that, now, I was a member of that, too. Perhaps it was the total surprise, but I was able to go through the whole thing without problems. I could get it up and shoot. Without fear. I felt like I was nine feet tall. It only took about six or seven minutes. Then he washed his mouth out in the sink. "We have to be careful," he whispered. "My supervisor is in back of the plane, in tourist, but sometimes she comes running up here. On this flight, I do first class."

"You do," I agreed.

He cracked open the door, and eased out. I stayed in, pissed, brushed my teeth, and washed my face. Then I made myself fairly presentable, tucking my shirttails neatly into my pants. Suddenly I remembered an older queen telling me that sucking a man off in a suit was always nice. There was something about it that satisfied hungers that even bare skin, wonderful as it is, often did not. I looked at myself in the mirror. I appeared relaxed. Kind of real. Then I went back to my seat.

Powars was up. I had thought he'd be asleep. He was on the phone speaking German. He stopped. "You all right?" he asked me, putting his hand over the mouthpiece. "Are you comfortable? Would you like a blanket?"

As if on cue, Sven appeared with a fresh pillow and blanket. Destry smiled at the handsome Dane, said *"Auf Wiedersehn"* on the phone, then hung up.

"Nice guy," he said, as Sven went off. I asked him whom he was talking with. "Just crap. Some Germans in South America. The Germans have funny deals all over, you know. Guys in Bolivia are pulling out a lot of silver and tungsten. But none of the money goes back into the country. Then some *mensch* in Africa wants me to do a secret deal with uranium from Somalia. It's an Arab country, so he tells me they wanna trade it for Cuban coffee—maybe to keep 'em up at night." He winked, then yawned. "God, I wanna go back to sleep again."

I looked at him. How could I not go out to him—even paddle with him to those places where the bad dreams came from? "You're really good at this, aren't you?"

He sat up a bit and shrugged his big shoulders. "The important thing is making these guys feel that they're in control—I'm just helping, see? You can't make 'em feel that you've got 'em by the cahoonies, even when you do. I learned that from a coupla Greek shippers. They always made you feel like they're humble, you're doing *them* the favor. They can have enough dough to buy and sell and buy you again, but you're doing *them* the favor. Americans always come off like the Three Stooges. They think that if they just blow enough smoke in your face, once the smoke clears no one's gonna see what they're all about." He laughed. "Dumb, ain't it? If we didn't have so much wealth in the country to begin with, we'd all be eatin' shit by now."

I nodded to him. What he was saying did not really make a lot of sense to me. I still had no idea how anything that Destry Powars did produced so much money. Even working in a bank, money always seemed like some kind of phantom material to me—I felt about it the way most people feel about computers. It's just there, but no one really knows how they work. I looked deeply into his eyes. I felt relaxed suddenly. I thought I should go to sleep.

He turned from my gaze. "You wanna see a movie now? You look kinda bored."

I shook my head.

"They got all sorts of stuff. But no gay porno. How'd you like Sven?"

"Excuse me?"

"Sven. Did you have fun with him in the john?"

I felt like I'd been slapped. That feeling of being tall evaporated. It seemed so evil of him to have known what I had done—what I had thought I'd gotten away with. "What did you do, tip him? Is Sven part of the service on Swissair?"

"Naw, come on, don't be so mean. He just does that with everyone who takes his fancy. I mean it. You're good looking, Allen. But you must know by now that I have this 'funny' feeling for you."

"Is that what you call it?"

He looked hurt. He leaned over and kissed me deeply, thrusting his tongue into my mouth. I thought my heart would stop, and that I had gone higher in the stratosphere than the Swissair jet. Then he stopped,

119

and I saw that all the rich Swiss were either sleeping, or staring at their business papers.

Powars ran his fingers through my hair. He leaned over and whispered, "I wish I could suck your dick right here."

"I'm not sure about that," I said and closed my eyes. I was tired, but could hear Destry's voice talking to me as I dropped off into the quiet night of the first class section.

"The Swiss are good at minding their own business," he said in a low voice. "They've made enough money doing it. Know how they got into banking? They started out as innkeepers. Overnight travelers would keep their valuables in their safes. Then they started to just leave their valuables there, especially, you know, before going into Italy. So the Swiss learned how to use them. They are good at using what other people bring them—chocolate, money, labor. They're famous for being tight little people, but they keep a nice country."

"Do they?" I asked, my eyes closed, charmed by him again. He was so smart, so big, so ....

Don't worry," he said softly, dropping off into sleep himself. "I won't mention Sven again."

We were wakened a few hours later. It was dawn. I did not feel like waking up, but Powars was already alert. Coffee and a continental breakfast was brought. Sven came back, completely businesslike, handing out customs forms. On the ground, I only had to say that I was with Mr. Powars and the young agent smiled, stamped the visa that Powars showed him, and waved me on. A large black car, an older one, was waiting for us, with a middle-aged driver in uniform. He and Powars talked in German together, and then our bags were put in the trunk. We sat in the back, as he drove us through the town, which was clean, very beautiful, and near a large lake. He stopped at a large hotel that looked kind of like the Plaza in New York, just neater, even more *luxe* in a bland, understated way. There was a park near it, with swans and people walking dogs. It was a little before nine in the morning, but everyone looked dressed and ready for business.

"We keep a suite here," Destry told me. "You can use it while I'm at meetings. There's a health club, or you can nap. You didn't sleep a lot on the plane, did you?"

I told him that I had slept as well as I could. Then we got out of the car, and a blur of people flocked to us. They seemed to hover around Destry in a flesh-colored cloud of faces, hands, and arms. A fat smiling lady with metallic-red hair emerged first, her thick bare arms wide open: the welcoming concierge. Uniformed porters were next, who took our bags; then men in business clothes, shaking Powars's hand and bobbing in front of me, ignoring me, followed by female secretaries, aides, and gofers. It looked like something out of a stylish, 1940s movie, updated a bit. Women waited in the hotel lobby, wearing little black hats with veils, and there were men in fat ties and big-shouldered jackets. Powars smiled and waved.

We were taken up to the suite. It was huge, on the fourth floor, with a balcony overlooking the park, a sitting room, a luxurious bath with butter-soft towels, and a king-sized bed. I sprawled out on it. Destry warned me not to get my suit rumpled. He hurried out of his clothes, then went into the john. "If you wanna go out," he said through the door, "the desk downstairs'll let you back in. They know you're here."

I got up and went over to the balcony, feeling as if all of Zurich had been put there for me. I heard him at the sink, washing up. He came out in a lush terry robe, already on his cell phone. "It's international," he said, smiling as he clicked off. He ran a brush through his thick hair, then put on a fresh white shirt, got into a dark suit and put on a new tie. This one was all pure gold. It glittered like hammered metal in the morning light. "I guess I gotta do this," he said, his face tightening into a mask, half concentration, the other half—it scared me. I'd never seen that face. It was like war. His fingers drummed a desk in the sitting room; he exhaled. "I gotta make these people see what they don't wanna see, and do what they don't wanna do." He kissed me.

"Good luck," I said. (What else could I say?) He looked at me for a moment, then left.

I was alone. I turned on the TV, all in German or Swiss or whatever, then decided to take a shower. The health club idea seemed ridiculous: I felt like someone deaf and blind suddenly released into an alien world: the very hushed world of Swiss money. I used the john and spent a long time in the amazing shower. I brushed my teeth again, then slept for several hours. I woke up really hungry.

There was a room service menu. The prices, even in Swiss francs, seemed unbelievable; but why not? I ordered the "American hamburger with French fried potatoes." I suddenly wanted a milkshake, very thick and chocolatey, but settled for a Coke. I got dressed, not in the suit, but in some khaki trousers of my own and one of my own shirts. I felt like I was myself again, like I didn't have to worry about spotting something with ketchup. The food came in about ten minutes, brought by a young man who arranged everything precisely on a table in the sitting room. He spoke halting English. I could tell that he was waiting for a tip.

I realized then that I hadn't a dime in Swiss money. So I gave him five dollars, and he just smiled, and left. I turned the TV on to a game show, then to an old *Seinfeld* episode dubbed in German. It was actually funny; I mean, I could get some of the jokes. Mostly it was watching Kramer and Elaine trying to squeeze all those funny German sounds out their mouths. I finished the hamburger and the French fries—they were great!—then took the elevator down. The lobby was filled with elegant little stores, but as soon as I got outside, I noticed there was a Beneton and a Gap nearby. I was on the street now, in a shopping section, and though no one looked American, the young people did not look terribly different from American kids. Just better groomed; their clothes pressed, their hair neatly combed.

122   I got to the park and walked around. The air was fresh and lovely for a city. I wondered what Powars was doing—and how was he doing it. I had nothing to read or do, and the time crept by slowly. I thought about

going back to the suite, just to sleep again. I crossed the busy street filled with cars, then saw Powars coming out of the hotel with about a dozen other people. It was hard for me to see, from that distance, what he was like, what mood he'd be in.

I hesitated for a few seconds, then walked towards him. As I got closer, I could see that two of the women were so starvation thin, so corporately mannish, that they reminded me of ruthless drag queens. They had glossy, helmut-clipped hair and wore nearly identical outfits with tight black skirts and four-inch pumps. I thought about that bitchy hostess on *The Weakest Link*, and could imagine them with names like Leona Spreadsheet and the ambitious Imperial Grand Dutchess, Ivana Kutchanuttsoff. I laughed for a second to myself.

Off to the side was a group of younger men in lighter suits. Clean-shaven; deadly serious; very dark glasses. One was glued to his cell phone and looked over suspiciously at Destry. A tall, stoutly built man with thinning sandy-blond hair, in a deep-olive Burberry trench coat, had a broad face with a little smile welded rigidly onto it. He was stationed between two older men in banker pinstripes. One had his head pointed down, as if he couldn't listen to anything else; the other looked up with a constricted, anguished face, like he had to swallow some big item that, no matter what, he could not force down his throat. The tall man patted the man with the pained expression softly on the shoulder, as his blond head bobbed confidently and he kept smiling.

Powars's tie picked up the sunlight and reflected it into the deep shadows on his face. He looked bored, anxious, and stifled. I could see the veins on his neck; his jaw jutted out. He cocked his head back and forth. I should have been able to decipher what was going on; it was too simple. But instead, stupidly—motivated only by my lack of purpose and direction, and that sense of being out of place in this foreign setting—I kept moving towards him. Like I was magnetized. It was insane: what made me think that I could just go up to Destry?

I pushed close enough for him to see me. Our eyes met. I smiled ner-

123

vously. He grimaced and shot his right hand out, flashing a "Halt" gesture at me; I caught it and froze. His look said everything: Not here. Not now. Not you.

I pivoted, and headed back to the park, crushed. The ground started to wobble uncontrollably under me. I pretended that I didn't want to know any more about anything; I didn't even dare look back towards the hotel. Several people came up and looked straight through me. I sat down on a bench. A teenage boy with a brown cocker spaniel strolled by. The boy was sweetly pretty and angular and freckled, with a little bronze on his face. He smiled. The dog sniffed at me, then licked my hand. I was alive; I was human, at least for the moment. I said good-bye to him, like we had known each other, without a word having passed between us, then got up and went back into the hotel. At the desk, I told them who I was, and they sent a bell hop with me to unlock the suite. Some of Destry's bags were still lined up in the sitting room, where the porters had left them. I went into the bedroom.

Destry was lying face up on the bed. I had not expected him. "I'm sorry about coming on like that," I told him.

He kept looking straight up at the ceiling, then shook his head and said, "Why didn't you wear your suit?"

"I—I—" What could I say?

I felt sick inside. I turned away from him and went over to the balcony and started to cry. I could barely hold the tension within me, but I had to. I didn't want to make any noise or look back at him.

"Are you hungry?" he asked, shattering the silence.

I hesitated for a moment, then told him that I could be; I could be anything right then.

"I think I need to take another shower," he said. He got up off the bed. I faced him. He was smiling now, like it was all behind him. "We'll go get some lunch then. Have a little wine. You know the food is pretty good in Zurich. Then we'll leave."

I nodded. He took off his jacket, then his shoes and pants. I went over and removed his gold tie. I kissed him softly on his nose and cheeks. "I thought you had another meeting later."

He shook his head. "No. I'll let them clean the fucking mess up. They took a lot out of me this morning, Allen. You don't know."

I wondered why Gwinny had not been there, and who the other people were, especially the big man in the trench coat, but I did not want to ask another question. He turned away from me, naked, and got into the shower.

I looked around the room. Suddenly it seemed sort of small—even Powars seemed small. Then I took all my clothes off and walked into the bathroom. He was hidden behind the shower curtain. "I've got a surprise for you," I said. He asked me what and I told him to close his eyes.

I got in and began kissing him all over. He opened his eyes through the fine, misting water and smiled. His smile was gorgeous and radiant. He could not stop hugging and kissing me. His mouth went down to my chest, literally devouring me. I thought he was going to bite into my skin. "Please don't hate me," he whispered. "Don't. I couldn't take all this if you hated me."

"Why would I do that?" I asked. It seemed like another stupid question, but I had to ask it.

"Because—" he hesitated, then said, "Because ... of what I've got to do."

Warm water was all around us. It was marvelous, like fine crystal, with clear light coming in through the high bathroom window. "All right," I promised. "I'll try not to."

"Good."

He got down on the floor of the tub, and started sweetly kissing my ankles, my calves. He stroked my knees, then brought himself up, and carefully put both of my balls into his mouth. He did not hurt me, but kept them there, gently, as the water fell in this shower of light around us. I looked down at his muscular, hairy back and his feet and his gray toe-nails. I felt that for a while I had tamed the monster within him, but I was not sure how long that moment would last.

NINE

We redressed,

I again in the black suit, and had a light lunch in a small restaurant a few blocks from the hotel. Powars took the small valise with him—and looked around regularly, as if he expected someone to join us. He had almost a whole bottle of red wine, and I had one glass. I was still feeling queasy about everything—those people with him outside the hotel; the coldness of it. He did not mention business at all, but gabbed on about Switzerland, how much he liked the place. He spoke German to the waiter, and got the check.

We went back to the hotel. The suite was completely cleaned up; our bags were ready, and a car was waiting. This time it was another car, a silver Mercedes, new and clean, all gray leather, with a young driver. Powars told me that we were going to a resort about three hours away. "We coulda gone by train," he said, "but this is really the best way to see Switzerland." We drove past the lake, then started climbing up and through the mountains.

The afternoon brought one breathtaking vista after the next. Mountains and waterfalls and lush green meadows brushed with colorful patterns of alpine wildflowers. No billboards, litter, or roadside fast food. I could see why the rich loved Switzerland. We took a main highway for a while, then got off it. It settled into a lovely, misty evening. There was champagne in the back and Powars opened up a bottle and poured some out into two flutes. "They call it here *sekt*. It means 'sparkle.'

They like German champagne, you know. I don't think it's as good as the French stuff, but why not?" He lifted his glass to me, and then winked in the rearview mirror at the driver, who smiled. He had small blue eyes and a fresh complexion. "*Etwas zu trinken?*" Powars called.

The driver shook his head. "*Nein*. Not on my job," he replied. "But go ahead. *Prosit!*"

"What does that mean?" I asked.

"Toast," Powars answered, his voice lower. "It's kind of like *l'chaiyim*, you know, what the Jews say. Here, mentioning the Jews can be kind of difficult. It's still an open sore to some people. They'll tell you they did everything they could." He winked at me. "We'll have a wonderful meal when we get there. Then we'll go to bed. You'll be really pooped by then—the high elevation and all this air—I know it."

I drank the glass of champagne, then he poured me some more. I became kind of anxious again. The long, winding road going up reminded me that I had no idea where we were heading, or what would happen once we got there. I downed the second glass, and felt sort of giggly and funny. Everything started to twinkle around me; just "sparkle," like Powars had called the German champagne. I rolled down a window and heard cowbells jingling outside. Cowbells! I was drunk—and we were in the real country now. Birds. Cows. Haystacks. Mountains all around us, like big black giants in the dim light, topped with fine white hair. Snow. Little Heidi could have lived there. It was pure fairy tale. I was going off to meet the gypsies, or the fateful Giant himself.

I hiccuped, and then could not stop.

"Hold your breath," Powars ordered. I did what he told me, and held it as the countryside rolled down behind us. "You're gonna like this place. You can hike. They got an indoor pool and an outdoor one that's heated. Wait'll you see the view from the pool—"

Suddenly I said: "Why'd you want me to come?" It just popped out of me, like another hiccup, as soon as I got my breath back. Maybe it was the German champagne, but I had to know, stupid as it seemed. I wanted to be there, I knew that. He could eat me alive, destroy me. I knew that, too. All of your life you dream, if you're fortunate enough to dream, about something incredible happening to you. Now it had, but I still had to ask him.

He shrugged. "That's a funny question. Don't tell me you don't want to be here!" His eyes darkened, full of disappointment.

"No," I said. I moved closer to him. "I just wondered, why me? You can have anyone, you know that. All those gym bunnies in Chelsea, those cute little yuppy types—you have just what they want. Money. Position. I don't have a great body or a—"

He laughed. "You really think *I* have what they want?"

"Sure."

"I don't, Allen. What I have is just an illusion, except when it's real. Then it's too real, know what I mean?"

"No," I answered. "I don't. It seems real enough to me. This car. That hotel in Zurich. Going first class all the time. Half the boys in Chelsea would do anything to—"

"Would you quit that shit? I hate those little gym fairies and the guppy-yuppy types. They look at me and want to spit. I'm too real for them, and I ain't even that real. All they can see is … anyway, they'd just be scared. That's all. You're not scared, are you?"

I nodded. "A little."

"Good. Maybe you should be—a little. So am I. This is a lot harder than you think, but I wanted you to be here." He nodded at me, then took my hand in his larger one.

Suddenly my hand felt ice cold inside his, and my head pounded. I started to puke. Maybe that fear had crawled all the way up inside me; but this really gross, green stuff shot out of my mouth and landed on his suit.

"Oh, shit!" he cried. He grabbed a starched linen napkin and drew it across his jacket, then scooped some water from the ice bucket and used

128 it on the stain. "I'll never be able to—"

He stopped himself short. He grabbed another napkin, dunked it in the water and put it across my forehead. I leaned forward with my head on his knees. "*Halten!*" he called to the driver.

We were at the side of a narrow road, with a mountain soaring directly over us. The driver opened the rear passenger-side door, and Powars rushed out, grabbing me with him. The crisp air felt good, as I leaned over and threw my guts up. He held me.

"I'm sorry," he said. He put his hand, which felt cool and very good, on my forehead. My head burned, but my hands were freezing. "German champagne. Christ! You shouldn't have had it. I should have had some iced soda for you, and maybe something for your stomach. The air here's thinner. This has been no way to welcome you to Switzerland, has it?"

A policeman on a motorcycle came up. He looked huge, in total black leather, like he'd come out of a Tom of Finland drawing. He and Powars said something in German. I remember hearing the word "kranken," which made me think, was I a crank? and then *krankenhaus.*

"He wants to know if you need a hospital," Powars explained to me. "That's nuts," he said, and turned to the cop and told him that I would be all right. He even used the word "okay," which is universal now.

The cop smiled, shook hands with Powars, then left us. I felt better and got back into the car. We kept a window rolled down, with a blanket thrown over me. The air smelled wonderful, all hay and crystalline freshness. You could have drunk it. I fell asleep with my head on Powars's lap. Then sometime later, as I came out of it, the car stopped. The door was opened. Two men in uniform grabbed our bags. Powars got out and handed some money to the driver.

The hotel was a beautiful stone and wood building in the most wonderful surrounding I'd ever been in—ringed with mountains, near a clear mountain lake. There was a swirling carpet of stars above us, more than I'd ever seen in my life. There was a wide veranda with comfortable chairs, and inside the place looked like an old mansion, decorated with stuffed animal heads, softly polished furniture, glowing lamps, and antique oil paintings of Swiss mountains and old farming scenes. A buxom blonde in her fifties in a dark dress was at the desk. She smiled at

Powars and spoke to him in heavily accented English. "Ve are zo glad you are back!" He smiled, thanked Ulma, her name, signed in for us. "*Willkommen!*" she cooed to me, then gave him a small ring of keys.

Our bags had already been taken to our suite of rooms, in the back, on the third floor. As I walked through the long, well-polished hallway with Destry, my heart pounded. There was something magical about being there. The sheer quiet power of it. The rooms were wonderful, warm and spacious and kind of austerely cozy. There was a bedroom with a double bed and a sitting room. Beside that was a smaller bedroom, kind of like a child's room, with one twin bed and my bag in it.

"The Swiss are like that," Powars said to me. "Very discreet. They don't assume anything. Don't worry. You'll sleep here with me." He smiled.

I was tired—he was right; the air was thinner—but he wanted dinner and it would only be served for another hour or so. "You might want just some soup, something like that," he said.

I unpacked my toiletry bag and went into the bathroom and splashed some water on my face, then brushed my teeth to get that awful taste out of my mouth. When I returned, Powars had changed into another jacket. It was like a shooting jacket, very handsome, in a heavy moss-green tweed, with leather buttons and patch pockets, like something a country gentleman might wear in the fields, bagging rabbits. He was on the room phone and brushing his hair at the same time. He smiled as he spoke, changing from German to English. "Na, na, *naturlich. Bitte*, it's nothing. Don'cha have *kein* fear. *Ja!*"—he turned to me, his hand over the mouthpiece—"One of those young jerks back in Zurich. Jeeze!" He spoke another sentence or two of German to him, then clicked off.

"Already they're after me," he complained. "And the fuckin' cell phones don't work up here, so I gotta use house phones." He shrugged his big shoulders. "*Sheisse!*"

130   I looked at him. Suddenly, this embarrassed expression appeared on his face, like I had caught him at something dirty. "Some people are just monsters. No matter what you give 'em, they want some ... other tiny

piece of shit more."

I asked who he was talking about. His body tensed. He tried to breathe a bit.

"Maybe we'd better get to the dining room," he said. "Once it's closed, you're on your own here. If you're lucky, you can find a cow out there to kill!"

I did not ask him anything else. As we walked out the room, I noticed that he took the small valise with him, and that he didn't use the key to lock the door. I asked him about that.

"Why bother? If they wanna climb up seven thousand feet to rob you—it's all here! Besides, you don't know the Swiss. There's a reason why they've never been invaded; even Hannibal couldn't do it."

The dining room was large, but only about six tables were occupied and they were far apart. You could hear nothing except a violinist, who played corny classical music off to one side. I felt again like I were in some kind of World War II movie, but I could see men flipping open little palm computers at their tables while speaking in that subdued Swiss manner, which was kind of like the way their watches worked. Discreetly expensive; never flashy; quiet. I noticed Powars's watch. It was thin and gold, and half hidden by the cuff of his shirt and the hairs on his wrist. He noticed me looking at it. "Swiss," he joked. "What else?"

He had a fabulous dinner of venison with crabapples, small potato pancakes, and chard. I had some light chicken soup and a salad. My stomach still did not feel great, but I figured that after a night's sleep, I'd have a good breakfast. He asked me if I wanted a taste of the meat. I had never had venison before. I was not sure. "I know," he said. "You don't want to eat Bambi's daddy. Just his cousin, the cow. Come on, try it!" He cut off a good chunk and I did. It was grainy, slightly tough, but richly flavorful.

"Have you always eaten like this?" I asked. "I mean, whatever you wanted to eat?"

131

"I grew up on Velveeta cheese, crap like that. Before they got to me, I didn't know what a salad fork was. 'Ya mean,' I used to say, 'you gotta have a' extra fork jus' t' eat ya salad wit'?'" He laughed out loud. It was hard for me to believe that his English had actually improved; obviously learning other languages had helped. His laugh seemed thunderous in the tastefully quiet dining room. I felt embarrassed: the polite, well-brought-up gay men I knew would never have laughed like that, certainly not in a place like this. But then, they never would have walked into a place like this; they could only dream about it. A waiter in a black uniform marched over to us to see if we "required" anything else. Powars asked for mineral water, coffee, and the dessert cart. "You should see what kind of sweets they got here," he beamed. "You think you're up to trying one?"

I looked at him and slowly shook my head. With my stomach in the shape it had been, I wasn't really in the mood for dessert.

"Destry," I said softly, "could you tell me—who are the 'they' you're always talking about?"

"*Always*? I don't always talk about nobody." He lit a thick dark cigarette. "This tastes wonderful. I know you don't smoke, but it's good Cuban tobacco. It don't taste like American weed at all."

The waiter came by with the dessert trolley. It was spectacular. There was enough heavy whipped cream on it to cause three coronaries. Per person. He picked an anthracite-colored chocolate torte chunked with black cherries and piled up, half a foot, with a Matterhorn of rich white peaks. I, virtuously, picked a raspberry tart, with no whipped cream. Powars grinned at me. "Chicken!" The waiter moved like a dancer— every motion perfect. The way he precisely hoisted a cake slice and slipped it onto a sparkling, gold-banded dessert plate. The way he aimed the steaming black coffee into those elegant little white, fluted, gold-banded cups. I had Earl Grey tea. It was lovely, the fumes, the steam rising into my face. The waiter left.

"Who are *they*? I mean it, please, I want to know."

"Just people. The kinda people I am now." He sipped his coffee. "You might not find 'em your"—he broke into his beautiful smile, with the dimples that disarmed me—"your cuppa tea." He shrugged. "But it takes all kinds, right? I mean a lotta people think I'm a weirdo. I'm just raw meat; a total asshole. But nobody knows what hurt is, like I do."

His eyes started to glaze over. He turned away from me. He still had not answered my question. "Who are *they*?" I repeated. "Those people you mention."

"Don't worry." He shook his head, his face still turned from me. "They're as ... good as people are gonna get, mostly. You won't deal with 'em—I mean, there's no way you'll ever meet all of 'em." He turned to me, a bit more in control now. "The big meeting," he explained, pushing his coffee aside, "won't be here. It's always, uh, strange thing. That's when we total up what we owe each other for the year: kinda like a big sales meeting, know what I mean?"

"Is that why you're here?"

He nodded to me. "It's not something you can avoid—lemme tell you. It'll be at this other place. The hotel's got a private lodge down the road, where we meet. It's really old—I mean *old*—and not for the public. The meeting's guarded, but, hey!, that's not for you to worry about. I want you to like it here. Really! What's not to like?" He took a big forkful of the cake, sloppy with whipped cream. A gob of white foam slid down to his chin that looked wickedly handsome now. He pushed it with his little finger into his mouth. He licked his lips.

He looked fetching, really. But if I were going to find out anything, I had to stick to my guns.

"I still don't understand why you brought me here."

That wicked-little-boy smile that he had, that was so adorable, fell immediately. His mouth hardened. "Oh, Jesus! What do you want?" His eyes closed. "Listen, if you wanna leave, I can have a car for you tomorrow. Tonight's too late, but if you wanna go, just say so." He turned away from me. He looked slapped. Hurt. "Didn't you like the flight and going to Zurich? Don't you like being here with me?"

133

I felt like an idiot. "Sure," I whispered, my heart pounding. He was right: what the hell *did* I want? "I don't want to leave." I took his hand, even though the rather grim-looking waiter with the dessert cart was looking directly at us and Destry had turned his face down to the table. The waiter was trying hard not to be noticed—that Swiss discretion, I guessed—but I could see his dark eyes roaming towards us from the coffee station. Finally, he was summoned to another table. "I don't want to leave," I whispered. "But there's something about"— I halted, then said— "about all this that frightens me. I'm sorry."

He turned to me and squeezed my hand. "I know. I do, Allen. I sure know. You wanna know what it's gonna cost you, at some point. That's what we all wanna know, ain't it?" He tried hard to smile, like he'd been caught in some small, foolish mistake. "I mean, *isn't* it?"

The fleeting smile fell. He was close to breaking apart. I hated myself. Why couldn't I just accept this—this "flight into change," into what seemed like my own dumbly belated destiny. "I want you to go back to the room," he ordered. "I don't like you to see me like this."

"It's okay," I said. "Listen, you already saw me puking up in the back of that car. It's alright."

He shook his head. He looked really stunned. I noticed that he did that sometimes, looked childish, rejected. I wanted to kiss him right there. I promised myself I wouldn't ask any more questions. Ever. I told myself that. He smiled again at me.

"Go back to the room. I'll be there soon."

I got up and walked towards the entrance of the dining room and the dimly illuminated promenade with its upholstered armchairs set up for quiet. A row of windows behind it were black now, but you could see the silvery points of stars and even the distant white tops of mountains outside.

I didn't feel like going back to the room alone, so I sat down. I felt puzzled, and really bad. I'd been picked by this extraordinary, very successful man, and shouldn't I have been simply…Then I saw the big man from Zurich—the one in the olive Burberry trench coat—striding through the promenade. He was now in an elegant navy blue suit, double-breasted, with a tightly knotted, yellow silk tie. I was sitting back in the dark, and he didn't see me. The polished wood floor vibrated heavily with his step. He halted at the entrance to the dining room. Our waiter came up to him; perhaps to tell him that the room was closed. I craned my neck to see further.

The waiter pointed him to where Destry was still seated by himself. I tiptoed over to a box tree in a planter, near the entrance in shadows. I saw the blond man with the thinning hair—he was actually getting to be quite bald—approach Powars.

Destry got up and embraced him. They were alone now, only the two of them in the big dining room. They started talking in German, then quickly switched into that strange low, unexplainable emanation—that weird noise, part click, part laugh, part release, that came in waves—that I'd heard yesterday in Destry's office. Meditation? Yoga? I shook my head. It lasted only for about forty seconds, and as it did, the man handed Destry a small brown paper bag. I had not noticed it in the promenade. For a few seconds Destry held the bag to his chest, then he picked up the small valise, took a clipped sheaf of papers from it, and handed them over to the man—who stuffed the papers into his inner jacket pocket—as Destry carefully guided the brown bag into his valise and eased the zipper closed.

Then the noise—that wordless language I could not place—stopped, and the man sat down at the table in the same chair I'd been in, and they started talking casually, in English, about the weather, the coming day. Destry mentioned my name—I was in bed, sleeping, he said. The big man smiled, leaned over, and gave Destry an affectionate pat on the cheek.

I could not see Destry's expression. His face was now turned away from me. But the man laughed out loud. Not with Destry's loud embarrassing laugh. It was different, a low, mirthless laugh; hollow, full of comfortable superiority. I had heard the same laugh in the corner offices of the bank. The sound always scared me, like a grotesque mask whose horror only serves to unmask the viewer. I felt as if my own weakness were now pursuing me. I got out from behind the shadows where I was hiding, and hurried as quickly as I could to the elevator, to get back upstairs and into our room.

135

TEN

I was in bed

when Destry came into the dark room. Even with the windows closed, the air was fresh to the point of aching coldness. He undressed in the bathroom, brushed his teeth, changed into a fresh pair of ivory-colored cotton pajamas and got into bed. He nuzzled me. I was naked; despite the cold, I never wore pajamas. He felt warm and good. I turned to him and pressed him to me. He started kissing my neck with his mouth slightly open, sucking the flesh tenderly. "You might wanna wear p. j.'s. It gets cold here. They left you a pair."

I told him I didn't know that. His hands went to my stomach, and then to my genitals. I was turned on. There is something about fear that can scare you stiff, as well as soft. He pushed the fluffy down comforter off me and went down on me, licking and sucking my diminutive penis, then he pulled me over him. I arched up a bit, so that he had my sex organ in his mouth, as if he were floating under me. He pulled his dick out from the ghostlike, pale pajama bottom and began jerking off while he sucked me. He made this wonderful sound ... like the wind rustling through pine trees. It didn't seem human. It was more than just a sigh; it was ... just this beautiful, natural sound. He brushed the short, dark shadow bristles on his cheeks across my tender scrotum. I whimpered with pleasure, with that uncontainable, conflicting mixture of ecstasy and pain, pulled by waves of desire and anxiety, that easily described everything about my being with him.

Then he started to bite into me again, while he cradled the slender tube of my penis softly in his hands, sometimes licking the nearby pink head of it. It was not even a bite like a regular tooth bite, but more like what I imagined a night moth's scouring tongue might make as it channeled darkly into the silken complexion of a gardenia blossom. Now, I felt ready. I cannot say I loved this, but it no longer terrified me quite so much, as he withdrew something deftly out of my scrotum and into his mouth.

I had no orgasm. I found myself going completely limp and strangely satisfied afterwards: I'd had orgasms before where you're thrown into the wonderful oblivion of complete release. This was not that. I was just delivered … like a present at Destry's big-toed feet; something that he could now call his own—and I knew it. He started snoring. He had not come, either. His large dark cock was safe now, tucked inside his fresh-smelling pajama bottom. He had turned from me and was sleeping soundly on his side of the bed. I had to see what I could get away with.

I got up carefully out of the bed, and went into the john. I kept the door wide open, and flushed the toilet. It made a much louder noise than I expected. Good. I flushed it again. Then I went back to him and watched him. He was still asleep. It was dark in the room, but I needed to know what was in the bag that the man had left with him. I had no alternative. I went back into the bathroom, retrieved a small box of wooden matches on a shelf above the sink, and returned. About ten feet away from Destry, I struck one. I waved the tiny light around me, until it revealed the small valise on a table, next to a window. I tiptoed over.

The valise was unzipped, revealing a few letters in envelopes. My match went out. I lit another, then with my thumb and forefinger, I opened the valise further. There was his palm computer and more papers …. Nothing else. I thought my heart had stopped beating as I withdrew my fingers. Then it occurred to me: he must have put the paper bag in one of the closets or a chest of drawers. There were two chests in the room, but I knew I could not go rummaging through them without waking him. The same for the closet, which was actually only a larger chest, but big enough for hanging items. I blew out the match just before the flame reached my fingertips, and, feeling very cold, hurried to return the matches to the shelf in the bath.

I got back into bed, but didn't touch Destry. I hugged myself to get warm again. I looked up at the ceiling and behind my eyes I saw his face. The bristly cheeks. His dark eyelashes opening to reveal the amber-gold of his eyes. I was crazy about him, and terrified again. I waited for the sun to come up. When it finally did, Destry was still asleep. I showered, making as much noise as I could, then walked out of the bathroom to dry off.

"You sure are up-and-at-it early," he said, yawning.

I smiled. "It's the air here. It makes you sleep like a log."

"Sure does. You want some coffee? They'll bring it to the room."

I told him no—why didn't he shower, and we'd go down for breakfast? "I've heard Swiss breakfasts are great."

"You heard right. I'm gonna take you hiking today. There are a couple of villages. We'll walk through them."

"I thought you had meetings," I said, while I slipped on some underwear. I still had that funny feeling in my scrotum, like it had been punctured. And I felt depleted, kind of weak. But I attributed that also to the jet lag and the higher altitude.

"Naw. Not today. I'll see some people tonight. It's okay. All work and no play makes Jack a jerk, right? Did you like the shower? It's got all these funny little jets in it like massage hands. I love it. I can spend days in it."

I smiled. "Why not do it now?"

"Naw. I never shower before breakfast, if I don't have meetings to go to. I'll just wash around a bit, then we'll go down."

He got up slowly, took off his pajamas, and went into the bath. I liked the way he looked with his pajamas off. That hairy, kind of butt-heavy nakedness of him. He seemed so totally real to me. I don't know why. Maybe it was because we were in a beautiful hotel room in Switzerland, and he was my only connection to the place—or even to the world. I watched him and he knew it and he smiled at me, melting me. I blinked. My heart was beating so hard and fast that I was sure he could hear it.

"You okay?" he asked. "I'm sorry you had such a hard time in the car."

I told him I was better, then he went into the bathroom and closed the door. I looked over at the chests and the closet. I opened the closet immediately. There were some drawers at the top, and I quickly popped them open. Empty. I shifted his hanging clothes about. Nothing. I had the suit, my one jacket, and a few pairs of pants. Powars did not travel light. Everything was freshly pressed, neat, perfect. There was still that distinct smell of laundry starch and expensive dry cleaning. No one would believe that everything had come out of a suitcase. I heard the toilet flush, then water run. He came out, wearing a terry robe. He walked over to the closet. "What were you looking for in here?"

"Excuse me?"

"You were looking in here. I can tell."

"I thought they might have left us some slippers. I only brought one pair of shoes, you know."

He shook his head. "Oh. Sure. I'll ask at the desk for some. It's no problem." He reached in, pulled out some dark pants and a fresh shirt, a beautiful gray silk-and-mohair one. "Wait a second. I just realized some-thing—you might want some hiking boots, too. They have a shop in the back. Mostly tourist stuff, but they sell good hiking equipment. We'll pop in after breakfast."

"Thanks," I said.

Breakfast was, of course, in a breakfast room. It was smaller than the dining room, with large windows overlooking the mountains and the lake that mirrored them. The vista went on and on, then disappeared into pure cerulean air, like a landscape in a Da Vinci painting. "Beautiful, huh?" he said when we sat down. "I been all over the place, I mean the world, you know; but no place is like this."

Breakfast was served by a young slender woman in a demure black uniform, who smiled shyly. Everything was either on a cart or a sideboard, and there was a dizzying assortment of food—meats, cereals, eggs, fruit, pastries. There was also champagne, Bloody Marys, some liqueurs, and even stout, I guess for British guests who could begin the day that way. "In Europe, they don't go with this You-Can't-Drink-Till-Sunset bullshit," Powars said. He ordered a mimosa, then had warm oatmeal and about six eggs scrambled with ham and cheese.

"You better eat," he ordered me. "We're gonna go out, and I mean *out*."

I was not used to eating so much in the morning, but I had a cheese omelet with sausages, muffins, and some fruit. Towards the end of the meal, the big blond man from the day before appeared. He was dressed casually now, but richly, in a camel-colored cashmere turtleneck and a light zippered jacket. Destry rose and they shook hands formally. Destry was all smiles.

"Allen, this is Ernst. Ernst Waldman." He pronounced the last name as "Valt-man," in the German way. Destry's voice sounded very different in German; there was a little heel click in it, that was not there in English.

The man took my hand. "*Sehr erfreut*," he said. "I am glad to meet you." He turned to Powars. "So, what brings you up here?" he asked, as though they had not met the evening before.

Powars smiled bashfully. "Usual. The meeting. Our friends." He said something in German, to which Waldman twinkled darkly, like it was an inside joke between them. I got up and excused myself. I needed to go back to the room.

"It's the good Swiss food," Waldman said, smiling. "I hope we will meet again soon," he added.

I smiled at Powars, who told me to take my time. "Ernst and I will talk a minute. Maybe go outside and have a cigar."

I nodded and slowly walked out the room. At the door, just beyond their sight, I heard Waldman say: "He seems like a charming fellow. Not like your usual—how do you say it?—*buddies*, Destry!"

"Screw you!" Powars boomed.

I did not wait another moment. I hurried up, using a stairway, and literally ran through every chest and closet. I even went through Destry's empty luggage, making sure everything was exactly back in place. I found nothing. Then I had an idea.

In the bathroom was a walk-in linen closet—the guests were always to have fresh towels, robes, soap; there was even a rack to hang washed-out nylons, and an ironing board. There were cleaning supplies for the maid. Of course, I thought. How silly: everything's in the linen closet. I went in, and pushed aside a stack of luscious white Turkish towels, the kind with tiny ridges that feel like massage mitts.

There it was at the back of the closet. I tried to pick it up and draw it towards me, but it stung my hands, like the simple brown paper was armed with fierce nettles. It toppled over, almost crashing to the floor—it terrified me. I used the tips of my fingers to prop it back up, then carefully nudged it back in place on the shelf. The bag was sealed with clear tape, but there was no way I could open it with my bare hands. Even picking it up was painful; my fingers vibrated with hurt. But I managed to replace it exactly where it had been on the shelf and cover it with the white towels, when—

"How we doing in there?" Destry called from inside the door to the room.

I had remembered to lock the bathroom door. I flushed the toilet and ran some water in the sink.

"I'm gonna need to be in there and shower soon!" he called. "You wanna shower with me?"

"I already did." I said.

"So?"

I opened the door. I still had my clothes on, but he was naked now. And very excited. He started to strip my clothes off, and a minute later I was in the shower with him. He was right about the massage waterjets. They could wake you up or lull you to sleep. We put them on a needle-fine but energetic wake-up. He kissed me, grabbing my mouth with his. I felt like Fay Wray with King Kong, he was so hairy and big. He tried to fuck me in the shower, but since I had not had a morning clean out yet, bowel-wise, I thought this would not work. I don't know why I think in those terms, but I do. Maybe too many years of working in a bank.

I ended up sucking him, on my knees. It was really wonderful—just submitting myself to him that way. He came in my mouth, great gushes of cum. Then he sank to the floor, with the water pulsing all over us, reminding me of the blood rushing through his dick. That's what causes erections, right? Excitement; blood; the stiffening, awakening of life. He pulled me to him and kissed me again. Like he was only half-conscious, still in that dark dream world of orgasm.

But I was not. I looked at him. There was something so odd about him. Kind of…primal animal; coarse. But it was stupid to have that revelation dawn on me then, because he was that. So why think of it? Why pretend to be smarter than I was? We got up, soaped some, quietly washed off separately, dried. He seemed almost abstracted now. He smiled distantly at me, his face cocked towards me every now and then. We dressed and he put on another fresh set of clothes.

We went to the guest shop and he bought me a pair of Swiss hiking boots. The beautiful rich chestnut leather was supple and soft, but sturdy, with that disciplined simplicity I associated with the Swiss. We went to the desk, where a very nice man offered us two small rucksacks filled with lunch. "You'll like this," he said. "Little sandwiches with salmon, cheese, and onion. And *naturlich* a little schnaps and mineral *wasser*." He also gave us a map which showed us a trail that would be good for this time of the year.

At his suggestion, we went out a side door: and there it was, the whole world it seemed. Mountains. Lakes. Streams. Trees. The air so clear on that beautiful morning that the mineral water seemed silly. Of course you could drink this air, I thought.

If you just knew how to pay for it.

The trail began as a regular country road. We went through a scrubbed little village of chalets, barns, a tiny church, a school, and a post office. "Every town has a post office," Powars told me. "The Swiss postal system is world famous. It kept the country together—all these little cantons separated by mountains. They needed a good postal system." I nodded. I really wasn't listening that much. I kept wondering what was in that paper bag, and why was it so difficult for me to touch it? We started climbing. The road became a dirt path, rocky, hard on the knees, twisting about; but every twenty or thirty feet, the view changed. At first we could see a nearby village and the hotel, then two villages, a stream, a river, and then what I thought was a forest.

"No, it's just a grove of trees," Destry said. "There are no big forests in Switzerland now. Every tree's been planted. It's very precise. If you want real forests, you need to go to Poland. That's where they still have forests—and wild pigs, bison. Amazing. The Polacks are so funny. They're not dumb, they're just funny."

"What do you mean?"

"In a lot of places, they won't go into the forests, because they still believe in … " He laughed.

"In what?"

"Witches. They think that witches hang out in the forests. It's a scream, don't you think?"

"Why?" I asked. I looked down. The view was dizzying. It seemed to swirl around my feet and actually disappear in places into thick mist. I sat down. "Why's that so funny?" I asked again. "About the witches?"

He shrugged his shoulders. "What witch would hang out in some dumb Polish forest, when you have," he paused, then said, "New York?"

"New York?"

"Yeah. New York. London. L.A.—lemme tell you, that would be a town for witches! If I was some kind of ol' witch, I'd hang out in L.A."

"But you're not," I said. "Are you?"

He laughed. "You sure you feeling okay? I think the air's gettin' to you. There's a ski hut further up. We can go in there and rest. There's a john if you need it."

My stomach did feel kind of funny. Probably it was the rich Swiss food, the altitude, and also that gnawing, panicky feeling that kept asking me, What the hell was I doing there; and what was really going to happen?

We trudged upward in the direction of the hut. We were now at the timber line. The sun was high; it was actually quite warm. I had worn a sweater and took it off. Powars was in one of his expensive T-shirts. It was a golden, buttery yellow that made his dark hairiness even more attractive. He had a thick Navy sweater knotted around his shoulders. "Why don't you take your shirt off?" he said. "You'll feel better. It can get very hot up here."

I did. He was right. I had become suddenly overheated. He put one of his hands on my chest, and tweaked my nipples. His hand was big and cool and felt wonderful. Impulsively, he licked some of the sweat off my chest and took one of my small nipples into his mouth and bit it lightly. Then he let go of me. "You're some guy," he said.

The hut was not too much further up. We made it in about twenty minutes. It was unlocked, simple and clean inside, with a stove for wood fires, a glass-chimneyed oil lamp, some wooden matches, and an old-fashioned hand pump for water. He told me that places like that saved lives; I believed him. There was an outhouse attached, and I went into it. It smelled fairly rank, but I needed to use it. The food—much richer than I was used to—had done a number on my stomach, but I felt better after a clean-out. I wiped myself with some toilet paper that felt like steel wool, pulled my pants back up, and came out.

There was Ernst, in very fashionable, Swiss-looking hiking gear, talking to Powars. He smiled at me. "Guten tag!" he said to me. "Nice to see you! How you like this country?! *Schön, schön, schön!*"

144   "That means it's beautiful," Powars explained.

"*Ja!*" Waldman agreed. "*Sehr schön.* I will hike with you some. I was telling Destry that I know a secret grotto around here."

"Sounds cool, don't it?" Powars said.

I nodded.

"First, *Mittag essen*," Waldman said. He also had a rucksack from the hotel and we sat outside at a table next to the hut, with the mountains all around us. Waldman started yodeling to show us how you could hear the echo. "There will be snow here in a few weeks—then you should be here. It's a fairyland. All—" His fingers started to dance about and then drift slowly down to the table to show me what it was like. I nodded and told him how beautiful it must be. "You don't know. There are secrets here. Great secrets. That's what keeps it so beautiful." He looked over at Powars, and I could see something moving between them, like a wink that did not happen. But I could see it.

We all ate sandwiches. Waldman took out a small bottle of *kirschwasser*, a cherry schnapps, that tasted sweet and bitter at the same time. He and Powars swigged it, while I took only a taste. They finished the bottle, then we all had some mineral water. Waldman went over to the outhouse to pee.

"Do you like him?" Destry asked me.

I shrugged my shoulders. "I guess so."

"Funny dude."

"Is he one of your…the people you work with?"

He looked down at the table. "Yeah. I guess you could say that."

Waldman returned. It was still warm there. I put my shirt back on, tied my sweater around my waist, and we started up again. I enjoyed the hike. Waldman chattered amiably with me and asked me simple, unthreatening questions about my life New York—"Do you go to theater? Do you like the new Central Park?" We stopped every few minutes to look at the gorgeous views as they unfolded around us. Then, at his suggestion, we made a slight twist off the main trail. You could have missed it easily, but there was a narrow passage between two large rocks, and after slipping through it we followed a dried stream bed up a steep grade for about a quarter of a mile.

145

Then there it was: a mouth into the mountain. Waldman waved us in, with a flashlight as big around as a fist. It was like something miners might use; it made a search beam in front of us, with Ernst appearing huge at the lead, sometimes looking back at us. The place was totally creepy. There was a trail cut into it, made by ages of trickling water with, perhaps, some man-made help, too. The land outside was dry from the fall weather, but inside it was putrid-oozy. Our footing was slippery. Maneuvering slowly through an eerie dark maze, with a bone-chilling bottom of wet moss and slimy rock under our feet, we wandered deeper in.

"What you call this place?" Waldman called back to me. "A cave?"

"More like a cavern," I answered. "But it's not like the caverns I remember seeing pictures of."

"No? No *pictures*?" Waldman said gruffly, aiming the flashbeam up at the humped top and then the pitted, water-seamed walls of the place.

Powars joked. "It sure ain't picturesque!"

"*Nein*," Waldman said, spinning the light around and hitting my face with it, blinding me. I had to clench my eyes shut. "Not from pictures. You got that right."

I opened my eyes. I could see Powars's face. He was happy.

"I think it's kind of cool. A secret cavern. Thanks for showing it to us, Ernst. I been coming to Switzerland for years, and you never showed me anything like this."

We stopped. Ernst set the light down. He smiled. A rising tide of genial superiority flooded his face. "Maybe you're not ready—and your friend is not either. You say it is 'cool,' Destry?" He shook his head. "I say it is *schön*. It is full of *geschichten*, secret stories. Not like such places in America, with all the big showy—how you say?—*kristalls* and stuff. I saw one in Arkansas. They have a church in it—real Hollywood, U.S.A." He laughed that big laugh again. Powars shrugged. Ernst picked up the light.

146   We walked further in, down even deeper, listening to the faint beep-beep seeping of water. The air became thicker, damper, and achingly chilled all at the same time. The beam of Waldman's light chased across

the rocky ceiling, then bumped into a huge colony of bats who were sleeping contentedly upside down—hundreds and hundreds of them—making this almost snoring sound until the light woke them.

Immediately they *whoooshed* out—a flying city of them, blacker than night—over us, their leathery wings beating only a few feet above our heads. They had this rank smell, like dirty, rotting hair. I clenched my eyes closed, afraid; their call made my teeth grate. It was a whiny, high-pitched scream, like a taut wire plucked in the wind. It followed them as they soared out of the chamber, and then returned.

They became quiet.

I opened my eyes; the bats settled in, their wings refolded like stygian moths over their small, squirmy bodies. Ernst had the light pointed up at his face. He looked like a jack-o-lantern. "They don't like it when you bother them," he said in a low voice. "But they are no problem. *Kom.*"

I was shaking, but followed them. Powars repeated, "Cool, cool," as we snaked around a pharaonic wall of rock, then came to a huge room. It was breath-taking, like something from a palace—but a palace where a monster, more terrifying in its grasp and strength than I could imagine, might rule. There was actually a throne, a raised ledge, for it, or him. I could see him sitting squarely on it, with an elephant-sized head and one penetrating eye that looked directly into you.

Ernst's single light poured over the vast space. "*Königzimmer,*" he declared. "It is the king's room. Even I—I tell you—am amazed here."

Destry nodded. "You're right. It's amazing. Why didn't you show me this before, Ernst?"

The bald man shrugged. That genial, deliberate smile that he packed away and took out when he needed it, came back on his face. He looked smugly at Destry. "Perhaps you were not ready, *bruder mein.* There are things, maybe, even you should not see."

I looked at them in the dim atmosphere as my eyes became more 147 used to being there. Waldman's light skimmed over Destry's face and his features froze for a second as panic shot through him. Then the light passed. "I see," he said stiffly. "And you think I'm ready now?"

"*Ja*, Destry. Sometimes we must make our own—how you say that word?—*itinerary*. Right?"

Destry looked away. Ernst kept smiling and waving the light over the dark vistas edged by even darker passages that spread away from us. Sometimes the towering rock formations were fluted in thick cobwebs, beaded with brilliant showers of diamonds from captured water. They sparkled. The waving beam of light made them dance; Destry and I watched and secretly smiled at one another. He gave me a quick kiss on the cheek, then grabbed my hand. For a moment, I felt that I was supporting him.

"*Kom!*" Waldman ordered. "Permit me, please, to show you the pictures."

"Pictures?" Destry asked cautiously, letting go of my hand.

"*Ja*. Very interesting. You'll see."

I became excited. "Cave paintings?"

I smiled. I felt like a discoverer myself. I was ready to see them.

"All right," Destry said. "Come on, Ernst. Let's see these pictures."

Ernst brought us up to a slightly higher area. It was colder, dryer, not so clammy. It felt like a raised chapel, carved out to one side. I shivered. My breath frosted up, and I pulled my sweater back on. Powars did the same thing. At first there was just starkly shadowed darkness with sentinels of menacing, upended rock columns, some cut short like seats or even tables. Then, at the furthest wall, isolated by Waldman's light, were his "pictures," some scratched into the rock, some painted with soot and a kind of reddish-ocher stain that could have been blood or squeezed berries.

Silently, we examined the wall. I became so immersed in it, that the vast, dark reaches around me disappeared and only the wall, in the vivid illumination of Waldman's light, existed.

The cave art depicted a ritual, perhaps to do with war or the spirits of the hunt. A powerful group of men, who were drawn so individually— so real in their detail—were killing a victim: a defenseless bound man who was smaller and offered like a sacrifice. The men looked hulking, slope-backed; I thought they might be Neanderthals, though it was hard to say. I'd read that Switzerland once had an ancient primitive population, which had sought safety in the mountains and caves, when the rest of Europe was being invaded by more advanced humans from the East. The men were all naked, carrying spears, though some had knives or daggers. The bound central figure, thinner, simply outlined, had vague, primitive facial features, but his hands and legs were clearly tied with rope or hide thongs. The killers were drawn realistically, with broad-boned faces, individual eyes, shaggy hair. Their big, well-defined bodies had pointed nipples, with large muscles and realistic genitals. They had just cut his throat—at that moment. My eyes followed a stream of dark blood, as it spurted in gushes from the fresh, jagged wound. I could feel the horror, the rushing, unfathomable pain of the cornered, terrified victim.

My heart raced. This was so graphic; so immediate. I had seen pictures of cave paintings, with bison and tusked woolly mammoths and stick figures for men; but nothing like this. This was savage, close to unbearable. Then Waldman's light fell on a lower section of the wall, illuminating a separate frieze of drawings done with a skill that turned my blood cold.

The hunters (I'll call them that) were now around other victims. These smaller bound men—I counted four of them—again were almost faceless, with dots for eyes, but they had more detailed bodies: starved ribs, tiny nipples, narrow stomachs; thin, shy penises. The naked hairy hunters were in profile, their heads situated just below the crotch of their victims' bodies. Waldman's light focused on those realistic faces. The pictures glistened. Those fearless eyes … mouths …were wide open; and the glistening teeth of these hunters—saber-sharp, more like animal than human teeth …were aimed squarely at the gashed, lacerated testicles of these bound men.

I felt dizzy. The light stayed on the pictures, but I couldn't look anymore. The place smelled disgusting, maybe from eons of bat crap; it nauseated me. I began to retch loudly, feeling helpless. I hated it. Powars put his cool hands on my forehead and then on the back of my neck.

"Ernst, he didn't need t'see this," Destry said. "We have get him outta here."

"Sure!" Ernst said, suppressing a chuckle. "Your friend maybe has *angst, ja*? All of life is not so pretty. It's no Disneyworld, right? We'll get him back to the hotel. Get him a little more schnapps. Make him feel good." Waldman smiled, then began patiently to lead me by the hand.

I felt sick to my stomach, weaker than I had imagined. Then I realized that I was being separated from Destry, who had taken the big light and was still mesmerized, by the pictures. His eyes would not leave them; while I found myself walking into the darkness of this terrible cave with Ernst.

"You'll be all right," Waldman whispered to me. "Let me take you, please." He drew me along with him. "I know this place like—how you say it?—like the back of my hand."

I nodded, but had this sensation that I had ceased to exist. That my fears, my reaction, so physical, to that barbarous painted scene, had made *me* disappear. Completely. The hand that Ernst now held was somewhere away from my real body—or my soul. I was still with Destry, over there, peering at those pictures. My entire being was there. I did not want to be so weak; I wanted to be another person. Stronger, whole—different from the man that I was. What, I wondered, was Destry getting out of those paintings, and why wasn't he with me? Was he deserting me? He couldn't, I told myself. The only thing that this bald man had was some physical part of me. Destry had the rest.

We walked farther. "Can you see?" Waldman asked.

I nodded involuntarily. I felt like a stick, a puppet. No, I couldn't see, but I could feel my way with him. I told myself that I was no longer frightened, because, really, I was no longer there. I was just in some kind of ... frozen shock. There was no need to be anxious, I kept telling myself: they were only cave pictures. This meant nothing, I said over and over inside. It had nothing to do with Destry.

150

But who were those people, the men of the cave? That question rang in my ears. Along with, who was Ernst; who was Destry, and—even more immediately, more frighteningly—who was I?

"Destry'll be here in a moment," Ernst said kindly. "Please, why don't you turn behind. You'll see the light. Still on the wall. He's looking. He sees maybe himself there in that old picture. We do that, you know...with old pictures sometimes. We see who we are in them, *ja*?"

I turned. I made myself glance behind me, and there it was: those ghastly pictures on the wall, focused in Destry's light. They looked huge now, illuminated in this darkness of death like some old drive-in movie screen watched from a great distance. I remembered them from my childhood, riding in the car with my parents at night and seeing, from a distance, a drive-in movie screen. Cowboy movies. Silent "Shoot-em-up!" Silent "Bang, bang!" That huge distant image of falling without sound. Destry reminded me of that. I was still looking back him, my hand was in Ernst's, when I heard the sound.

That crashing noise...of the slippery, sucking, downward-sloping stones beneath me, surrendering, plunging ... giving way. The cave floor was gone. Thick darkness fell over me like a pair of wet black rubber gloves, choking my throat, squeezing my eyes, nose, mouth. Water poured in around me. Swirling, flooding, solid darkness, rushing into my lungs. I was being sucked into a vacuum. What a way to die, I thought. Alone. Where was anybody—Ernst?—anyone?

I jerked about, trying to get my body to the top. I'd seen a large dog once, cruelly thrown by boys into a flooded drainage ditch, flail as I did, desperate to survive. But the water kept rushing over me, pulling me under. My guts were heaving up anything now, air—whatever—I was going to die: I knew it. I felt strange bits of light around me, like fluttering butterflies. I watched them flickering, even in that horrifying darkness. It was diverting, weirdly comforting.

My body must have had something left in it, because in some split-second that I cannot account for, the panic stopped. I relaxed. My body 151 went into a kind of crushed ball; then the water surging under me pushed me up into air. I gasped, got water into my mouth, spit it out. Then more water came in. It was all total blackness.

Then I saw a light, bouncing jerkily towards me. I heard Ernst's loud voice say, "Sorry! Sorry! He fell in the stream. He's dead. Your friend he is dead!"

"Come on, Ernst!!" Destry shouted over the water's booming surge. "You can't take him from me! I won't—"

"*Nein, nein,* no one takes, but *Gott!* You know holes—how dark it was—"

I could hear Destry screaming—"You won't let me have him! You shits! You wanted me to have no—!

"QUIET!" Waldman raged. "I'll kill you, Destry. You know that!" His voice quieted. Then he said: "*Bruder mein.* Give me your hand, it's okay."

"NO!"

Waldman had grabbed the light from Destry's hand and was pointing it away from me. I could see its beam ignoring me. My energy was zapped. I might last in this thunderous surge of numbing water for another minute, then be sucked deeper into the cave; they'd never find me. I prayed that if I were going to die, I wouldn't know it. I was a coward—I wanted my death to be easy...

More water poured in. My eyes closed and I felt this watery light pouring through them, as if through smoked glass; the lids were now translucent.

My lungs stopped hurting. I could no longer feel my body. I was sinking. The butterflies of light had stopped, too; the light was now way up at the surface—I could see it drifting just over the water above me—cool, detached, and yet warm at the same time. I was dead cold.

Something hard stopped me. An arm. Then a body. A whole body. Powars. The water again must have pushed me back up again, and he had gone in and managed to grab me. With Waldman's help, he got me over to a ledge or some piece of rock. Destry pushed at my stomach, with his mouth directly over mine. He blew a straight shaft of air into me. I was horribly cold all over, but alive. Shivering, but breathing again.

"We thought you were a goner," Ernst cried. "*Tot.* Dead. Nothing I could do. I did not like Destry to risk two lives by going in. Destry, you are ... how you say, a hero. *Ja,* a hero. Allen, you owe—"

"He owes *nothing!*" Powars shouted. "Nada. He's soaked. I hope he doesn't die here of some fucking cold. Take off your jacket, Ernst, and give it to him—"

"My jacket. Na, *I'll* be cold. I am an old man—I helped save him, too!"

Destry was fuming. He was soaked, too, but did not show it. "Take off your damn jacket, Ernst!"

"This is unusual, Destry. The others will hear of this. I am your—"

"Take the fucking jacket off, or *I'll* kill you."

"Okay, okay. Americans. *Mein Gott.*"

Destry had taken my sopping shirt and sweater off. I still had my hiking boots on. Although they were wet, they were waterproof and my feet were not freezing. My pants were soaked, but who cared? Waldman threw his expensive suede jacket, still warm from his body, over me. Destry put his shoes back on. I lay there, relieved for a moment. Then the cold began eating through me again. My teeth started to chatter, but I was so tired that I could hardly open my eyes.

"We'll have to get you up," Powars said. "Come on."

Waldman was angry. He'd been deprived of his Swiss jacket, and he went on cursing and muttering in German and Destry would growl back at him, but not loudly. They were like two dogs circling each other in these echoing reaches. I was so tired I could barely keep my eyes open. Powars managed to get me up and somewhat on my feet, supporting me, while Waldman led the way with his flashlight. We had to stop every couple of feet. At one point I started shaking, coughing violently, and going into dry heaves. I ended up buckling to the rocky floor. Powars knelt down and held my head up. Waldman kept his head turned from us, beaming his flashlight at the high wet ceiling of the cave.

We started again and finally reached the mouth. I could see light outside and the soft bluish shadows of the approaching sunset on the distant snow. Powars took Waldman's jacket from me. My guess was that he had heard enough bitching already. My pants were sopping and since he was going to carry me, he didn't want Waldman's jacket to get wet. He tossed it back at him, then put my wet shirt and sweater back on me.

Powars knelt in front of me and told me to grab his shoulders. I did. He arched over, hooked his hands behind him, around my butt, and carried me like a sack of potatoes on his back. It was slow going. We stopped often, but he managed to get me back to the hut, with Waldman walking in front with the light.

Evening had settled in. Waldman lit the oil lamp and started a fire in the wood stove, then told Powars that he was heading back to the hotel and would send people back for me.

"Sorry the cell phones don't work here," he said, smiling in an almost genuine way. "You think he needs a—?" he mimed a stretcher.

"No," Destry said. "Just some warm clothes. I'll be here with him. I'll see you later on this evening. Tell Gwinny that I'm here. I'll want to speak with her."

Ernst shrugged his big shoulders. "Gwinny's smart. She knows what to do."

"She's always been on my side," Powars said bitterly.

"Don't be stupid. You forget who has done what for you—"

Powars looked down at me. "Maybe you'd better go, Ernst. It'll get cold here soon. *Danke für allis hier.* Thanks."

Ernst shrugged again. "*Bitte sehr,*" he said, then walked out the hut.

Powars and I were left alone. The hut had a steady cheery glow from the lamp and the stove. I could see stars through the windows, and the tops of mountains and drifting, blackening clouds. Working quickly, Powars took everything off both of us and arranged our wet clothes to dry on the floor near the stove. By the wall was a narrow, thin cotton mattress on a platform, with some bedding, army blankets and sheets in a cupboard. He made up the bed and put me in it, tucking a sheet and the blankets over me. I thanked him.

He looked at me softly. He rarely ever looked at me like that, with none of his defensive arrogance. "I was scared," he admitted. "You don't know how scared I was. I hate being so scared." I could see that he was getting cold. A line of chill bumps went over his upper chest.

"He tried to kill me, didn't he? Why didn't you just let him?"

Powars moved closer to the stove, warming himself with his broad back to me. I liked looking at him. It was something I could not stop doing. "Ernst's Swiss. He's different. Why'd you think he wanted to kill you?"

"Because I'm not stupid."

He moved back a bit in his bare feet. I could see him rubbing his hands together, though he still would not look at me. "Okay," he said calmly. "I know you got freaked out by those strange pictures. And the cave; it was dark. Caves have dangers in them. It was an accident, it was—"

"I heard what you were saying, Destry. Like I keep asking you, what's going on here?"

He hesitated; his body started to shake. "And like I keep telling you, Allen, I'm just a businessman. I do deals with people. I set things up all over the world. You don't know anything about business. I work with lots of people—I—"

"And some of these people are here?"

He turned to me and licked his dry lips. "Some."

"Where are the rest?"

"All over the world ... like I said."

I closed my eyes. This was too big for me. Waldman had just tried to murder me. I was in way over my head, like I had been in that water. If Powars had not pulled me out—maybe he would not be there the next time. What the hell was going on? He'd never answer me. I'd been stupid. Who did I think I was—I was just this little queer with polite queer friends, who worked in a bank and was going noplace. I thought I could kind of hitch a ride with ... but who was *he*? I opened my eyes.

"I've got to go back to New York," I said.

155

"You can't."

"Why not? You said I could go last night. Why can't I go now, as soon as we get back to the hotel?"

"You're sick. You could get pneumonia. What do you want me to tell you, Allen? The people I work with would never let me have anything like you in my life. They'd stop it."

"Why?" Suddenly it seemed that he was giving me a real answer. I sat up in the bed as best I could.

He couldn't look at me; his face was aimed towards the floor. "Allen, they made me what I am. I was just a piece of shit, I told you that—I was trash from New Jersey. I was the type you'd see with prison tattoos burned on my butt. I just sucked dick, that was all. But..."

His eyes welled up. He really looked naked. He was. He started to shiver badly.

"To get out of me what they wanted, they had to take everything from me, Allen. Except just one thing. One tiny, little thing."

"What's that?"

"I can't tell you, I swear, but you've got it. That's why I just ... feel like I want to worship you. I mean it."

What was he talking about; worship me?

"I mean it," he continued. "You've got that one thing they still want to take out of me, but I won't let them have it."

I felt bad, like I had really hurt him. It seemed impossible, how could I ask him any more, without doing more damage?

"Is it ... in my balls? Is that why you do that? Those paintings, in the cave, were they—"

He seemed suddenly very small, like he had contracted into something else, something closer to what I was.

"If I tell you, it's over with for me. Completely. I'm as good as dead.
156   You gotta know that. Please don't ask me."

He did not say another word, but knelt in front of me, on the dusty wooden floor, so that his bowed head was below my face. I reached down and pulled him into the narrow bed with me. I kissed his mouth, his neck, his chest, then lower. My mouth found his cock. I sucked him, made him wet as I could, then pushed him into my ass and let him fuck me. Fuck me like we were joined together, like we had become one thing, some animal newly created, of unspeakable origin. Whatever we, or it, was, it was so far away from the sad existence I had tried to make for myself, alone in New York, that I couldn't even name it. I just knew I was now his; to be worshipped or destroyed.

I hated the thought of it. I should have drowned in the cave. I felt that torn up; conflicted; desperate. He came inside me. It was like all those butterflies of light had landed. I could feel him coming, his entire, immense orgasm, all the way through me. Through every cell in me. Every cell was now lined up with him—with his cells. I could see them. Know them. It was that intense. Nothing, not a single molecule, could be held back.

He slept, snoring slightly, his mouth open, his white teeth catching glints of light from the sharp, brilliant, three-quarter moon outside. I got up and washed myself at the creaky, old-fashioned pump. My clothes were dry enough to put on. Then I heard distant feet crunching outside—it was so quiet you could hear it from a long way off—and I saw the faint movement of lights. I got Powars up, and he dressed.

It was really cold now. Two young men in brightly colored ski parkas knocked at the door. One was tall, blond, very fresh-faced. "Ve hear you haf problems," he said. His friend was shorter, with raven hair and darker cheeks, but built like a gymnast. They had brought a first aid kit, a collapsible stretcher, two pairs of clean drawstring pants, flannel shirts, and two coats for us. They smiled while we put on the pants and shirts, which felt much better than our old clothes from the cave. Then we put on the coats and left the hut.

"Ve haf fear you vud need a doctor," the tall one said. His friend spoke no English, and Destry said something to him in German. The short one smiled. I was sure they were prepared to carry me if they had to. They had big flashlights. I was feeling much stronger and we made it fairly quickly down the mountain into the village, where a hotel car was waiting. Destry and I got into the back, while the tall blond drove up front with his friend. I suddenly realized how hungry I was and told Destry. He said that he'd have dinner sent up to the room.

ELEVEN

I took a warm bath

in the room. Afterwards, wrapped in a thick terry robe in a comfortable chair, I felt incredably better. Destry was by the bed, on the phone with Gwinny. Sometimes he called her Rose, sometimes Rosie. He was smiling, nodding; this beam of warmth came out of him. He hung up and came over to me.

"She's always on my side!"

I asked him what he meant.

He turned from me. "I need allies. She's my ally here."

"I thought I was."

He nodded softly, then turned his head slightly and gave me a strange, distant, almost hostile look. But I could not tell where the hostility was aimed. It was also fearful. Was he afraid of me? That seemed impossible.

There was a knock on the door. Two men in white jackets brought in dinner on a cart. It was extraordinary. Lobster, white wine in an ice bucket, asparagus, small potatoes with parsley and fresh dill. We ate it in the sitting room, and Powars, barefooted, still in the drawstring pants, poured the wine.

"You're looking better," he said. "How d'you feel?"

"Okay."

"Good." He smiled at me. His mouth was so amazing. I wanted to swim in it. There were moments when I felt drunk with desire for him.

159

But I had to hold that back.

"Can you tell me about these people?" I asked.

"I can't. I wish I could, Allen, but I can't." He reached towards me and felt my head. "I still think you're a bit feverish. Lemme get you something to lower the fever."

He went into the bathroom and shut the door. I had this horrible feeling that he was going to get it out of the brown bag. He came back with a glass filled with slightly amber-colored water.

"Here."

"What is it?"

"An old Swiss remedy. It's just herbs."

I told him I did not want it. He insisted. "If you don't take it, I'll worry about you. You wouldn't like that, would you?" He smiled again.

"Okay," I said. "But I want you to take half of it."

I was rarely so forthright with him. He shrugged his shoulders.

"All right. What's good for the gander is also good for the other gander, right?" He guzzled down half of it, without grimacing. "Here."

I sat on the bed and took it. It wasn't bad actually; it had a slightly sweet, licorice flavor. I looked at him and nodded. He smiled, then kissed me. "I liked fucking you in the hut," he said. He sat beneath me on the floor, cross-legged, and grabbed my feet. He kissed the soles of them. "You don't know what my life's like, Allen. The loneliness; the pressure. Not flipping out's the hard part."

I asked him why he didn't leave it.

"That's easy for you to say! You just don't know, really!"

I told him he was right. I started to feel flushed, like a wave of heat was coming over me. He looked up at me, then sprang to his feet. His face, beard-shadowed, wobbled.

"Let me get you some more," he suggested. "That dose can kind of 160 screw you up. You need some more to balance it out. That's the way these herbs work. They're little pissers, I can tell you."

I tried to laugh. *Little pissers*! The way he said that, like we were talking about Excedrin. But I couldn't resist him. I'd have to take it now. I felt too good, kind of warm and…beautiful. Yes, that was the word. *Beautiful*. How could I deny him anything? He'd saved my life—or had he?

He returned from the bathroom with another glassful of liquid, this more deeply colored, closer to garnet that amber. I got up and he handed it to me and I drank it down, without another question. Then he led me back to the bed. I had wanted to brush my teeth, but I realized I could not get up. Gently, he unbelted my terry robe, lifted it from me, and helped me get into bed. He plumped some pillows for me and made sure that I was comfortable. The room felt so secure and warm. He went over to the door and opened it; I could see him talking to a woman.

It was like looking through water. I could hear her voice. She came towards me, and I knew instantly that it was Gwinny.

I smiled. I could smell her perfume. Sweetly Oriental, with notes of night-blooming jasmine and mandarin orange. She looked lovely. Lovelier than I had seen her, only briefly, just two days before. What a two days, though; what a strange two days. She approached me and I saw her face, her beautiful, lacquer-smooth features and small, jewel-like nose. It was thin at the tip, very elegant; she pressed her soft lips to my cheek.

"Hello, darling," she said. "I heard you had a hard time."

I told her I was glad to see her. She turned to Powars, and said, her mouth now creased, saddened, "No wonder they want him. You must do—"

"No, Rosie, don't. Don't say that. He doesn't—"

"Doesn't what?" I wanted to scream—but couldn't. I just stared at her. She seemed apparitional, like she had only glided in, or was it those "herbs" that Powars had given me. For a moment, Gwinny looked transparent. I thought I could see her whole body. Her large breasts, her shoulders, thighs, legs.

"I'm going to get dressed," Powars announced. "I can't go out like this."

"Of course not." Gwinny looked down demurely at her softly buffed nails. She was sitting now at the edge of the bed. They were talking, as if I were not there. "Did you have dinner in your room?"

"Sure. Lobster. Real nice. Rosie, he had a bad time up in those mountains."

"I heard," she said. "From Ernst. He's pissed at you, you know?"

"Yeah, I know real good." He was sitting next to her now, with his head down.

She sighed deeply. "Destry, darling, I'm afraid that what you had— that they first wanted—well, maybe they're not so sure they want it now."

"They *gotta* want it! I had to be mean for them. They wanted that."

"I know, but you know how grubby Ernst can be. He may try to get even with you. Very soon."

He put his head in his hands, running his fingers through his thick hair. "You think?"

I could see her touching him, stroking his stubbly face. She turned to me. "How's he feeling?"

"He's coming along." Destry put her hands inside his, and brought them up to his mouth. "This is an eat-or-be-eaten world, Rosie. There better be enough of us on my side—"

He started making this awful high squeal from sheer tension, like a child being hit, then he released her hands. She got up. She was wearing this beautiful gown, all lustrous white, with simple panels of silk. It reminded me of the moon outside on the snow-capped mountains. She wore a single strand of pearls and had brushed her long black hair straight back. I watched her passively, her eyes a lovely green, like glimpsing a distant planet as clouds of stardust opened. She looked at me with the glimmering lights from the room bouncing around her face. I was dreaming, I was sure of it; this woman was visiting me in a dream. Then she said, "Are you sure, Destry, that you have enough on your side?"

His face tightened into a mask of fury."Fuck 'em all!" he exploded.

She put her soft, elegant hand on his cheek. "Destry…." She sighed. "The difference between us is that you never really understood what the game was. Someone like I—"

"Gwinny!" he exploded, jumping off the bed. "Cut the shit! I know your parents were half gods and half royalty and half—"

"I never said that, Destry. It's just that where I came from, compromising yourself for something was"—she shrugged—"normal. We played the game. But some of us knew how to keep more of ourselves back while we did it."

"Sure, Rosie! Your shit don't—"

He stopped. He looked at her in this funny, cold, indirect way, as if he were only half present. And the other half? In my state, I had no real idea what was going on. Then he said, "Okay. Maybe you just had more t'keep," and went into the bathroom and shut the door.

Gwinny came back to the bed, sat on it and held my hand. I loved the way her hand felt. Cool, soft. Beautiful nails. She sat there for a while, thinking, watching me. I could hear Destry in the shower. I thought of him in it. I tried to smile. Sometimes she touched my forehead, then she returned her hand to mine.

"Allen," she said softly, "I wish you could understand what I'm saying, but maybe it's best you can't." I couldn't answer. I felt like I was in a coma, able to hear, but not speak. Sometimes, though, people in a coma can respond. I grasped her hand slightly tighter. "He loves you," she said; her softly colored eyes, like emeralds, on me. "He's going to die."

Why? Why? *Why?* I wanted to say. But I couldn't.

"He'll play the game, until … " She shook her head. She was wearing little diamonds earrings, which sparkled in the light. Pins of light dashed around the room. "You're so nice! I didn't think Destry would ever have such good taste. No wonder Ernst tried—"

Destry came out of the bathroom. He had shaved, and was dressed handsomely in a dark wool suit. He had on one of his spectacular ties, this one in an aquamarine blue that looked like it was spun out of precious stones.

Gwinny kissed me quickly on the forehead and got up. "Well, aren't we flashy?" she said. Destry beamed at her. "Do you think he'll remember any of this?"

"I dunno. I didn't want him to feel any pain from what's going to happen to him." His head dropped. "I had to offer him, you know."

"To—?"

Powars turned out the lights. He was about to usher Gwinny into the hotel hallway; I could not keep my eyes open any longer. Still, whatever dream I was having, took on a very different quality with the next words he uttered. "Yeah. To Ernst."

I was asleep. Knowing you're asleep, when you're asleep, is one of sleep's mysteries. Sometimes you don't know, and when you awake, it's like you've been traveling. You ask, where was I? But I knew: I was asleep. Those ol' Swiss herbs were working. (I recalled that song: "Those ol' Swiss herbs have me in a spell. / Those ol' Swiss herbs that you ... grow so well. / Those icy fingers—") No icy fingers. No. Just this velvety sleep. In New York, I never slept like that. My neighbors upstairs, stupid jerks, were always making noise. Two disco queens, they'd decide at three a.m. that now was the hour to crank up the volume. "Oh, dearie! Did we wake you?"

Nothing's as vacuous as vacuous fags. They make those Jewish princesses born in the Calvin Klein shop at Bloomingdale's look like Benedictine monks. Or was I being too bitchy from those ol' Swiss herbs? Anyway, the shut-eye was lovely. I dreamed about swimming with porpoises in this warm Caribbean water—one of the great queer totemic dreams, I think—naked, phallic water creatures who adore you. Who lift you up and nuzzle and kiss you. Who could ask for anything more?

They were now kissing my genitals with their warm, sea-puppy tongues. I was smiling, there in the arms of that lovely dream. In that lovely sleep. Just doing ... lovely things in the water. Soft voluptuous movements in intimate tandem with hunky dolphins, who reciprocated my every wish, thought, desire. I was breathing with them. Bubbles were coming out of my nose and we were kissing, as they nudged me and I felt them tickling my crotch, my small seashell of a dick being licked by them, now sucked lightly, along with my toes, my fingers, my nipples...their mouths, though, were strangely grating. Kind of like a cat's. Or, was that a catfish's?

Or a … anyway, they were armed with whiskers that could cut like a knife. They were now at my testicles. I was hard. My small dick—it always seemed like a kid's dick, not a man's—was hard, while all these strange, aquatic things were sucking me from *inside* my balls. They were now *inside* me. I was bleeding, but softly, warmly. Kind of like the way a warm salt bath feels as the temperature starts to penetrate the delicate area around your scrotum. I was not frightened. How could I be in this warm bath of a dream, surrounded by gentle dolphins "nursing" at me? Oh, sweet creatures, I called. These sweet, sweet, *sweet—*

SMACK!—I jumped straight up from the sting of a slap across my face. I bolted awake.

Ernst Waldman had slapped me. He was laughing that full, ghastly laugh I'd first heard in the dining room. Four men had surrounded me, holding me down while faceless mouths sucked eagerly on my wrists and fingers, and this small being that looked like a dwarf was wedged at my thighs. I saw only the black-collared back of its neck, as its mouth sucked lamprey-like at my testicles. I started screaming. "No! No! No!"

Ernst raised his hand and slapped me again twice. He rammed the corner of a plump feather pillow into my mouth, and the almost mechanical chewing and sucking continued. It was like being sawed open by this thing's needle-sharp teeth, while it made triumphant, piercing little shrieks and gurgling moans. My head was killing me—the drugs; the slapping. I felt like a plaster doll that had been banged against a concrete wall until its head cracked. My eyes brimmed with tears. I managed to glance through their glassy prisms at the four dour men in funereal evening suits; then at Waldman, with that revolting, genial, superior look on his face that I'd seen now too many times. And finally at the creature lapping at me, who now turned on my chest and looked curiously into my eyes. It had a smooth, dark, almost featureless face that glistened with a soft, oily sheen like a newt or a salamander. I could see almost nothing of him. Only his bright, bottomless eyes that smiled intensely at me, fiercely happy. I wanted to vomit. I wanted to die. I wanted this dream—vulgar, insistent, stupidly violent—to stop.

It did not. The thing continued sucking at me.

Where was Destry? I still could not speak, or cry out. Only weep. But I wanted Destry.

"Are we having a nice time?" Ernst asked. He was so big; his face looked as blank and lifeless as some asteroid from deep space. "The service here to your liking? *Gut für* our American friend?"

I closed my eyes, tears were burning them. I was choking on the feathers from the pillow. Then I heard: "Cut out the bullshit, okay?" and smoke filled the room. It was Destry. His voice, his presence. "You don't have to be so ugly, Ernst. They got what they wanted."

I opened my eyes. Destry seemed to float among the gauzy, curtained shadows by the window, with Gwinny materializing next to him. She looked so fresh in her white silk gown, as if she were made out of the Alpine air itself. Her slim hands went up to her black hair, arranging a few errant strands at the sides of her face. She pulled a tiny compact out of her purse, flicked out a tube of mauvish-red lipstick, and carefully applied it to her lips. Powars puffed at a new thick cigar. The smoke drifted around his head like a white cloud. It cleared and I saw his eyes, soft beams of light, pure gold and bright now; the brown in them had settled, and all that was left was an intensity of gold.

"Yes," Gwinny said, shaking her pretty head. "He doesn't really know what we're doing to him, Ernst. Why do you have to be so...brutal?"

Ernst smirked. "You call *me* brutal? Ugly? You two think you're real big, don't you? We pulled you both from *sheisse*. One was a cocksucker, and the other a whore—"

Destry's eyes narrowed and darkened. He blew smoke right into Waldman's face. "Ernst, I hope they take you fast. When it's decided, it'll be all over for you, too."

Waldman laughed. He waved the smoke away. "*Nein, nein*. Not so long, *bruder mein*, as *I* do the deciding. Remember, I chose *you*, little-boy-acting-like-a-big-big-man."

Destry lowered his head and took another puff on the cigar, then let the smoke dissipate. He shrugged his large shoulders. Gwinny placed her hand on Destry's arm, as he said to Waldman, "Haven't you finally taken enough out of me, Ernst?"

Ernst smiled, then opened his arms and walked towards the couple. He kissed Destry softly on the mouth. "I love you both like *kinder*," Ernst admitted, though I could see a visible shudder run across Gwinny's face. She seemed so different when she was serious, drawn into herself. "On the morrow," Ernst said, trying to be sweet, "he'll forget all this. And you will, too."

Destry approached me. My eyes were still filled with tears, but a light now poured from him, like that first moment at the baths in New York. Except that he was dressed now. He looked handsome; and tragic. I looked at him and began to feel strangely blissful. The dwarf creature sucking at me either stopped, or I could no longer feel it. I didn't want to look down at it again. I grasped Destry's hand.

"It'll be over soon," he promised. He kissed me on the brow and ran his fingers through my hair. He pulled the corner of the pillow gently from my mouth. He knelt by me, holding my hand and kissing my fingers, one by one, and then in groups. The herbs had so incapacitated me that I felt light-headed. I could have floated out of that quiet, beautiful room. I could have floated over the Alps even. He stayed there for a while, kissing and caressing my hand, then he rose.

He was right. The strange small creature, dressed in a shapeless, black sack of an evening suit, rolled away—that's the only word for it. He and the other men left. Only Destry, Ernst, and Gwinny remained. Ernst approached Destry with a glass of the garnet liquid.

"Give your friend this to drink. If he doesn't drink it, he knows I'll take him back to that hole in the mountain and kill him. He's not stupid, right?"

"No, he isn't," Gwinny said. "He's not. Certainly not any dumber than we are." Her face brightened; I could tell it was an effort. She smiled at Destry, then at Waldman.

"*Gut!*" Waldman shouted. "Now it's over. Come out with us, *lieber freunden*. We'll discuss our business. Dance. Take on the whole night! There's so much to talk of. All over the world, people need what we can give them. The edge, *ja*? That—how you say it?—*that certain edge*."

"Yeah," Powars admitted. "That fuckin' edge."

He took the glass from Waldman, and put it to my lips. I drank about half of it. What else could I do? I wanted to forget this as much as anyone. But the terrible thing was that I could not.

"*Ganz gut!*" Waldman said. "Now he'll sleep, and we'll go out."

Gwinny stroked my forehead. I closed my eyes. I wanted them all to die. But the truth was, I could not really hate anyone. I knew that I had fallen into this … and what could I really expect?

Powars nodded. "Yeah, Ernst. We'll go out. You, me, Rosie here. Some of the others. When you're in Switzerland, there is nothing like the night, right? It's so big and clear." Gwinny giggled, Ernst gave out a chuckle that seemed more like a belch, and Powars took up his cigar again. "There's some more shit I need to go over with you, Ernst, before the meeting tomorrow."

Ernst gave Powars a little love pat on his cheek. "The meeting … of course. *Naturlich*. Business is business always. Business comes first in this world." He nodded, pleased with himself. "You can meet your nice friend afterwards in the morning. *Ja?*"

Powars nodded. Bleary as I was, I could feel coldness coming into him, from that contact with Waldman. Ernst left with Gwinny, slamming the door hard behind them. I felt locked on the bed.

"Why don't you sit up," Powars said coldly, his voice strained close to breaking. "You can."

I did, and he sat next to me and handed me the rest of the glass. I drank it. What else could I do? He held my hand. I felt very heavy and slumped back on the pillow. The sheets were freshly ironed. I could smell 168 the prim, lovely hint of starch in them. "I had to do all that," Powars said, breaking down, crying, sobbing horrible tears. "So did Rosie."

"Destry?" I asked, finally able to say something, just before I became too tired to speak. "Will they kill me?"

"Naw. Not a worry; not now. It's me they want, honey. Not you. They're not such a bad group, really. I mean, sure, they can get jittery at times—a bit, you know, evil. But it's all business, and, sometimes, you have t'give a little just to take a little. Know what I mean?"

I didn't. Not one bit. But I nodded anyway. My head no longer pounded, it just felt like it was too heavy to be on my shoulders. My "private area" felt as if it had had a hole burned in it. I managed to reach under the duvet and quickly pull my hand out. There was no blood at all. Had I been hallucinating all of this?

Powars kissed me on the cheek, like he was putting a child to sleep. "I better go," he said. "We'll have a few drinks at the bar. There are these funny South Americans we're gonna be dealing with. They need the kind of things we can bring 'em. Also, a whole lotta stuff in Africa. You can't believe how mean those guys in Africa play." He smiled and got up. "The good thing about a business that floats from place to place is that it's always hard t'trace. Your houses, your cars, your big apartments—they can all just disappear in a minute. And show up someplace else."

He went to the door, and turned around. "That's why these funny folks here in Switzerland are so nice. They funnel all the good stuff to me, then it either disappears or goes someplace else."

He now looked so distant. He could have been the strange dwarf, for all I knew. Maybe they were all dwarfs, and only appeared to be bigger.

"Get some rest," he said seriously. "You had a hard day, Allen. I'll be back in the morning, and then we'll have breakfast."

TWELVE

True to his word,

Destry was there when I woke up. He looked somewhat tired—I had no idea what the night, with these strange creatures who seemed more like hallucinations than humans, had been like for him; but he seemed actually kind of...wondrously glamorous. Self-assured and glowing, like a movie star. He had showered and changed for breakfast into a rich nut-brown, cashmere sports jacket, a soft green shirt open at the neck, and heavy moss-gray twill pants with tiny leather buttons at the pockets. He leaned over the bed. "How you feeling?" he asked.

"Okay." What else could I say, really?

"Feel like breakfast?"

I told him I did. I was hungry, strangely enough. Very hungry. I felt like I could have eaten a cow. A horse! I got up, a bit groggy, sure, but at least I'd had some sleep. "What did you do last night, after you left me?" I asked him.

He broke into a big smile. "Oh, you know—we caroused. Talked business. Deflowered a few virgins—just joking! Sometimes I don't sleep at these things for days. Or I just conk out. My friends up here keep you up a lot. I mean, they like the night. It's when we do our most creative planning. Real thinking!"

I nodded. *Thinking ... Creative.* "You haven't really told me much about your work," I said.

"What's to tell? There are situations all over the world for us. Greedy people who want to look away; they want to blink hard. Get it? You can get away with anything, once you find people willing to blink hard enough—and long enough. We do most of the dirty work while they do the blinking, and now they all want to blink. It's part of the great 'opportunities' of our time. Governments. Businesses. Mega-*mega*-businesses. They blink and blink; sometimes the blink lasts for years."

I looked at him, nodding. He had never told me so much.

"Drugs, deadly metals—with all sorts of everyday things thrown into the bargain. In the old days they sold slaves and put the money into rum. Now, they sell all sorts of stuff—humans, too—and put the money into... hey, you'd never believe it!" He shrugged. "Come on! Get dressed. We'll go down for breakfast."

I didn't even shower, but got into some pants and one of my own shirts, a sturdy oxford cloth button-down, white with gray stripes. I went into the bath, splashed some water on my face, brushed some of the night out of my teeth, gargled, ran a comb through my hair and came back out to the sitting area of the room.

Destry was on the phone. "Naw, Tony," he said. "We're just gonna eat breakfast. Why don'cha come eat with us?"

Pause. He winked at me, then pulled me to him and kissed me on the cheek. He had shaved. He smelled wonderfully fresh with just a lemon and vetiver hint of his expensive Bond Street cologne. It had a kind of tang to it, like expensive stationery. One of my bosses at the bank, a young woman, had her own embossed stationary that had that same kind of fresh light smell. Every sheet cost dollars.

"Good," Destry said. "I'll order. See you." He hung up. I asked who he was talking to.

"Tony. Remember, I spoke to you about him in New York? Funny type of Brit fag. He was kinda like you."

"What do you mean?"

"Didn't know his ass from a hole in the wall." He lit a cigar and started to puff at it. "Mind? I'll go out on the balcony if it bugs you."

I shrugged. "Is that what you think of me? That I'm just stupid?"

"Naw." He let out some of the smoke. I choked lightly on it. "I'll put this out, okay? I just mean, you never learned how to live in this world. You're innocent. You ain't like me, at least like I am now."

He put out the cigar. He got up and I held him to me. "What are you doing to me?" I asked. "What's this all this about, Destry? I mean it, these strange people? This strange place?"

He smiled. He had such beautiful dimples when he smiled. He sat down again, then pulled me to him so that I was on his lap. I loved it. I even loved being smaller than him. I wanted to get lost in him. I was frightened; I needed him.

"Allen, I was what they call a *ginzo*, know what I mean?"

I told him I didn't.

"Poor white trash immigrant types. Just ripe for that ol' American dream. And I was a queer who didn't like, let's just say, your other type of queer men. You know, New York pretty boys who think they're so hot-shit cool."

"Yeah, sure." About them, I did know.

"Then these people, nice people, really, in their own way, found me. They took out of me what was necessary to take out, and left what they could use. They did not leave a whole lot, that's the truth. But when I met you at the baths I just knew that, inside, we had something that—"

"*What?*" I kissed him immediately. My whole mouth went right into his. What did he know?

He smiled. That wonderful smile again.

"Gosh, maybe it was just something we both had. But the truth is, I'm scared to say what it is."

"Why?"

"What d' you mean 'why'? Why do you have to know? Just be glad, just—"

"But you *do* know?"

"Yeah."

"Will you ever tell me?"

He nodded. "At some point."

I kissed him again; he moaned. "Good," I said. "Because I want to know."

He pushed me off him.

"Let's have breakfast. I'm tired of talking like this. I'm tired of talking period. How're you feeling? Headache, or anything like that?"

I told him I was okay. I did feel pretty good, considering how badly I'd felt when we left the mountain, and later, when something happened that I knew we were not going to talk about. He went into the bathroom again, and came out with another glass of liquid. "You need to drink this."

It was that same garnet color, but deeper this time. I asked him again what it was.

"Just herbs. Come on. You really need it, I swear. If you don't take it, Allen, you're gonna get some very strange 'psycho' effects. I mean from the air here and all this energy and shit. I mean, we kept you up last night. I know that. I apologize."

"What are you talking about?" I took the glass from him.

"We came into the room, started messing with you. Having fun with you. You were asleep. You never did fully wake up, but stuff like that can screw up your head. They did the same thing to me, when I first got involved with these guys."

I started to drink the liquid. I put it to my lips, but didn't get any into my mouth. "The guys?" I asked. I walked over to the windows in the room. There was a nice house plant on the sill. Some kind of ivy that trailed almost down to the floor. I turned my back to him, and carefully, out of his view, lifted the glass up to the plant's pot.

"Yeah, the guys. The ones I work with. They did some funny things to me. Hey, you 'bout ready?"

I told him I was.

"Hey, don't water the plant with my herbs! I know what you're doing."

173

I turned to him. None of the liquid was gone. I smiled, drew the glass up to my lips, then the phone rang again.

It was Ernst this time—"Ernst, *mein mensch!*" Destry turned away from me, and they started palavering in German. I swiveled around to the ivy plant and dunked half of it in there before he could see anything. Powars was smart, but not that smart. Then I took a very showy swallow of it, getting none of it down my throat, and told him, while he was still speaking with Ernst, that I'd had enough.

Breakfast was served by a man this time. He was middle-aged, had thinning dark hair, and was dressed like a funeral director. He smiled shyly at Powars.

"This is Luke," Destry said to me. "How are you, Luke? *Wie geht es Ihnen?*"

"*Gut, und Sie?*"

Powars nodded to him. "Wait'll you see this breakfast. I need it this morning."

Coffee was served immediately, and orange juice. Then a pudgy, youngish-looking man, maybe in his early thirties, burst through the door. He was about two inches taller than I—but still shorter than Destry—and macaroni-white, with a black-as-ebony rug on his head. He wore a splashy, long-sleeved Orlon shirt, all Day-Glo pink-and-black flowers in a jungle design. As he got close enough for me to smell his stale morning breath, I saw deep lines etched into the pale mask of his face.

"Dez darling! You warm me like the first flush of spring. But you always do!"

Destry started to laugh uncontrollably, as the gentleman settled into a chair next to us. He leaned over to me and introduced himself.

"Tony Winzor here. Not like *the* Windsors. Ac-shully, I think the way *we* spell it—with a 'Z'—is older than they. They're just Germans, y'know. I shouldn't announce that *too* loud, should I?"

He looked at me seriously, then winked.

"Nice t'meet you, Allen. A little new blood in these parts never hurts." He winked at Powars, who raised one eyebrow, nodded, and continued laughing.

I smiled warily at Tony.

"Is he one of the guys?" I asked Powars. "You know, one of your friends?"

Powars ceased laughing; Tony stared at me with a razor edge under his buoyancy. "What's he going on about, Dez?"

"It's early, Tony. We had a hard time up in the mountains yesterday. He's a bit confused, naturally, about the business."

"Ahh." Winzor sighed. He started *tsk*ing annoyingly with his tongue. "It's the elevation; this bloody elevation." He stretched his thin Orlon-clad arms out over the table. His hands were bloated like steamed white sausages, without a single line or wrinkle on them, unlike his face. "Got in late *late* last night m'self, see? Afraid I had no idea *what* he was blathering on about." He stared at me like he was pulling sections of me apart and then pinning them down. "Tell me, Allen, do you like organ meat?"

My mouth fell open. "What?"

"Ah, our breakfast!" Powars exclaimed.

And so there it was: Luke hurried in with three gleaming white plates piled with what looked like raw ground meat on them. I asked Destry what it was. He laughed.

"It's our steak tartare! I need it after last night."

Tony winked. A ripple shot up his forehead and met the black thatch up there. "That's it. *Tah-tar!*"

I looked at the plates. This was no steak tartare. I'd had steak tartare before. This was bone pale and kind of grayish, with streaky, runny grains of dark pink in it. I couldn't stand the smell of it. It had a rotten stench.

"I can't eat this," I insisted.

"You've got to, darling!" Tony Winzor jumped in. "Come on, a little bit of it'll do you worlds of good. We eat it every time we come back here; it helps you get over the new environment. The staff makes it up just for us."

Luke hovered over us. "Something not *gut*? You don't like?"

"He likes!" Tony insisted. "Right? You don't want to hurt the poor man's feelings, do you? There's over a thousand years of Swiss pride here!"

I sat silently, my mouth clenched shut. All I could think of was why was Powars doing this to me?

"Yeah," Powars said, shoveling the chopped stuff into his mouth, after heavily salting and peppering it. "Once you get past the way it looks, it's cool. What's that word you've got for it, Tony?"

"*Fortifying*, darling. Fortifying. That's the word Mum used t'use for anything we kids thought was detestable. But this is awfully good stuff. Luke"—he looked directly at the waiter, into his narrow beady eyes—"he's fine! He'll eat it. Rightey-oh?"

All of their eyes were on me. Luke glared at me like an insulted vulture. I thought that if I didn't eat this, he would eat me. I pushed my fork into it, and managed to force some of it into my mouth and chewed it rapidly. My guts started rushing up into my throat. I had to swallow it, before the damn waiter left. Tears fell from my eyes.

"Now, try a little more," Tony said sweetly. "Come on! Mumsey's waiting."

The plate seemed mammoth. I'd seen manhole covers that weren't so big. I drank some coffee, then some orange juice, then tried more of it. If I just swallowed it without chewing, I could do it. It wasn't so much the taste as the smell.

"What is this?" I asked seriously.

"A little concoction they do," Winzor said. "My mum served something quite like it, but not nearly as good. You have to learn to separate all the fine flavors in your mouth."

"Yes, you're right," I said. "Separate them."

But the only flavor I could detect was raw blood, and something that tasted like…pork? Or was it really like what I imagined human flesh tasted like? Not that that was particularly an item on any menu I'd ever experienced, but…maybe it was just the sight of it. I'd read once that the Arabs believe the eyes of animals are a great delicacy, especially the eyes of a camel or a goat. At a feast the most honored guest is presented with that, sometimes on a fresh bed of lettuce, also, in desert countries, a delicacy. The guest scoops up the eye—they are roasted carefully—on a single green leaf and then chews it, savoring each moment. Like an oyster, kind of. It was all in what you knew, I figured.

"Yeah," Powars said, as if he were reading my mind. "Now, the Arabs, they'll eat anything. Eyes, intestines; they love the testicles. They eat those kinda things on lettuce, you know. Just scoop 'em up and eat it."

He made a scooping gesture with his left hand—how did he know what I was thinking? But then, maybe he always knew. He looked at me and dove back into it with his fork.

"This has got a lotta organ stuff in it. Pancreas, liver, that kinda stuff. It's brought in from all over. When you work hard like we do, it just pops you right back up!" Powars smiled gamely at me.

I nodded. I pushed it around on my plate and made a noise like I was chewing. Then I pretended to swallow it, and asked, "Does it have testicles, too?"

"No, no!" Tony protested. "God, that's gross. Raw testicles—who'd eat anything like that?"

Powars laughed. "Maybe some of those Wall Street types, they'd eat 'em if they could get 'em. Seriously, some of those boys work eighteen hours a day for their money. They should try this. They'd love it."

"It's a pure pity," Winzor said. "A tragedy to mums and wives all over the world. Most of those young men just work themselves to death. But to our delight, there's always another one. They think they're so indispensable, but we know exactly what to do with them."

"Don't be a meany," Powars warned. "I have friends like that. They're really easy to deal with. You just let them think they're important. Let 'em think they're the big deals. Then you—" he took a silver knife from the table and made a decisive cut into what I decided to call his breakfast dish. "Then you cut *their* nuts off."

Winzor laughed loudly. He opened his mouth while still chewing on the raw meat. He had that same bone-chilling, hollow laugh as Ernst. Where did it come from? They finished their plates; I'd barely made any progress on mine.

Luke came back, shook his head disapprovingly at me, but cleared the course. Afterwards, they had soft-boiled eggs, rolls, coffee, fruit, and pastry. I had some more orange juice and a roll and butter. I could not believe they could eat so much. Powars settled in with a cigar. Winzor started to smile. He asked Destry about Gwinny.

"She's recuperating from the night. Ernst and his friends here, you know how they are. They don't let up. Gwinny just ain't a party girl like I am." He smiled contentedly and twirled the cigar in his fingers. He put his expensive shoes up on an empty chair; I could see the waiters at their stations registering a faint disapproval. His eyes were brown again, with thin slips of gold rimming them. "She's scared of the meeting, Tony. Why should *she* be scared? Tell me. What am I missing?"

"Loose lips screw a ship, luv." Winzor glanced over at me, with those steely pins ready in his eyes.

"Sure," Powars agreed. "But sometimes, Tony, you need a—" he paused. He blew a cloud of richly scented cigar smoke up to the tall ceiling. I watched it rise. "You need another soul in this life."

The white smoke curled slowly around a crystal chandelier, then disappeared. My eyes went back down to the two of them. Powars and Winzor were exchanging looks. Cold, knowing looks. I hated Winzor's guts. Could he read my mind, too?

"What now, darling?" Tony finally asked.

Powars shrugged. "The hotel has these hot springs that are nice. What do you think of that, Allen?"

178   "Fine," I said. As long as it did not involve a cave, it sounded all right.

"Good. It'll be relaxing. I could definitely use a little relaxation." He lifted his foot from the empty chair and got up. "We'll go back to the room and change. I need to read some newspapers. Get some email off my palm gizmo. You got one of those, Tony?"

"Sure," Tony sniffed. "But I didn't bring it. It didn't seem right, for this meeting with the—" he stopped himself. "I'll see you at the springs, say, after noon?"

He smiled, winked at Powars, got up, shook my hand briefly, then left us.

I asked Powars what Tony meant when he said it did not seem right for "this meeting with the—"

"The boys. Our friends, you know. He wants his head clear for it. They ask a lotta you, Allen. The truth is, Tony's a bit less ballsy than I am. He's more nervy, more *strung*, you could say." He started to laugh. "In our fun little circle, he's no loose cannon, but the nut they use to screw the rest of us in with tighter."

"He doesn't sound trustworthy," I said.

"You have to understand, when they took him in, they had even more work to do with him than with me. He's tacky. I know he's a tacky English queer, but his mother was a waterfront prostitute. He didn't even know who his old man was. I always felt bad for him. Sometimes people like him have even less going for themselves than I do. They have less inside."

We went back to the room. He hung up his sports jacket and took his elegant polished shoes off. He was really tired now, even I could see that. He got on the bed, and pulled me to him. We lay there on a beautiful gray brocaded bedspread. He put his head on my chest. I ran my fingers through his thick hair.

"Allen, if anything happens to me, I want you to go back to New York and just live at my place. Karl and Winchell'll take care of you. I won't let you down. I mean it."

"What could happen?"

He shook his head. "I dunno. I wish I could tell you." He looked up at me and smiled softly. "When you make your bargains and keep your promises, you don't know how much it's gonna cost you." He yawned. "I guess you didn't like the breakfast much, did you?"

"It was ... strange."

"Strange?" He sat up and laughed. "So, does strange scare you?"

I put my hands together anxiously. "Sometimes."

He nodded. "It's okay. It scares me, too. Sometimes."

He unbuttoned his shirt and tossed it on a big chair. In the soft light, the hair on his broad chest appeared onyx-black, with glowing tips of red in it. "These guys," he said, yawning, hardly able to hold his head up, "they ask a fucking lot from you."

"I'm sure. When will you have the—" I hesitated; I was actually shy about asking. "When will you have the big meeting?"

He yawned. "Soon. Then we'll go back to New York. I want you to live with me, Allen. Will you? When we leave here, I want you to be mine. I mean it. I do. Will you?"

I hesitated. He took my hand and pressed it to his chest. I could feel his heart. What could I say? I was his. He owned me. It was painful. As much as I detested so much that had happened—and I did fear him, yes, I did—I was his.

"Will ya?" he asked me again. "Please."

"Yes." I finally said. "I will be yours. I mean it. Always."

I felt like I was throwing my entire life into a pool of hungry sharks.

He kissed me, drew me right into him, then he yawned again. His eyes closed.

"Fuck the newspapers, the emails. We're gonna have a nice time today. You'll like the hot springs. They got a pool, too. Tennis. Oodles of rich people come here. You should see 'em. Jeeze, it's the kind of place I used t'dream about when I was a kid. You know how kids dream? They wanna be movie stars and ride around in limos, or rockstars; football 180 players, maybe. Well, I wanted to be in business. Talk the money talk, the way big money talks. It's a language, see? But I was just a little shit. That's what I was. My dad was a drug addict, my mom—she used to walk the streets, too. I was beaten, hurt."

He looked so different now. It was like all the warmth inside him was coming out, towards me.

"Everybody thinks they're so alone in the world," he said. "They are … and they'll do anything to stop being that way, even—"

He paused, and turned from me. His eyes could no longer look at mine.

"What?" I whispered.

"What I had to do."

I pulled his face towards mine and started to kiss him. I could not help it. Now the strange esoteric books in his office, his own weirdness, everything about him, started to have some kind of logic. Maybe I just wanted it to make sense. This huge wave of unfathomable feelings—I was so moved, so wiped out inside by him—hit me. "Yes," I said to him; then said, to myself, *if* I had to swim with the sharks, then I wanted *this* one with me, even if it meant him eating me.

"I went to school at night," he said, the words spilling out of him. "Baruch College"—he pronounced it *Ba-rooch*—"in the city. Damn heavy business school. I hit the books. Tried to learn everything I could. Then I finally learned something. It just wasn't gonna happen. Ever. There was always *something* between me and what I wanted. I felt like I was four feet tall. That tiny. Frightened. I felt bad. Maybe you feel like that, right?"

"Yes." I said. "I do."

"Then I met these guys. There were bunches of them. It was funny: they didn't frighten me, really. I just fell in with them. They took me in, trained me, and somehow I believed I was meant to be one of them. They brought me along and put me into positions I never could have got into myself. Doors opened for them. Doors on the top floors of those towers you see in midtown: the big corner offices with long black limos waiting downstairs. They said, 'Don't be afraid, we're behind you.'"

He started shaking. I held him closer to me. He calmed down a bit. 181

"I never thought I'd end up like this: Rich. A lot smarter. Sure, I can fly around the world. Talk the money talk. Dress well; eat like they do. I can do all that. But they took so much outta me. They did." He yawned. "I'm tired, yeah, but lemme tell you, they didn't take that one thing that I know you have." He put his hand to his yawning mouth. His eyes closed. "The turds couldn't take it."

Now I was the one trembling. He'd never been so real to me, never drew me this close to him. I was really frightened now…too scared to ask what it was that I've got. I'm this shy, polite guy with a kid's teeny dick who never fit into anything. I'd been scared all my life. I'd been a sissy, a little dickeater, I always felt like the one Cracker Jack box on the shelf that came without a prize.

"You have it," he whispered, reading my mind. "Underneath all your fear. Under all that stuff inside you that keeps you from being what you want, it's there. It's … Jeeze. Shit!"

"What," I pleaded. "From being what?"

His shoulders shrugged. His face which had seemed so close, so touchable, became distant. He smiled.

"Y'know, I'm pooped. Last night was fun—the guys can run you ragged, lemme tell you. Right now they're still at it—at that lodge about a quarter mile from here. That's where they meet. You won't get to see it. The meetings are secret, and, well, to tell you the truth, they can get rowdy."

His eyes closed. He was withdrawing from me. I knew it. "Shit," he said, yawning again. "I been talking too much."

I kissed his ear. I wanted to know, *had* to know, what he meant … from being *what*? Why was he changing the subject now? He started to giggle.

"That tickles!"

"What—what did you—"

"You wanna know what I did, right? How I got to be a big—make a lotta money, climb up from garbage; that stuff? Well, I learned what they taught me. I learned to stop being everything that was what I was—we made promises. We—"

"No," I said. "That's *not* what I meant. I want to know what you meant when you said, 'Under that stuff inside' that keeps me from being what I want ... is *what*?"

"Oh." He smiled. He took my hand, and turned and kissed me full on my mouth, inside my mouth. Then he said it, whispering very softly to me. "Just ... inside you, is me."

He fell for a couple of hours into a stone-deep nap. He talked sometimes in his sleep. Mostly it was numbers; maybe assets, stock trading numbers, I don't know. They came out of him in slow, whispered reels, as if there were a computer tape inside him, unwinding. Finally, when I was sure that he was really out of it, I got up stealthily and went into the bathroom and opened the linen closet door. There, behind the towels, was the small bag. When I uncovered it, it glowed, casting a saturnine light on the luxurious terry towels around it. I could feel heat coming from it, and that stinging sensation.

With the tips of my forefingers, I drew it carefully towards the edge of the shelf. I started to feel sick, like a wave of blood was lashing up into my throat. I managed to pick the sack up; then, with both hands, and despite the pain, I untaped the flap and opened the bag's brown mouth. I lifted it cautiously to my face, to get a better look.

It seethed. It started to rage. An entire storm seemed trapped within the simple brown paper. A fierce red powder, deeper, darker than any ruby, with a scent like dried animal blood mixed with the roots of rotting lilies, exploded in tiny, grainy pellets before me. Some hit my cheeks; others went directly into my nostrils. It stung my eyes and shot into me. I couldn't let out a noise—I could hardly breathe—but I would not let it go. Despite the pain, I held on to the bag.

Then my aching fingers found it, rising before me: another Nicky, the small effigy even more hideously naked than the one in the office; gripping by the neck in its tight, oversized hands a strangely humanform lizard of the same form as the repellent, mummified thing on Powars's desk in New York. It was struggling in Nicky's hands, writhing in its final death twitch, as the dwarf's coarse mud face looked directly up at me with an expression of disdain, loathing, and ultimate power. I could feel the life force, the struggle, going on within the two creatures, as the pain in my shaking hand, increased horribly. Finally I could take it no more. I lowered the effigy back into the bag—which, in spite of my efforts, skittered away from my hands and dropped.

It cracked loudly, like a shotgun going off. Powars came roaring in.

"What've you done? *SHIT*! What have you done!"

He was out of breath. His face swept the room, his eyes darting over the floor, the towels, the entire bath. His chest shook. Then—so quickly I could hardly believe it—he snapped back into control. He exhaled deeply, rubbed his hands firmly together, and calmly ordered me back into the room.

As I left the bath, I turned and saw Powars kneel, gently pick up the brown bag, and gravely kiss it. My heart stopped. He glanced over at me with a look that I could only see as revulsion. Then he pushed the door closed in my face. I sank into a nearby chair and buried my head in my hands.

I heard that noise again, a low, wavering echo, that sound like a spastic laugh and a kind of moan and cry, all at once, coming from behind the door. All I could think about was leaving—running, racing, tearing back to New York, to my old life. Never being near these strange people again. I'd return to the bank. To my polite friends. To the cheap little dinners we all paid for ourselves. Sometimes I'd indulge myself in a glass of white table wine. That was all. I was not ready for any of this. I knew it.

Powars clicked open the door to the bath and advanced towards me. He looked as if he were carefully preparing the case for my execution. I wanted him just to strangle me, like the lizard; I would have been happy if he'd done that. But no, it wasn't fury anymore. It was something else.

Now he was ready to ask *me* the real questions. It was time for my final interrogation. Who *was* I? What was *I* doing to hurt him? Why could I *never* trust him? I waited in disgrace. The insides of my stomach shook.

"You ready for the hot springs and the pool?" he asked.

I nodded.

The springs were partially indoors, with big thermal windows, sparkling white tiles, and beautiful lapis designs near the ceiling. There was a natural, outdoor spring as well, and a changing room in the *Badehaus*, as it was called, with a bar in it and quick waiter service. Powars was drinking a lot, mostly Italian drinks, the kind that taste like strong cough syrups with a splash of soda in them. Sophisticated people said they were "an acquired taste," and I always felt kind of stupid for not having acquired it. I had soda with lime, and watched him. He was beaming, seemingly sublimely confident. But it was only a mask.

Lots of rich people were out in the resort then, wearing wonderfully tasteful expensive clothes. Through the big windows of the *Badehaus*, you could see them parading. Nothing too ostentatious—just casual silks and cashmeres and worsted woolens. We walked in terry robes to the outdoor spring, all hot and gurgly, surrounded by formations of lava rock. In the cool air, the spring felt stinging at first, almost like that stuff in the bag. Then you got used to it and it felt relaxing. I needed it. I had never been in a situation as complicated and frightening as this.

We took off our robes and settled into the steaming water. The water hissed and gurgled. Destry put his big arms around me and kissed the back of my neck. I was sure the rich, comfortable Swiss disapproved of such public displays of affection between men, but for a moment, neither of us cared. He let go of me and I could see his face. Now he was ringing with happiness.

"I been coming here for years—and never had anybody like you to bring with me."

I looked around. I knew we would not have very long to talk. "Did you ever try to bring others?"

"No."

"Why not?"

"The time wasn't right. And I never thought I could trust anybody enough to bring him."

He looked around. From a corner of my eye, from a considerable distance, I caught a glimpse of someone who might have been Ernst, walking through the hotel's beautifully manicured park, with six or seven well-dressed people. Then he disappeared around a bend, behind a group of shaped trees.

"Was that Ernst?" I asked Powars.

He nodded. "I guess they're getting ready."

Then Tony Winzor came rolling towards us in the water.

"Allen, luv!" Tony called. "How are you after that breakfast? I feel like a tiger. A real tiger!"

In the stark light of the spring, Tony's soft, hairless body looked even more shockingly white, like some peeled, overboiled Irish potato. Or a corpse. His belly sagged; his wrinkled nipples were like the patches on an old, deflated inner tube. I realized that he was even older than I had thought. He might have easily been in his late fifties or sixties. His loose pale bathing trunks did not hide the rolls of veiny goose tallow at his hips, or the aging flesh on his upper legs.

"He's fine, Tony." Powars said. "We're both cool."

Tony laughed. Beads of sweat poured down his brow into the hot spring. "Even here?"

"Sure," Destry answered. "Even here!"

I looked at Powars. There was a quick, wary look in his eyes: paranoia, certainly. I glanced behind me and saw Gwendolyn. She was dressed for walking outside, in an elegant black, quilted jacket, but not dressed for the springs. She leaned over and called to Destry. He got out of the steaming water and put on his robe.

Tony gave me his cat-gulping-the-canary leering smile. "Did you get your nap, Allen, with Destry?"

I told him I had.

186   He gave me a loaded wink. "You're a lucky boy to have him. He's a hot item, isn't he?"

I just smiled.

Tony and I got out of the spring and joined Powars and Gwinny. Powars quickly introduced us, as if I had never met her.

"We know each other," she said, smiling softly, "from New York."

Destry shrugged his shoulders.

"We saw each other las—" I blurted out.

She waved her hand casually. "I wasn't sure you'd remember. You were kind of under the weather."

"He had a headache," Destry explained to Tony.

"Ahh!" Winzor agreed. "This place'll do that. Between the schnaps and the altitude—and don't forget all the attitude!—one can get huge headaches here."

"Yeah," Powars said. "A lotta headaches. Maybe we should sit for a while."

We went over to a group of deck chairs. It was fairly warm in the sun. Tony threw a terry robe over his white dripping flesh and a waiter brought him a light blanket when he brought us drinks. The talk quickly went to Ernst, and I could tell that Powars wanted me to leave—just the way he acted. Maybe too polite with me. I finished my soda, and he suggested I try the pool. "You'll like it," he said. "The water temperature's perfect. I'll meet you in a short while."

I got up. "I'll go with him," Gwinny said. Powars asked her why, and she said, "Just for the short walk. I'll be right back."

Gwinny smiled at me as we moved towards the heated outdoor pool filled with hearty people jumping in and out of it. "I'm sorry, I didn't think you'd remember me," she said. "Do you remember much of what happened?"

"Some." I looked at her. She was very pretty. Could I possibly trust her? I had to trust someone. "Who are you?" I blurted out. "Who are these people?"

She shook her head. "Friends of Destry's. That's all." She stopped walking and bit her lower lip for a moment. "He really likes you," she whispered. "I've never seen him so happy."

"What's going to happen to him, can you tell me?"

"Ernst, the others—they'll tally up what he owes. That's all."

I shook my head. "*Owes*? What does that mean?"

We were almost at the pool. "Just that, Allen. It's a business situation. These people are good at what they do, but they play rough—and for keeps. They came to him, just like they came to me. They offered us something and we took it. It's what they always want: that you'll take it. You *have* to take it. You have to be *willing* to take it. The truth is, they choose you because they *know* you'll take it. Do you see what I'm getting at?"

I nodded to her. Yes, I did.

"There are people all over the world, Allen, who'll sell anything to anyone. You must know that. We use those people; it's as simple as that." She looked down at her slender hands. "I can't tell you any more."

"I see," I said. I thanked her for telling me what she did.

She looked up and smiled at me. She seemed radiant. She must be in love with Destry, I realized; but whatever they'd had, had not worked out. I took her pale hand briefly. I felt suddenly very fortunate.

"You must let him love you," she said. "And don't question it."

She paused, then looked over at Tony Winzor, who was gesturing about something to Powars.

"He's changing here," she added. "One way or another. But I can tell you this: he won't leave here the way he came."

She turned and hurried back to Tony and Destry. I felt this lump in my throat, but got into the pool. There were heat lamps around it, but I felt this chill run all the way through me. Some German children started bouncing around me. They were all freckles and adorable, but their noise, the normal sounds of children, sounded like the whip crack explosion that the bag had made.

188   I got out and went over to the pool's heavy iron fence, painted a cheery blue. It came up to my waist. Destry, Tony, and Gwinny were still talking by the spring. Tony's face had lost its glued-on English smile. Gwinny looked drawn, her face now incredibly old, on the verge of cry-

ing. She lifted her hands up, palms out, in a gesture that seemed charitable and so out of place there. Why, I wondered, was she more human than the rest of these ...what were they? I did not know. I just knew that one of them held me, and always would.

She got up, and with her shoulders rounded away from me, returned to the hotel. A moment later, Powars came to me by the fence. I could see Tony on his deck chair, starting a new drink. "How about the steam room?" Destry suggested. "They have a sauna, too."

The spa area was over a slight hill, with a long deck connecting it to the pool and the spring. The steam room was large; its strong eucalyptus smell opened my clogged sinuses and cleared up some of the lingering aftertaste of the mysterious breakfast "tartare." There were several Swiss men in it. They didn't really look at you, but had a way of making you know that they knew you were there. It wasn't rude. They didn't snub you—it was just a quick nod, then it was over.

We went into the adjacent small redwood sauna. It was dark and relaxing and we were the only ones there. We took off our bathing suits. Powars pulled me to him and kissed me. His tongue went all the way into my mouth and stayed there. Then he kissed my neck and my nipples, making this noise, somewhere between a sigh and a barely repressed sob. I had never heard him make that sound before. I didn't want him to say a word—I felt so close to him. He must have brought me to Switzerland, I decided, for a honeymoon. He would claim me openly in front of all of his friends. That was what he had wanted to do. That must have been the "change" Gwinny was talking about.

The other things, the things Powars did to me, the strange apparitions in the room—the whole oddness of being there with Ernst and Tony—I could make nothing of that. I didn't care. I only wanted him. He made me tremble all over.

He broke off kissing me. "Like I said," he whispered, "if you have to, I want you to go back alone to New York. Stay at my place. I mean that."

"What's going to happen?" I asked.

189

He did not answer me, and now it was too hot and close in the sauna. A Swiss man in his late thirties came in, looking absolutely starved. He was tall, almost bald, with a high forehead and a thin nose. You could see the bumps in his bone-white shoulder blades. He took off his loose black swim trunks and casually nodded at us. He looked like a racing hound shorn of all its hair. His hipbones jutted out. He had almost no pubic hair. His long penis dangled limp, uncut and featureless. He sat quietly on a bench with his head in his bony hands, reminding me of a long list of repeated numbers with no explanations to them.

"Do you feel like some tea?" Powars asked. I told him I did. We left the sauna—the tall man did not look up at us—and we went back to the room. We showered quickly, separately; Powars seemed withdrawn. He changed clothes, into a beautiful, deep red polo shirt that was so silky it glowed and a pair of dark burgundy wool slacks. I wore the pants of the new suit he had bought me, and one of the expensive white shirts.

"You look beautiful," he said, sighing. "I think you're beautiful."

I laughed. "Me?"

"Sure. Maybe we should have the tea in the room. I can call for it."

I asked him why.

"I don't know. Just—let's do it, okay?"

Tea was brought up by a nice girl in a dark uniform who arranged the table for us—tea in a pot, some beautiful crescent-shaped lemon cookies, and small tea sandwiches—and left. Powars began munching the sandwiches. "These are real good. Salmon. You should try it. You like salmon?"

I told him I did, but asked him why we were having tea in the room. It started to rain outside, a dreary, sad drizzle after the pretty sun-swept morning and afternoon.

"Because I don't want to share you," Powars said. "I don't want to be in any more bullshit with people for a while. Can you understand that? We're going to have the big meeting—the one you asked about—tonight."

I had started on one of the sandwiches, and now its crustless white bread stuck on the roof of my mouth. "*Tonight?*"

"Yep. About eight bells, like they say. So I won't be around for dinner. I'll come back later. We'll have a late supper. We're leaving tomorrow. I'm taking you back to New York."

"I'm ready," I said. "I hope the meetings here have been good for you."

He turned away from me. "Yeah. They been good. About as good as they're gonna get."

He ate some of the cookies and had some tea. Then he poured himself a small glass of one of those medicinal-tasting Swiss liqueurs. A pale grass-green color. He held it up to me and asked if I wanted one. I nodded. He poured me one. "I trusted you, Allen. I want you to know that. I don't usually trust people, at least not regular people."

I laughed. "Am I that regular?"

"No. Like I said, you're like me."

"I'm sorry about the bag falling—"

He nodded his head. "Why'd you need to get into it?"

"Fear," I said. "Fear. Curiosity. Maybe both."

He nodded and took some more of the liqueur. "I understand. I do. I understand a lotta stuff. That's why I wanted you here. I guess you know that things aren't—" He quit talking. I waited, my eyes on his very serious face, then he said: "I need for you to do something for me. Will you, please?"

He looked bashful and uneasy. I had never known him to be so handsome. Almost angelic.

"What, Destry?"

"I need for you to take some more of the herbs. Will you?"

"Why?"

"Because I'll be afraid if you don't. I'll be really afraid."

THIRTEEN

It was really raining now.

He came back from the bathroom with a new glass, with the herbs dissolved in water in it. This time they were not red, but rusty brown. It reminded me of the evening outside, the rain, the sunset.

I took it from him, and reluctantly started slowly to sip it, scared of what it might taste like after the breakfast. The flavor was like a heavy vegetable-beef stock. I decided not to think about it; whatever it was, I began to take it. Powars reached for my hand and tilted the glass, forcing the whole concoction down my throat. It felt warm as it moved into my stomach. I had been feeling chilled after my swim and coming out of the sauna into the cooler air. Hot tea had helped, and so did the liqueur, but now I felt so warm that I took off the expensive white shirt, leaving my T-shirt on underneath. But I still felt too warm.

"Here," Destry said. "Let me help you." He slipped the T-shirt off over my head, then untied my shoes and pulled off my pants. I was now only in my Jockeys. He ran his hand inside them. My genitals were really hot. He pressed his mouth to the cotton that separated him from my cock, then yanked my underwear down and sucked my dick into his mouth. He was still fully dressed and seated at the tea table, with me standing.

192   I felt like a doll again. Like something he was playing with. Even though I was erect and the head of my penis was surging with heat, I felt strangely detached from him. He pulled me from his mouth, then lifted

me up and put me on the bed.

My head started swimming. I'm not sure where I was, but I was not there. He did that weird thing to my balls again—like a moth sucking at whatever flower I had become. Whatever it was, I was not myself. I only knew that I was aware of the rain outside, of streaks of lightning, of distant thunder, and of some swelling, calming darkness that had overtaken the room.

He stopped doing it.

I felt tired, but relieved. Not satisfied, like after an orgasm. Just relieved. Kind of like you do when you finally urinate, after holding it in for a long time.

He stood over me with the paper bag in his hand. Its presence seemed completely neutral to me now.

"Are you still frightened?" he asked me.

No, I told him. He could have been in an aquarium, he seemed that distant from me.

"Good. I'm going to head out now." He put on a camel overcoat of beautiful soft wool. "If I have nothing to offer them, you're gonna have to go back to New York alone. I want to keep all my promises to you, Allen. I guess you don't know what I'm talking about, but it'll all be taken care of."

He leaned over and kissed me lightly on my lips. He stayed there for a moment. I had this feeling that if there had been wallpaper in the room, it would have kissed me like that. Slanting towards me, kissing me. But he was not wallpaper. I smiled blankly at him, again like a doll. I had no idea what he was talking about. But I was so out of it, it made no difference.

A moment later, I heard the door to the room close. The snap of it was deep, kind of symphonic. Like Brahms. The door closed like Brahms. I closed my eyes. Then the door opened again.

Or did it? Was I asleep? Dreaming?

People started to walk into the dark, quiet room. Ernst. Tony. Everyone I had seen at the hotel: all the waiters, the maids; Ulma, the blond woman who had greeted us; the skinny, naked man in the sauna with his pale bony shoulders and a dick like a limp white snake. He smiled a weary, Swiss half-smile. They all were waving.

"Hello, Allen," they said. *"Guten tag. Wie geht es Ihnen?"*

"Gut!" I said. *"Und Sie?"*

Suddenly I was speaking German. Then Spanish, *"Bueno,"* then French—*"Bon. Tres bon!"*

I stared at them, and they became my friends from New York, all those polite gay men that I used to have dinner with. We would talk about opera and Broadway shows and split the bill afterwards. "You've been away," they said. "We hardly recognized you, Allen." I smiled and waved back.

Then Powars walked in and they waved at him, like they were saying good-bye. All of them, even my friends who had never met him. "Gee," Destry said to me. "They like me, and they don't even know me! They recognize me—I feel like a real celebrity, a big shot!" He grinned at me, the most wonderful, open grin, filled with lilies and poppies, and vast fields of wild flowers.

I just watched him, like I always did. I was a watcher; I knew it. Powars had been the participant, the doer, the monstrous, unpredictable saint whose energy had brought me here and who now possessed me.

The others surrounded him, all of them naked now, doing this satanic frenzied dance. Tony, with his soft, boiled-potato body, was next to him. Then there was Ernst, grotesque, with a huge chest and great swirling shags of clay-red hair on his shoulders, thighs, and stomach. He turned all the way around for me, gloating, with that knowing, self-satisfied smile that I hated. I looked down and saw Waldman's big toenails advancing like thick vines, steadily creeping through the red hair on his toes. The nails were black, glowing like polished onyx. I watched them as he danced, the light glittering on the twisting, growing nails.

I could not possibly be dreaming—it was so real. Dream and reality had merged: I was now watching within my own brain. Dream, reality; and, even worse, my own history, that small person I knew myself to be.

Ernst's big black, advancing claw-nails scooped me up like a child and threw me into the whirling, convulsive ether of time. I was treading through it, trying to keep my head above the violent rush taking me farther and farther back. Objects of revulsion collided around me. Strange effigies, images, and faded pictures ripped from old books jumped out at me, then gave way to thin, twisting bits of light, like the eerie lights through the transom; like the fluttering lights through the waters in the cave.

The raging stopped.

I was in Powars's office: the green lamp illuminated the dark, bent claws of the small reptile on his desk. I am fascinated by this thing, transfixed by a mixture of revulsion and my own transformation. I abhor it— and adore it. I have dissolved the fearful space between me and it. I am the watcher who has removed himself in the watching.

I am on my knees, worshipping this strange dead thing. I look at it. The lizard's large, glassy eyes have opened, staring at me, cold and real. They are smiling—inviting me into the world that I wanted, the frigid, threatening world of Powars, with Destry himself waiting at the beginning and the end of it.

I am falling into it.

Tony and Ernst appear before me.

I feel terribly worn, perhaps from fighting my own fear. How could I be so tired, I think, even in my sleep?

Tony is so clever. Like an aging, but well-practiced ballerina, he is all limber wrists, fingers, and elbows that move the air in graceful figure-eights. He and Ernst perform a charming minuet, measured, elegant, despite the spreading nails on Ernst's awkward feet. Their arms weave slowly in and out to a music I can not hear. Without warning, it stops. They smile, jaws thrust aggressively open, their shark-like teeth fully bared. Tony, delightfully enthusiastic as always, pulls Destry into their open, waiting arms and they are ready now… to eat him.

To devour him entirely.

They'll do to him what he's done to me in bed; but entirely, leaving nothing of him. Nothing.

Nothing.

My heart races as I watch Destry's blood, great pools of it, fill the room. A bright red glistening brilliance comes spilling down from the ceiling, as Powars attempts desperately to swim, to climb up through it, to escape.

But he cannot.

I feel sick. Utterly fearful again. They rip him to shreds, then eat him with their fingers daintily, with a snort and a revolting, slurping licking. They burp and giggle, so pleased with themselves. The gathered staff of the hotel applaud—all the disdainful waiters, the shy tea girl, the man at the shop.

Why do they hate him so? He would soon enough be gone.

Now more of the strange men appear, the creatures Powars referred to as "they," who had trained him and pulled him from nothing and nowhere. With them comes the strangest, most repugnant character of all. He resembles a wingless insect, a small, glistening, naked, grayish pupa turned revoltingly human, all wrinkled and leathery. And he is coated in the slimy mixture of blood and half-chewed flesh that had once been Powars, wearing this as a kind of decorative covering, like torn pieces of a shiny body stocking. Even so, he seems to be all cock and eager face and eyes.

He watches the entire gathering satisfied. All he had wanted has come to pass. All his underlings—"they"—nod quietly. Then, having fulfilled their promise, all of them, including Tony, Waldman, and their leader, leave.

The rose-colored light that Powars had tried to climb fills the hotel room like a cleansing steam, obliterating everything in its path. It swirls and eddies, making patterns of beautiful rosettes.

I watched it, enthralled. Relieved, even. Then the red light started to dissipate. When it cleared, there was Gwendolyn Hong Rose, dressed in a deep blue outfit with long sleeves and a string of moon-white pearls. It was like something you might wear to a sedate wedding. She reached for my cold hand. The wind howled outside.

"You've been so good for him," she whispered. "What you are, they can't take away." The warmth of her hand pressed all the way through me. Then she let go and walked out the door.

I jerked awake, and bolted out of bed, crying. This had been no dream. No hallucination. But a warning.

I was covered in goose bumps. I had thrown up on the bed. I felt horrible; there was still the odious taste of vomit in my mouth. I felt like I had defiled the room. I could not stop being afraid; my guts, in every sense of the word, had failed me. I'd been taken into this rich, proper European place and I had failed Destry miserably. I looked at the evidence, the mess on the bed, and felt like a shit. What would Destry say to me? What could he possibly say?

Naked, cold and weak, I managed to strip the sheets from the bed, then went into the bathroom, threw some water on my face, and flicked on the light.

I looked in the mirror. I could barely believe what I saw. There was Powars, staring back at me. That same look—intense, desperate, yearning, but at the same time, despite everything, openly in command—was there. What he had said all began to make some kind of warped sense: "If I have nothing to offer them—"

I had no time. I had to go get him. Even with my own weaknesses, I had to pull him out of this. I got a washrag, flushed some cold water on it and washed myself as best I could. I put on my white shirt, black pants, shoes and a sweater—I had to appear normal; I had to appear presentable—and went out to the front desk. I asked the young man there where the lodge was.

"You cannot go. *Es geht nicht.*"

"Why?"

"A meeting ist there. Important. For—" his English failed him. "For big men in the company. *Verstehen?* I mean, sir, you understand?

He looked like a boy, with a long thin neck and his Adam's apple choked inside his tie.

"I must go," I insisted. "Mr. Powars needs his medicine. He's been sick. He forgot it. Do *you* understand?"

He disappeared into an office and an older man with a mustache, in a better fitting suit, emerged. I had the strange feeling that I had seen this man in the ... I can only call it the "experience" I'd had in the room.

"I am Herr Einsatz," he announced. "Can I help you?"

I told him I needed to go to the lodge. Einsatz repeated what the young man had said. I told him that Mr. Powars was sick and I had his medicine.

"I'll call a doctor," Herr Einsatz said. "Ve haf a very good *arzt*—a doctor, I mean—here at the hotel. I've been gifen orders not to permit anyone to the lodge. They meet once a year and cannot be disturbed for any reason."

I nodded, smiling broadly.

"If you haf the medicine," Einsatz said seriously, "I vill deliver it myself."

He extended his hand. It was very thick with huge nails. Despite the elegance of his suit, the nails looked blackened. My body began to quiver.

I told him that I had left the medicine in our room. "I'll run and get it," I announced.

I turned and walked down the long clean corridor, to a side exit. The door clicked locked behind me. It was really dark out, and raining steadily, and I had no hat or even a coat. I hurried to the front driveway, with rain slashing down on me, to a waiting taxi. Its lights were on, and I jumped inside, then realized that I had no Swiss francs, just some American money.

The driver turned around. He was dark with the handsome shadow of a beard on his cheeks, and definitely not Swiss. "*Wo?*"

I looked at him.

"Where do you want to go, sir?" he asked in perfect English.

I sighed. "Where are you from?"

"Not here!" He smiled. "I'm from Argentina, but my parents are Italian. And you?"

"New York."

"Love the place. So, where you wanna go, dude?"

He opened a window and lit a cigarette, then asked me if I minded. I told him not at all.

"You like N' Sync?" he asked.

I told him I didn't even know who they were. "Good. So, dude, where to?" He took a deep drag.

"Do you know where the lodge is, of this hotel?"

"Sure. No sweat. You could walk it in maybe ten minutes, but it's a bitch of a night out there."

He threw down the meter flag, and I noticed that it jumped about every three seconds. It was completely dark outside, except for some distant lightning that lit up the far mountains and the somber face of the hotel. He told me that he loved Switzerland in a storm. "As long as you're not up in the mountains. Then it's really *sheisse. Habla Español?*"

I told him I spoke nothing except a bit of high school French. He asked me why I wanted to go to the lodge, especially in this weather. I told him there was someone in it.

"Ah, a woman? A romantic rendezvous?"

"No. Not a woman."

"Then it must be business. In Switzerland, everything's business. It's good for me. I make a lotta money here, though the Swiss are a pain in the—"

The lodge loomed up in the dark ahead of us, like a fortress from another age, all tiled gables and deep eves and dark, heavy stone pillars. No light came from it; the shutters had been drawn, as if the fortress had pulled itself in for the night for sleep.

The driver stopped the cab. "You sure you want this? I can't see anyone here. Should I wait?" He turned back towards me and smiled. "I can for a short while, you know." I was really too anxious to make a decision. "I'll turn the meter off. Just come back in a minute and tell me what to do."

I nodded and went out. The rain was coming down harder, and I felt bone cold as soon as it hit me. The eves of the roof sloped close to the driveway, and I was quickly deep in their shadows. I couldn't see the door, but I heard a low constant stream of noise within. This had to mean talking and people inside; many people.

I went back and opened the passenger door of the cab. "I'll be all right," I said. "But I don't have any Swiss money."

He laughed. "And you think that's a problem? What you got— francs, marks, bucks? This is Der Schweiz. We take anything!"

I had sixty dollars on me, and gave him a twenty dollar bill. He totaled it up in Swiss francs, and offered to give me change. About four dollars. I told him to forget it, then he drove off. I went back to the lodge.

I waited under the dark sloping eves, to get my courage up. Not to feel so frightened, empty, and sick. As I became accustomed to the lack of light, I noticed a door. It was of the same heavy, dark-timbered wood as the lodge walls, slightly recessed and bound in iron. I was sure it would be locked, and I would stay out in the cold, until I had enough brains to walk back, defeated, by myself.

I tried it.

It opened silently. I entered a small hallway, like an antechamber, lit by a table lamp made of stag antlers, with tiny light bulbs and thumb-high silk shades. The yellowish light made the gloomy room appear bigger and threw the old pewter hunting pistols with stag horn handles on the walls into dim relief, along with one narrow door to the right and one to the left. And another door, a little wider, directly in front of me. I heard that noise again, wordless, just wavering spikes of sound. I tried the third door.

I was now in a long corridor lit with low-hanging ceiling lights, glass-shaded in old Norse-looking designs. As I proceeded forward, the noise became louder. A heavy black door at the end of the hallway creaked opened, and a man appeared.

He was the oldest man I had ever seen, covered with wrinkles etched into more wrinkles, with two bird-like eyes that could barely peer out from the aged map of his face. He was dressed in a long, stiff black mourning coat that ended in swallowtails. His white shirt, yellowed with age, had frayed dirty cuffs at the sleeves. He was hardly there, he was so small and bent over.

"Do come in," he whispered. "You're the guest, right?"

I nodded. He took my right hand in his. His hand was thin and bony, with long curled blackened fingernails, and he led me through another heavy door, to a huge room. The windows, as I had seen from outside, were tightly shuttered. It felt cold, yet strangely stuffy.

The noise was unbearable. It reminded me of the frantic hum at auctions, with people buzzing greedily, their individual words lost in hysteria. There were signs about, in many languages. Some, in English, said: "Take What You Can, While You Can Take It!" "We Brake for Suckers." "The Market Is Our Buddy. Don't Forget It!"

Ernst and Tony, both dressed properly in conservative business attire, nodded to me, smiling knowingly, as if they had expected me all along, then they started to laugh loudly. They pointed at me with extended index fingers, convulsing with laughter, until this ugly, clay-red color rose into their faces. I realized that the noise I had heard before, that rose in shrill peaks, was a chorus of this horrifying laughter, emitted from all the teeming, carrion creatures I saw around me. They were all laughing— some of them even spitting uncontrollably.

In the middle of all of this, down on the age-darkened, scarred wooden floor, stripped totally naked, was Powars. Hunched over; sobbing pathetically. His strong, hairy body was pale, as though his blood were draining from it ounce by ounce. That same paleness made him seem to glow. I drew closer to him; he looked up at me.

"What are you doing here?" he whispered. "I didn't want you to go through this. I swear. I wanted you t'go back to New York without me. They can't make me do what they want. Not now."

I knelt down with him. The noise was ear-piercing. This constant ringing laughter. I looked around. They were all pointing: Ernst, Tony, this large gathering of shrunken old men and other bizarre, rapacious-looking individuals, some even female perhaps, others grotesque beyond description, beyond anything I'd ever seen in my life. I bowed my head.

"What do they want?" I asked Powars softly.

He shook his head. "I was gonna offer 'em something else. Look at them. They have no mercy, Allen. You got mercy, but they have none."

I put my hand on his cheek. I had no idea that Destry could cry like that. He looked like a little boy who'd been hurt so badly he could put no words to it; the way at some point we've all been hurt. "What do they want?" I asked and waited for an answer.

"I can't say it. Please, Allen. I can't—"

The noise started to rise, inhuman, like ravenous birds. Then I realized that these creatures were somehow communicating with each other. They were gleefully passing things back and forth—tokens or fiduciary documents or bits of money. Pieces of paper, at any rate. Some of the attendees had smaller signs they raised and lowered, while they laughed and made that harsh noise.

Then, out of nowhere, this silence spread from face to face, this awful vacuum of silence.

I knelt on the floor next to Destry, waiting.

From the back of the room, came a creaking sound, like some ancient machinery. A large wooden wheelchair, of some very antique sort, was being pushed towards me as everyone watched in silence. Then I saw Gwinny, just as I had envisioned her, dressed in deep blue, with large, moon-white pearls around her neck, pushing the chair.

She nodded to me, and with her slim hands bade me stand up. I looked into the chair, and saw that in it was sitting the actual Nicky, the live version of the small, murderous effigy in the brown paper bag. Nicky, the last and most gruesome of these creatures, whose wrinkled nakedness I had seen in my vision. Only now, instead of in the slimy bodystocking of Destry's torn flesh and blood, he was dressed neatly in a small gray suit, like a nice little boy at a dress-up party. He even wore a pink, clip-on bowtie.

He looked up, gleaming at me. His nose, like an old Punch puppet's, was somewhat bigger than I remembered. His top lip had a little curl in it that softened the hardness of his mouth. He surveyed the gathering. "Hi!" he exclaimed, spitting that one syllable at me.

I nodded to him. Powars was still on the cold floor. He could not look up at the two of us. "Stay down there!" the dwarf ordered from the chair. Then he grinned at me, like a lethal, unstoppable, salesman.

"Hi, babes! Good t'see ya! How ya doin' tonight?"

I did not answer him or smile.

"Come on, why th' serious kisser, huh? This ain't so bad. We wanted ya friend down there to hand you over to us. Plain and simple. Know what I mean?"

I shook my head.

"Another dummy! He's gotta give us something every year, see? We picked him up outta the mud and made him what he is—but he's gotta give us something. That's called 'the natural law.' You get picked up; you give out! That's what the mud's all about. We gave him my little Kewpie-poopie doll for safekeeping. It was like a final pledge, dig? His last chance. Cute, ain't it? And pretty! I made it myself. But you, Allen, you little dumb shit, screwed up! You got curious and you cracked it good. So now it's *you*. It's all about *you*! Understand?"

I looked down at Powars. All of his bravado was gone. "What did you give them before?" I asked him.

"Every piece of me," he answered, "till there was nothing left. My conscience; my being. My soul. Really. That's why I loved you. I recognized in you—"

"Oh, no!" Tony screamed. "Is *she* getting silly again? Powars, you're just a little wart with a dick attached, you're—" He started laughing, shrieking, once more with Ernst behind him.

I couldn't take it. I turned around and slapped Winzor as hard as I could. I didn't even think about it—I had never done anything like that in my life—I just did it. He shut up instantly. They all looked at me now.

Every one of them. Powars got up, crouching, his hands over his genitals.

"I'm willing," he said to them. "You can have me."

"Destry!" Gwinny cried. "Oh, Destry… please."

"*Ganz sheisse*," Ernst said. "Once a whore always a whore, right, Miss Rose?"

"Would you two stop!" Nicky ordered. "I hate it when my people argue." He motioned towards Gwinny. "All right, let's have that other little doll now."

"Please, I don't want to do this," she said.

She had a small brown paper bag cupped to her chest, so that the blue material of her dress glowed against it.

"Give it to him, girl," Tony ordered, the smirk back on his face.

"*Ja*, it's out of your hands now," Ernst agreed. "If you cannot make good on your promises, then it happens."

Gwendolyn handed Nicky the small bag.

"That's a nice girl," Nicky said. He took the crumpled brown bag, opened it and placed his fat little fingers inside. He pulled his hand out. It was covered with some of the reddish powdery herb Powars had been giving me. Nicky licked his reddened fingers, smiled devilishly, then thrust his hand back into the bag.

"Maybe you shouldn't see this," Gwinny said to me. "You might want to turn your head. What happens in our world is not always pleasant, it—"

"Oh, God!" Tony shrieked. "You're as bad as Powars. We all come from the same filth—the same common shit—one way or another. So it does you no good to think you're above it. Let him see. Come on, Allen, *girlfriend*! Take a damn good look!"

Nicky's hand emerged from the bag, and with it came another small figure made out of simple baked mud, like you might see at a river bank, with the fecal leavings of animals, or lowly wanderings humans, barely submerged in the slimy ooze. The figure had this soft, unnatural glow, like it were covered with a fine dusting of powdered sugar. It was Powars; the face

204

was his, even though the body resembled some of the dwarfs in the room.

Gwinny ran her hands over Powars's thick hair. "I tried to keep it as safe as I could, Destry. I was your friend; I loved you, I only wanted—"

Nicky jumped off the old wheelchair and stood, the small mud figure raised high in his pudgy hand. A noise went about through the room, a churning, wavelike "Awwwww!" sound, a real recognition of the seriousness of what Gwinny had just done.

She gave me her hand, trying to comfort me. "I guess he'll have to do this," she whispered to me. "Maybe … you should just watch."

"Don't!" Powars screamed. "Please don't look, Allen. Whatever you do—"

Destry stood up fully now, showing everything to the crowd. They gathered in close to watch, their shifting eyes looking him up and down. The muscular little Nicky, one hand still gripping the statue, used the power of his other arm to push Destry back again to the dirty floor, where he crumpled, his head in his hands.

"I'll do anything for you, Nicky," he cried. "I swear! I'll make you lots of money. I'll screw people till they just—"

Nicky shook his head. "It's too late, Powars. You don't belong to us anymore."

He lifted the mud thing up as high as his short arms could take it— the "Awwwww" sound, mixed with volleys of razor-keen laughter, flooded the room—then he smashed it to the floor.

It was pulverized. The dust was disgusting; the smell like some pungent Asian herb mixed with dried dung. Some of the dust got into my eyes, and I tried to clear it out. Some got into my throat. I couldn't stop coughing and they only laughed more.

The old man who had led me in came up to me. "Drink this," he said, offering me something.

My eyes were tearing terribly, but I managed to see that it was a glass, with that familiar reddish color in it.

"You need to drink this, sir," he said. "I'm afraid it's the only way that you are going to get out of here."

"Please," Destry said. "Don't drink it. Whatever you do, don't drink that now."

Nicky came over to me. "It's up to you, babes. I don't care. Drink it—don't—who cares? But if you really wanna save what's left of ol' Destry—and of yourself—you will. See, I guess you figured out by now that no one in the hotel even knows you're here. The Swiss are so discreet. You've been a guest of ours; Destry brought you here, but you're actually our guest. The problem is, we don't always treat our guests so nice. Right, Tony?"

Tony smiled. "You're being characteristically too modest, Nicky. We've treated this gent just as he deserves. They all think they're going to get something for nothing. Those are the type of people we adore!"

Gwinny shook her head. "You're being a real jerk, Tony. There's no need to be quite as ugly as you are."

"Oh, *mädchen*," Ernst cackled. "Perhaps he *is* just ugly. Destry knows what's going to happen. What *must* happen." He looked at me, then grabbed the glass and thrust it into my hand. "Now, drink this before you really get hurt."

Destry got up—naked, defeated, shoulders hunched. "I don't know why you have to be so evil," he whispered to Waldman.

"Reality gives you many lessons," Waldman said. "This is merely one of them." He pushed the glass to my mouth. "Now, drink."

The laughter, loud as a the whip of a tornado, started again in full fury. I looked at Destry, nodded briefly to him, and managed to get the thick liquid down my throat without regurgitating it. I had to clench my eyes shut to do it. Then I re-opened them. Immediately, I experienced this unexpected lightness that felt almost good. A little disorienting maybe, but ... for a second, I thought: perhaps they did give me this for my own sake. Perhaps it was to stop *me* from dying. This unexpected smile began to bloom on my face. Waldman nodded at me; he approved. Then I looked at Destry.

His hunched shoulders began to shake. I realized, then, that somehow my drinking had been ... possibly ... a death warrant for him? Had it given them permission, in the most sordid way, to do even more horrible things to him? That shaking, with violent twisting and jerking, went all the way through him, down to his toes, out to his fingertips. His mouth opened, his tongue darted out ... and he began to get smaller. Smaller and smaller, until he reached the stature of Nicky. His skin did not shrink, it shriveled. He became wrinkled and ugly. The only part of him that did not become smaller was his penis. It seemed huge, like the big phallus on one of Nicky's hideous mud effigies.

A chill went all the way through me, but I stroked his head anyway. I still loved him. I could not help that.

"Come closer," he whispered, and I bent down to him. He placed his cock in my hand, just offering it to me. It was soft and icy. I kissed it.

There were tears in Powars's eyes. "They'll do something awful to me, these little turds."

"Watch your language," Tony warned. "We put up with a lot from you. Any other chap would have been a grateful. You were just a little dirtball when we first got to you. You never really changed that much inside—but you've changed now!"

"He thought he was too smart," Ernst said. "They all think that. The ones we take in. The ones we train. They think it's easy. They'll get what they want—we tell them everything. How to manipulate people. How to listen. Exactly what words to use. How to strike when you need to." He shook his head sadly. "If they only knew the full price. But who does?"

Gwinny nodded her head. She understood; she knew. "I'll help you," she whispered to me. "I'm here for you. Please know that."

I stood up. I felt tall, taller than I had ever really felt, maybe. I smiled; everything seemed so absurd that I started laughing, too. Maybe it was from that stuff they had given me to drink, but I wondered, did my laugh sound as horrible as theirs?

I did not know. How could I; who can really hear himself? I looked down at Powars, and he looked up at me and grabbed my sleeve.

"I need to have a word with you," he said softly. "They'll only give me about a minute, before the final change happens, so we need a word." He looked at Nicky.

"Sure," the little monster said. "Have your fucking word. Why not? We always get the last one, anyway."

"It's all right," Gwendolyn said, forcing a smile. "Go with him. I'll be right here. Then I'll take you back to the hotel, I promise."

We walked a few paces away from the rest of them, as they stared at us with vile, rapacious glee, like evil children, incapable of moderation or consideration. They started eating, lapping and slurping at the food that the hotel caterers had brought. I saw the same waiters from the posh hotel dining room circulating about, with silver trays of elegantly presented, colorful delicacies. I noticed that some of those present in the room were as big as I was. Others were small, kind of wormish, like caterpillars who had somehow turned into human beings. Some were meticulously dressed in a modern way; others looked slovenly and out of style. But they all grabbed at the food, stuffed it into their eager mouths, spitting out some of it, choking at it, pushing more back in. I glanced over at them, barely able to believe this, as Destry tugged at my arm, to get my ear closer to his face.

"I knew you were like me," he whispered.

I nodded. I was afraid of what he was going to say. It seemed inevitable, like waiting for a certain moment in a symphony that you know will come. I was only one of a million drab people in New York. The ones who crowd the subways, who manage just to survive the day and the year, who never get into the papers. I wanted to say, "You don't have to say it, Destry. I knew all along." But I didn't.

208   "Under," he whispered, "all of your fear and turmoil, is a simple heart. A kind decency. People think that's just weakness, I know. I couldn't really be what they wanted. I could do the fast money thing, but inside

I wanted to return to you."

I kissed him. I was sobbing. Tears flowed from my eyes.

"Gosh," he said. "I'm so cold. I wish we were back in that room having tea, then getting under the covers."

"Whatever happens, I'll wait for you," I whispered.

"Will you?"

"Sure."

"You won't be afraid?"

"No."

"You may have to do things that you—"

He was yanked away from me. This violent stream of bodies rushed at him with a noise that attacked my eardrums like a million dive-buzzing wasps. A snowy white blanket was thrown over him; it began to quiver and shake as they carried him off.

"We won't let you see this." Nicky said sweetly. "Although—"

"Although he's almost one of us now!" Tony smirked. "Welcome to the family. Right, Ernst?"

Ernst smiled and shook my hand. "True, true," he agreed. "*Bruder mein*, you are, *wirklich*, a brother at heart. You'll do so well. I know you doubt it. But there's so much you wanted in your life, and we'll bring it all to you. We'll teach you what to say, exactly how to listen—and when to stop listening; how to go into meetings—"

I felt myself floating off for a second. I looked around at the bobbing heads, the strange faces. "Suppose I want Destry?" I asked, landing myself back in reality.

There was a second of silence, then I felt as if I had fed them the punch line of a huge joke. The shrieks, the wails of laughter—this hysteria that spiraled around me.

"Sure!" Nicky screamed. "You can have that right away! Come!"

The nasty little man pulled at my arm, and with about a dozen of his followers in tow, we left the hall. The others would not stop stuffing their faces and guzzling down foamy steins of beer, or tossing back elegant little crystal glasses of liqueurs.

We walked through the dim hallway to another room. A small one, immediately to the left, with a little more amber light in it, from a half dozen wall sconces of old darkened antlers with the tiny silk shades. There was Gwinny. She was kneeling with a corner of the white blanket scrunched into her hands, gently humming. She dropped the blanket and stood up. "The Chinese," she said to me softly, "have a song my mother taught me. It's about how your children leave you, but they never really do." She pointed to the blanket. "He's down there, if you want to look."

I was afraid. I cringed. My hands were locked into fists at my sides.

"Come on," Nicky said patiently. "It'll do you a lotta good. You said you wanted him. Now you'll get to keep him, like I promised. But first—" He removed the blanket slowly, drawing it past the thing that was under it. It was no longer Destry. This man I had loved so much, this powerful storm of urgent needs and energies, was in transition. The flesh, the hair, all the limbs and soft-hardness that had drawn me to him, were now contracting before me, into another being and form. It was still breathing, but with a slowness and difficulty that reminded me of a locomotive engine on its last drop of fuel, trudging uphill on a dry, freezing night. I could hear distinct gasping.

I knelt over it. I could still see a few traces of Destry's physical self under this shrinking, translucent exterior. Gwinny put her hand on my shoulder. "I'll take you back to the hotel. I didn't want you to be shocked. Some people never get over this. You won't be … shocked, will you? Will you promise me you won't be shocked?"

"He won't be shocked!" Waldman's voice behind me answered. "He'll learn. We all do. Me; you; Destry. All of us learn, somehow."

"Is he cold?" I asked. "Maybe he needs the blanket."

"No, no," Nicky said, his voice low and calm. "Just watch. It'll be 210 over shortly. Then you can have him."

I pulled the blanket's fleecy white material towards me. I was the one shivering. And I watched, on the floor, as a form emerged into the soft amber light. I could barely contain myself. I thought I would faint. How could I not be shocked? How could I stay…composed, after I saw what was happening… as the strange, primitive form contracted further and its difficult, gasping breathing slowed and then almost ceased before my eyes?

"He's yours," Nicky said, smiling brightly. "You wanted him! Come on, babes, take a good look—pick him up now!"

I could not. I felt frozen. How can I say this? How can I tell you, that the only remains left me of Destry Powars was a small, almost lifeless… lizard? A reptile of the palest, mottled jade green, like old porcelain, its shriveled skin so delicately thin that even the faint light from the walls penetrated it. Nicky held it up tightly, by its pathetic throat, presenting it to the approving room like a trophy. They stared at it, gloating, and smiled.

I watched its little tail twitch slightly; then, in one final attempt at life, its lower body curled hesitantly up. At that, Nicky squeezed the last breath from its neck, as the rest of this strange "family" looked on and nodded.

Only Gwinny and I were not cooing approval.

I could see all of the poor creature's insides, like the glowing stems of water lilies pushing up through the wet murkiness around them. I kept hoping that it was only a trick—and Powars himself would walk into the room soon, wearing something costly, something wonderful. Smelling of that expensive cologne I liked so much. He would take my hand, and run his big fingers through my hair.

I could not stop looking. A face slowly emerged beneath the thing's dead features; and I saw him, Destry, clearly. There, below the greenish, thin skin of its head, was the sensuous mouth, the firm brow and nose; even, under clear parchment lids, his own brown eyes, ringed with their entrancing gold—all captured under the reptile's skin. I began to sob. It was true. He was reduced to this; his greyed toneails reduced to tiny claws.

The dwarf laughed. He grabbed the dead lizard by its tail and tossed it over to me. It landed in my arms and I pulled it to me, and kissed it.

FOURTEEN

The rain had stopped

and the clouds had begun to drift apart. The air was placid and won-
drously clear. I could see the mountains with their caps of snow and ban-
ners of stars above us. Gwinny and I walked slowly back to the hotel. She
had on a warm coat and scarf. She put her hand on my arm.

"You have to be brave," she advised. "He was brave. He came from
so little. Just like I did, really."

At the hotel, everything was taken care of. Gwinny saw to it, and the
staff was as courteous as ever and treated me in the way that, before, they
had treated Destry Powars.

I didn't have to worry about the bill, or the trip back to the airport in
Zurich—a driver had been arranged for this—or the blissfully quiet first
class flight on Swissair. This time, Gwinny flew with me. Sven was there
again, but there was no hanky-panky in the john. He seemed almost rev-
erential towards me; perhaps in some obvious, even physical way that I
could not see myself, I'd changed in what were really only a few days.
Mostly I slept. I was extremely tired. I did talk on the plane phone to a few
people. Gwinny gave me the numbers of some key people to call and told
me what to say. At first, I felt reticent. It was difficult saying that I, rather
than Mr. Powars, was calling them. I had to have a kind of tone that I had
never taken with my voice, and I can't really say I knew what I was doing.
All the pieces didn't exactly fit or match up in my mind.

Then I started to think that this was what Destry would have done—and I began to talk like him, run my fingers through my hair like him, drum the arm rest of my seat like him. My voice became edgier. A bit rougher. But in certain, unforeseeable ways I actually became smoother. Less tentative. Less anxious.

I knew I could do this … I must have known it, all along.

We got back to Kennedy, and everything went perfectly through customs. It was like they were waiting for me, and had forgotten about Destry Powars. Now I had my visa myself. I was dressed nicely. Gwendolyn smiled, took my arm—that is always helpful, that you have a "girlfriend," someone on your arm. Winchell was waiting for us with the car. He was wonderfully helpful and, of course, discreet. He didn't ask about Destry; had Destry briefed all of them before we left? I don't know, but the ride into Manhattan was quiet, luxurious, merciful. It was the kind of ride that rich men take for granted.

Mostly now, when I think about it, I have this feeling of relief. You could say, for the first time in my life, a feeling of being taken care of. And I understand what it was like to be "employed" only for being "yourself"—or some infinitely subtle impersonation of it.

Suddenly, I didn't have to "prove" my niceness, my "worthiness," to people anymore. In my insignificant past position, I had always to be polite, obsequious, vigilantly grateful. Now I could be a perfect shit if I wanted to, and no one could get to me. At least for a while—and who knew how long that while might be?

The thought of this life-saving cushion that Destry had arranged, that Gwinny helped to keep in place—the thought that I could just float on it, like something you pulled from under your seat on a plane and used in case of a crash—made those first few days alone back in the large apartment on Central Park West bearable, in fact, close to nice. Karl was there for everything. He gave me the key to Destry's old office and showed me his huge 213 Rolodex. Gwinny came in and explained things, went over the books with me, told me whom to trust and whom to watch. I saw, finally, Destry's mistakes. Where he had cut people off, or where he had been too nice. Where he had offered things—money, aid—that were not really his to offer. Where he had become arrogant, and where he had become just too soft.

Gwinny showed me all of this, sighing, sometimes crying. I dried her tears, held her hand. Sometimes I argued with her, but nicely. I needed her—I would need most of "them" now. I understood, then, like Destry, what it was like to have people who work to make you richer and more powerful. It is a good idea, I learned, to make them feel appreciated, yet slightly insecure at the same time.

I'm sure Destry was good at these games of force, manipulation, and, occasionally, insight. He had learned the secret language of power and money very well, though even that did not save him from himself: something I am very aware of. Learning all of this is not something you do immediately and it will take me a while to understand how he did it. A week after I got back, I had my first meeting with the Bolivian people and a few of their German friends, and also some edgy Peruvians who were blessed with silver and copper, as well as a great deal of oil to get out of the jungles.

I was the representative of a money source, and we talked about money like it were simply water: a natural resource. A group of people turn it on, and they can also turn it off. Even working at a bank, this was something that people like I, in my menial position, never got to experience quite so firsthand and graphically. I started to know that there were good years and bad years, and years when you had to provide the rain and the clouds—and even the pipes the water goes in—yourself.

I said almost nothing. I smiled. I nodded. Gwinny wrote down a few notes. We made a "modest proposal," for which the people from South America were grateful. I noticed several courteous young men in tasteful dark suits waiting around the big, tastefully appointed room we were in

214 near Wall Street. At certain points, they brought in coffee and little sandwiches which no one touched. I thought about just grabbing one and eating it, then realized that was not the thing to do. The coffee was sipped

black with lots of sugar in it. At the end of the meeting, the Germans smiled and the Latins all embraced each other and then came over and shook my hand. I felt like a god. I had done nothing, mostly what Gwinny informed me I should do.

Things went on like that for a month, then the bitterness, like the aftertaste from the dark coffee, came in. There was the loneliness and also the sense, that I could not avoid, that I was only a pawn—or at best a knight—in this game.

I had the fabulous apartment with its wrap-around views; Karl; Winchell; two nice cleaning women who came in when I was not there; the car. There was a house in the Hamptons waiting for me in the spring, and Karl could easily arrange a trip to the Caribbean if I wanted it. But I didn't. There was this awful hollowness in me in the big bed. I would look out sometimes in the middle of the night and see Destry's face, smiling at me. He would say, "What's the matter, Allen? Ain'cha happy?"

And the odd thing was that I knew I was. But happiness, I have learned, does not always fill that hollow feeling, it just rides over it. The hollowness is under you and the dazzle of the happiness—of things you've wanted, success—glitters over it. But in my past "normal" life, I'd had to pretend about so much for so long, that I could pretend that this hollowness did not hurt. Often at those moments, I would go into the office, turn the green desk light on, and look at his books. I got acquainted with the mysteries, the lurid Egyptian sources, the spells. I took the herbs, some of the powdered powerful ones in the brown paper bag they'd given me just before we left the secretive lodge; and I felt better.

I guess you should know that I have a brown bag of my own now. And in it is a crude, baked little mud figure that is there for my own safe-keeping. I hate to look at it. One difference between Powars and me is that he could look at his and laugh. I haven't developed a hard enough crust yet to do that. Those few times that I've taken it out of its bag, it has sent a chill up my spine. It's like there's something of me in that bag; and I still have no idea how this strange creature got it in there.

Gwinny has told me that the bag itself is significant. "They're always kept in simple brown paper," she explained, "so as not to draw attention to the figure within. It's kind of like us. You can never tell what we're really like, once you get past the external."

Nicky handed it to me before we left the lodge. We were about ready to go and I was in this completely shocked state, when Nicky chirped up, "One more thing!" then handed me the bag and made me look at what was in it. Then they all started in with that shrill, echoing laugh, that carrion chorus, like the spiteful *yip! yip!* of vultures, that I still can't do. I can't even imitate it. Gwinny can, but I can't. They whooped and cackled as we began to walk out, and I hated them, the little shits; God forgive me, but I really hated them! Destry never did. He would not—could not—hate them. Not the way I did. Chalk it up as yet another difference between us.

I almost dropped it, but the little creep steadied my hands. "We done as good of a job as we could," he said modestly. "We hope you like him."

My hands were shaking uncontrollably. I had seen the sad little reptile emerging, and now this. "Of course, you'll have to bring it back," he explained. "I mean, when we ask for it. But we'll give you another one after that—if you're a good boy!"

The shrieking laughter was deafening. Their little hands tried to push it back into the bag; it was too dangerous to keep it out. But at once I noticed that there were hairs baked into it, and, yes, bones, too. I could see the fibrous surface of cracked bones. My hands rattled; Nicky supported them.

"Come on," he ordered. "Look at the care we took."

I looked at the object again. The chorus whooped and shrieked. But Gwinny simply looked away, sparing me at least that embarrassment. Then Nicky began to push it safely back into the bag.

"How did you know?" I asked, crying.

216   "It's just our little secret." He smiled. He nodded to the others and they winked and nodded back. But anyone, really, could have seen what it was: that the little figure's head bore an immediate, unmistakable likeness

to me. The face baked in coarse, disgusting river mud—that face as violently primitive as one of those pictures in the cave—was, indeed, all in all, Alwyn Barrow. I could hardly look at it. It was too painful—and truthful.

"You two can run along now," Nicky ordered, once the bag was squared away, and the shocking reptile was safe in a pocket of Gwinny's coat. "Our meeting's not over, but your part is. Take no offense. It's got nothing to do with you. We have reports to make. Agendas. Run along now, you two. But don't go too far!"

"Yes!" Tony said. "We'll come by your room. We'll tell you what will happen and make one last—" He halted and smiled.

Ernst laughed. "*Extraction*. We will make one last extraction, *bruder mein*. Just a little something—you won't miss it at all."

"No, darling," Tony said. "Don't fret. We'll give you a little something to calm you down. The hotel staff's ready; everything's been set in place! What a *lovely* first trip to Switzerland this has been for you! Tra-la!"

Then Nicky bent my head down, and said, his voice hardly above a whisper, "Go on. You don't need to wait up for us. And, oh, yes, we have keys, just in case you decide to lock up the room."

I guess that was why Powars never locked the hotel door. I was sure they had keys to the apartment, too. They employed Winchell and Karl; I never saw their paychecks. In a way, I worked for them, but it was hardly any different from working in the bank or any other major corporation, which will be owned by one group of faceless unseen financiers one day and another the next day. You never know who's making out your paycheck now—or which country it comes from.

I started going to the baths again. Like Destry, I would take a cab there. I did not want Winchell to know what I was doing. I went through a noticeable transformation, and it hit my body, too. I no longer had a problem getting it up. I was harder—all over. I became more confident. More, you could say, "cocky," which I learned had nothing to do with the size of my dick. My walk changed. I kept my shoulders tightly squared, and my chest rigidly out. I took on that hard-edged New York attitude, the one that said your time was too valuable to waste on anything that was not exactly what you wanted. I had a lot of sex. I rejected a lot of men, too.

Why Powars had wanted me was still a mystery. Except, of course, that he saw how pliable I was; how needy. How I might submit to him immediately and hold so little back, just as he once did. The fact that we had something inside both of us that was sharable, that's too painful now for me to think about.

One night I did it with seven men. Seven! A lot of contact. A lot of activity and stroking and holding. But none of them were Destry Powars. I left in tears, I swear. I got a cab back uptown. The doormen greeted me. It was raining, lightly; spring was happening—the lovely beauty of spring rippling across New York, across Central Park, across the world. I went out on the terrace that overlooks the park from the living room. Night, soft, luscious, cloaked in warm mist now—the rain had stopped. I would have to get some sleep. I had meetings the next day and people to call. People to make offers to, or even discreetly threaten. You had to do that sometimes in my new occupation, in that business of those lucrative encounters where evil and greed meet and only the dead are witnesses.

I put my forearms up on the beautiful old balustrade. There was no peace within me. Funny little dollops of happiness, maybe, like the whipped cream on bakery cupcakes, but no peace. There was not even the basic sustenance I wanted, under that new hardness, my new confidence. That awful hollowness came back to me, that thing that tore at the pit of my stomach, especially after a night of sex without any real connection, any deeper emotional gift handed, even temporarily, to me.

I thought how, with no big effort, I could hoist myself up to the top of the balustrade and just ... hop over.

218   I'm sure someone had done that before in one of these beautiful old apartments. Someone who had been offered everything except that one slip of human love that keeps us going. Infants need it, or they die. We

never really outgrow the need. Perhaps men like I, inherently polite, decent, have the need in us ... more distinctly.

Or, do we?

My hands were on the nubby rough old balustrade, and I did a little hoist—just to feel what it felt like—when I saw it. Him. The lizard. The dead creature I had smuggled back with me, inert and still, from Switzerland. I had kept him in what had been Destry's beautiful room that was now mine, next to the brown bag, with my own figure in it. At those times when my fears of failure, of being only an imposter in this hard world, came back, I held him, watched him. Seen that wonderful old face locked within its reptile head.

It had known. It had come to take me. It bore itself in life again, just as Destry had told me it would: the pupè, the mud effigy of bone and river slime, had brought this distant form of the dead back to life again.

He scampered over my cold fingers and jumped onto my neck. I could feel the little sucking pads of his feet, his tiny, skillful claws. I took him into both my hands, his little heart pounding as hard as mine. He had loved me truly. As I had edged towards death, he would bring me back now. I had promised him I would wait ... I would earn him. My eyes filled with tears as I took him at once into my dark bedroom and lay with him on the big bed with some distant, soft moonlight outside, as he found his way, immediately, down into my pants.

the end

Perry Brass

Originally from Savannah, Georgia, Perry Brass grew up, in the fifties and sixties, in equal parts Southern, Jewish, economically impoverished, and very much *gay*. To escape the South's violent homophobia, he hitchhiked at seventeen from Savannah to San Francisco—an adventure, he recalls, that was "like Mark Twain with drag queens." He's published twelve books and been a finalist five times in three categories (poetry; gay science fiction and fantasy; spirituality and religion) for national Lambda Literary Awards.

He has been involved in the gay movement since 1969, when he co-edited *Come Out!*, the world's first gay liberation newspaper. Later, in 1972, with two friends he started the Gay Men's Health Project Clinic, the first clinic for gay men on the East Coast, still surviving as New York's Callen-Lorde Community Health Center. In 1984, his play *Night Chills*, one of the first plays to deal with the AIDS crisis, won a Jane Chambers International Gay Playwriting Award. Brass's collaborations with composers include the words for the much-performed "All the Way Through Evening," a five-song cycle set by the late Chris DeBlasio; "The Angel Voices of Men" set by Ricky Ian Gordon, commissioned by the Dick Cable Musical Trust for the New York City Gay Men's Chorus, which has featured it on its new CD *Gay Century Songbook*; "Three Brass Songs," with Grammy-nominated composer Fred Hersch; and "Waltzes for Men," also commissioned by the DCMT for the NYC Gay Men's Chorus and set by Craig Carnahan. His three-man performance piece with music, *The Death of the Peonies*, directed by Australian Peter McLean, was been done at numerous performance spaces in the Northeast. His newest musical collaboration is "The Human City," with Houston Opera composer Mary Carol Warwick.

Perry Brass is an accomplished reader and an internationally recognized voice on gender subjects, gay relationships, and the history and literature of the movement towards GLBT equality. He lives in the Riverdale section of "da Bronx" with his partner of twenty one years, but can cross bridges to other parts of America without a passport.

Other Books by Perry Brass

SEX-CHARGE

" ... poetry at it's highest voltage ..." Marv. Shaw in **Bay Area Reporter**.

Sex-charge. 76 pages. $6.95. With male photos by Joe Ziolkowski.
ISBN 0-9627123-0-2

MIRAGE
ELECTRIFYING SCIENCE FICTION

A gay science fiction classic! An original "coming out" and coming-of-age saga, set in a distant place where gay sexuality and romance is a norm, but with a life-or-death price on it. On the tribal planet *Ki*, two men—in the spirit of an ancient pact—have been promised to each other for a lifetime. But a savage attack and a blood-chilling murder break this promise and force them to seek another world where imbalance and lies form Reality. This is the planet known as Earth, a world they will use and escape. Finalist, 1991 Lambda Literary Award for Best Gay Men's Science Fiction/Fantasy. This classic work of gay science fiction fantasy is now available in its new Tenth Anniversary Edition.

"Intelligent and intriguing." Bob Satuloff in **The New York Native**.

Mirage, Tenth Anniversary Edition 230 pages. $12.95
ISBN 1-892149-02-8

CIRCLES
THE AMAZING SEQUEL TO *MIRAGE*

"The world Brass has created with *Mirage* and its sequel rivals, in complexity and wonder, such greats as C.S. Lewis and Ursula LeGuin." **Mandate Magazine**, New York.

Circles. 224 pages. $11.95
ISBN 0-9627123-3-7

OUT THERE

STORIES OF PRIVATE DESIRES. HORROR.
AND THE AFTERLIFE.

"… we have come to associate [horror] with slick and trashy chiller-thrillers. Perry Brass is neither. He writes very well in an elegant and easy prose that carries the reader forward pleasurably. I found this selection to be excellent." **The Gay Review**, Canada.

Out There. 196 pages. $10.95
ISBN 0-9627123-4-5

ALBERT

or THE BOOK OF MAN

Third in the *Mirage* trilogy. In 2025, the White Christian Party has taken over America. Albert, son of Enkidu and Greeland, must find the male Earth mate who will claim his heart and allow him to return to leadership on Ki. "Brass gives us a book where lesser writers would have only a premise." **Men's Style,** New York

"If you take away the plot, it has political underpinnings that are chillingly true. Brass has a genius for the future." **Science Fiction Galaxies**, Columbus, OH. "Erotic suspense and action…a pleasurable read." **Screaming Hyena Review**, Melbourne, Australia.

Albert. 210 pages. $11.95
ISBN 0-9627123-5-3

Works

AND OTHER 'SMOKY GEORGE' STORIES
EXPANDED EDITION

"Classic Brass," these stories—many of them set in the long-gone 70s, when, as the author says, "Gay men cruised more and networked less"—have recharged gay erotica. This Expanded Edition contains a selection of Brass's steamy poems, as well as his essay, "Maybe We Should Keep the 'Porn' in Pornography."

Works. 184 pages. $9.95
ISBN 0-9627123-6-1

THE **HARVEST**
A "SCIENCE/POLITICO" NOVEL

From today's headlines predicting human cloning comes the emergence of "vaccos"—living "corporate cadavers"—raised to be sources of human organ and tissue transplants. One exceptional vacco will escape. His survival will depend upon Chris Turner, a sexual renegade who will love him and kill to keep him alive.

"One of the <u>Ten Best Books of 1997</u>," **Lavender Magazine**, Minneapolis. "In George Nader's *Chrome*, the hero dared to fall in love with a robot. In **The Harvest**—a vastly superior novel, Chris Turner falls in love with a vacco, Hart 256043." Jesse Monteagudo, **The Weekly News**, Miami, Florida. Finalist, 1997 Lambda Literary Award, Gay and Lesbian Science Fiction.

The Harvest. 216 pages. $11.95
ISBN 0-9627123-7-X

THE LOVER OF MY SOUL
A SEARCH FOR ECSTASY AND WISDOM

Brass's first book of poetry since *Sex-charge* is worth the wait. Flagrantly erotic and just plain flagrant—with poems like "I Shoot the Sonovabitch Who Fires Me," "Sucking Dick Instead of Kissing," and the notorious "MTV Ab(*solutely*) Vac(*uous*) Awards." **The Lover of My Soul** again proves Brass's feeling that poetry must tell, astonish, and delight.

"An amazingly powerful book of poetry and prose," **The Loving Brotherhood**, Plainfield, NJ.

The Lover of My Soul. 100 pages. $8.95
ISBN 0-9627123-8-8

At your bookstore, or from:

Belhue Press
2501 Palisade Ave., Suite A1
Bronx, NY 10463
E-mail: belhuepress@earthlink.net

Please add $2.50 shipping the first book, and $1.00 for each book thereafter. New York State residents please add 8.25% sales tax. Foreign orders in U.S. currency only.

How to survive your own gay life
AN ADULT GUIDE TO LOVE, SEX AND RELATIONSHIPS

The book for ADULT gay men. About sex and love, and coming out of repression; about surviving homophobic violence; about your place in a community, a relationship, and a culture. About the important psychic "gay work" and the gay tribe. About dealing with conflicts and crises, personal, professional, and financial. And, finally, about being more alive, happier, and stronger.

"Wise … a book that looks forward, not back." **Lambda Book Report**. Finalist, 1999 Lambda Literary Award in Gay and Lesbian Religion and Spirituality.

How to Survive Your Own Gay Life. 224 pages. $11.95
ISBN 0-9627123-9-6

ANGEL LUST
AN EROTIC NOVEL OF TIME TRAVEL

Tommy Angelo and Bert Knight are in a long-term relationship. Very long—close to a millennium. Tommy and Bert are angels, but very different. No wings; sexually free. Tommy was once Thomas Jebson, a teen serf in the violent England of William the Conqueror. One evening, he met a handsome knight who promised to love him for all time. Their story introduces us to gay forest men. To robber barons, castles, and deep woodlands. Also, to a modern sexual underground where "gay" and "straight" mean little. To Brooklyn factory men. Street machos. New York real estate sharks. And to the kind of lush erotic encounters for which Perry Brass is famous. Finalist, 2000 Lambda Literary Award, Gay and Lesbian Science Fiction.

"Brass's ability to go from seedy gay bars in New York to 11th century castles is a testament to his skill as a writer." **Gay & Lesbian Review**.

Angel Lust. 224 pages. $12.95
ISBN 1-892149-00-1

You can now order Perry Brass's exciting books online at www.perrybrass.com. Please visit this website for more details, regular updates, and news of future events and books.